MY END IS

MORIS FARHI (1935–2019) was b[orn in Turkey and moved]
to the UK. An international human rights advocate, he campaigned
for Amnesty International and was both Vice President of PEN
International and Chair of the International PEN Writers in Prison
Committee. His novels include *Children of the Rainbow*, *Journey
through the Wilderness*, *Young Turk* and *A Designated Man*. He also
published a poetry collection, *Songs from Two Continents*, and wrote
for the theatre and screen. A Fellow of the Royal Society of Literature,
in 2001 Farhi was appointed an MBE for services to literature.

'Farhi is fuelled by a powerful imaginative gift.'
New Statesman

'Like a Truffaut of the East, who prefers the pen to the camera.'
Elle

'His is a quicksand sort of storytelling that sucks you in.'
Big Issue

'A powerful, eloquent writer.'
London Magazine

'Writing of this quality and passion is a gift.'
Time Out

'Farhi speaks powerfully and movingly for the oppressed.'
Jewish Chronicle

'Moris Farhi shames the willed littleness of British fiction. In Farhi's
writing there is a distinctive collision of traditions which results in
something funny, political and unique.'
David Hare

ALSO BY MORIS FARHI

Novels
The Last of Days
The Pleasure of Your Death
Journey through the Wilderness
Children of the Rainbow
Young Turk
A Designated Man

Poetry
Songs from Two Continents

My End
Is My Beginning

MORIS FARHI

SAQI

to Sonsie (Elaine Freed)
and in memory of Asher (Mayer)

SAQI BOOKS
26 Westbourne Grove
London W2 5RH
www.saqibooks.com

Published 2020 by Saqi Books
Copyright © Moris Farhi 2020

Printed and bound by CPI Group (UK) Ltd, Croydon CR0 4YY

A full CIP record for this book is available from the British Library

ISBN 978 0 86356 130 6
eISBN 978 0 86356 135 1

NOTE FROM THE AUTHOR

This narrative is set in a country that reflects some aspects of those countries ruled by dictators who see themselves as Saviours, perhaps even believe, like Pharaohs and Chinese Emperors of olden times, that they are gods.

I have not focused on the iniquities suffered by every country oppressed by a Saviour; there are so many reported in responsible journals and newspapers that it would take an encyclopaedia to accommodate them all. Readers will be aware of some of them and of others beyond those known to me. I have chosen to offer *some* narratives that reflect *some* of the policies of *some* of the modern Saviours.

PROLOGUE

Our planet, once the only azure dot in our galaxy, is now the colour of ash.

Nothing lives.

No Saviours.

No souls.

No Dolphineros.

No Leviathans.

No immortal works.

No breaking news.

Certainly, no Paradise.

(Or atoms.)

It's as dense as the Universe was after the Big Bang.

Only a neutron or two lies in a dry riverbed and dream of plants, habitats, music, stories, paintings, sculptures, animals, insects and children.

Shortly those neutrons, too, will be shadows in stones.

FRIDAY 15:04

Today the sun's axis shifted. Its marigold luminosity fell into thick Arctic darkness.

The Saviours killed Belkis.

Our mentors, the Leviathans, submit this truth: 'Death is a lie.'
I should believe that.

But aren't there other truths that are *not* lies? Such as fire once doused can't be rekindled?

The Leviathans warn us constantly: these days the Saviours, determined to claim their godhood, will hunt us, the Dolphin Children, relentlessly.

But we're young. We think time is on our side. Hubris – a tragic flaw.

Today is History Unbound, a national holiday bombastically decreed by Numen. It will inaugurate a duumvirate – a joint governance – that will put our country in a pastiche confederacy with the other regional power, an oil-rich Islamic Republic striving to emerge under its Transcendent Leader, Grand Mufti Hajj Qutaybah Abd ar-Rahman.

The duumvirs' propagandists forecast that the alliance, systematising Numen's progressive Western politics with the Grand Mufti's piety, will create a new age that will finally cure humanity's fratricidal disposition.

Whether the duumvirs believe in such an oxymoronic future is a moot point. Many pundits intimate that this aspiration conceals a new dark age as its main agenda, namely, the degradation of Numen's subjects into lotus-eaters and the Grand Mufti's into theoleptics.

The Leviathans are more forthright: since the duumvirs enslave their own people and lavishly support various terrorist groups as proxies for their end game, the alliance will last until one duumvir liquidates the other.

◉

Early this afternoon, having broadcast the mandatory Friday sermon from his Russian-built aircraft carrier, the Grand Mufti, surrounded by his personal warriors, the *Ghazis*, arrived regally arrayed in *bisht, ghutrah* and *agal*.

Numen and the specially invited leaders from neighbouring countries – all prospective Saviours prowling in the wings – welcomed him with red-carpet protocol. Belkis and I, endowed by our Leviathan mentor, Hrant, with the ability to perceive the invisible, murky, auric fields enveloping the duumvirs. We identified some of these spectres as their own role models – prominent among them, Batista, Idi Amin, Pol Pot and Saddam Hussein.

Eventually the tyrants, waving blessings to the crowds, boarded a festooned statemobile – a light armoured personnel carrier projecting Numen's martial credentials. Escorted by a long tail of outriders, half-tracks and limousines – and a flight of helicopters – they set out for the Presidential Palace, Xanadu, where the Grand Mufti would be staying. Xanadu is an eyesore of 1150 rooms built by Numen with misappropriated public funds. A cartoonist once drew it as a Ziggurat, with the caption, 'Mr Tickler's Shack' – an allusion to Numen's Hitler moustache. The cartoonist withered in dungeons, but his derision lives on.

About today's demonstration: Hrant and his peers agreed that History Unbound would be an appropriate occasion for it.

But Belkis and I disagreed where and when to mount it.

Belkis insisted that a protest during the Grand Mufti's arrival would rouse the superpowers which, even as they condemned both despots' dismal Human Rights records, indulged them as useful also-rans.

I maintained that since Numen, flaunting his machoism, persistently disparaged the superpowers as neutered dinosaurs, our demo would be more effective if it occurred on the Sunday afternoon when he and the Grand Mufti signed their concordat at Xanadu. Our clamour would goad the superpowers to re-evaluate the duumvirs' agendas. Moreover, as Numen would aim to show the democratic countries that his subjects have the freedom to demonstrate, we would expose his brutal rule by provoking his Security forces to react heavy-handedly.

The Leviathans agreed with my rationale. But Belkis, impetuous as ever, remained inflexible. In the end we yielded to her and tabled my proposition as Plan B.

Leaks about our demo galvanised the people. Defying Homeland Security, they thronged the cavalcade's route.

Homeland Security has six forces: Pinkies (Informers), Police, Riot Gendarmerie, State Intelligence Agency, Scythes (National Guards) and Dragon's Teeth, Numen's personal bodyguards. The last outfit, recruited from various terror groups and famed for their barbarity, are supposedly inconspicuous in neat suits; but with machine-pistols bulging under their jackets, they look like Robocops.

No banners or placards; they'd be confiscated as weapons. Just seasoned demonstrators with techsets trumpeting the nation's grievances. Then the Houdini act: slipping into anonymity like herrings in shoals.

As the best location, Belkis chose Genovese Plaza, a landmark for state visits.

In bygone times, the Plaza's Great Tower kept vigil for fires, armadas and floods. The Plaza itself, a Romanesque rialto, was where citizens could personally vent their grievances to their rulers. Latterly, however, politicians had appropriated it for demagoguery – prompting the people to call it Fartheads' Pulpit.

Today some illuminati – internationally esteemed therefore as yet unpurgeable by Numen – are trying to reinstate Genovese Plaza as a Global Forum. Belkis, embracing this vision, predicted that one day the Tower will be reconstituted as a Tower of Babel which, unlike the one in the Bible, would solve the world's problems and enrich us with umpteen languages and cultures.

According to a legend Genovese Plaza is also the one place on earth where gods, alerted to oppressors' iniquities, would rush over and cast the despots into hell's cauldrons.

This morning the gods stayed away and let the Saviours kill Belkis, soul of my soul.

@

I think Belkis knew she'd be killed. She started the day not as *La Pasionaria* of previous demos, but like Joan of Arc calmly waiting for the English to ignite her stake.

While we blended with the crowds, she kept watching the Scythe snipers on the Tower's observation platform. Did she see them as a warning that her time was up?

I tried to distract her but to no avail. Silence imprisons thoughts.

Then, as the cavalcade approached, she caressed my cheek. 'Sorry, Oric, I wandered into limbo. All our missions, all the countries we went to became one. Now I'm back on the earth. The earth I know. The earth that knows me. If it's my time to be killed, I'll be glad it'll be here.'

'Nonsense! We'll waft away like we always do.'

Again she scrutinised the snipers on the Tower. 'Life is everlasting. Even stones say so. If only Saviours understood that. But they can't … all they know is carnage. They worship it. It's the god they've chosen. The god that demands the sacrifice of untold innocents. That anoints their hands with blood. That tells them the more they massacre, the more godlike they'll be.'

'Only until the day they see how deluded they've been.'

'Why can't that day be today, Oric?'

'If only.'

'Let's forget if onlys. Let's *make* it today. Let's stop them today!'

I grimaced. 'With slogans?'

She rebuked me. 'With our example.'

I should have looked into her mind then, but I was scanning the Plaza. The cavalcade was approaching the arched entrance. We'd switch on our sound systems when it reached the middle.

She held my hand vigorously. 'We met in this beautiful city, Oric. Fell in love here. Became Dolphineros here. Home turf – best place.'

I looked at her quizzically, still unable to read her mind.

She kissed me fervidly, reading the doubt in my face. 'Death is a lie! That's the Truth!'

The cavalcade entered the Plaza.

She slipped out of my arms.

I froze.

Somehow, she scrambled past the Riot Gendarmerie at the barricades, past the Grand Mufti's retinue of hajjis distributing copies of his favourite hokum, *The Protocols of the Elders of Zion,* and past his Ghazis. She managed to avoid Numen's outriders, ran into the road and stopped not far from the duumvir's statemobile.

I tried to run after her.

I couldn't move. I was cemented by fear. Hidebehind had me by the throat and was choking me. The ancients called Fear Hidebehind. Ascribed to Him countenances of spiked scales, ogre heads, bats' wings, ophidian hair – the usual phantasmagoria to depict a demon that's never seen, never shows chest or testicles, never exposes an inch of sinews that one can spit at or strike.

Belkis switched on her sound system.

Her voice filled the Plaza. 'No to despotism! No to this duumvirate! We want Liberty! Equality! Justice! Social Care! We want Life!'

The Scythes on the Tower opened fire.

Belkis crumpled.

I watched, still paralysed by Hidebehind, as Numen shouted

orders at his Dragon's Teeth.

He needn't have bothered.

Burning their motorcycles' tyres, they were making for Belkis.

Still waving her tiny speaker, Belkis was trying to stand up. 'No to Big Lies! No to Post-Truths! No to mass catacombs!'

Then thuds. One, two, several as the Dragon's Teeth outriders tossed her about.

Finally, Numen's statemobile ran over her broken body.

I bellowed and bellowed.

Some Riot Gendarmerie veered towards me.

I should have confronted them.

Instead, winged by Hidebehind, I fled.

FRIDAY 16.07

Here I am now in our grotto.

I don't know how I got here.

On the other hand, our island lies only a few miles from the City. Did I swim? Take the ferry? Tack into the wind?

Uncanny how deserters can waft like sleepwalkers.

There's Hrant, our Leviathan. Droves of luminous silhouettes are gliding in: other Leviathans. My son, Childe Asher, with amber almond eyes stops paddling his Moses basket, climbs out of the lagoon and hugs me. I push him aside and stoop over Hrant. He looks soulless. Uninhabited. Scorched earth. I shout. 'Did you see?!'

His dolorous eyes are imprinted with Belkis's crushed body. 'Yes.'

I wail. 'She wanted to repair the world. In one day. Today!'

'Yes.'

'Why couldn't she wait!?'

He mumbles. 'Sometimes long waits cause despair. The soul gets battered by impatience. Staying on as human becomes unbearable.'

'Dolphineros are supposed to be immune to despair!'

'Supposed to be – yes.'

I am wretched. 'Then you – Leviathans – shouldn't have made her one!'

'We didn't. She was born one.'

'And I'm not? You mean that's why I abandoned her?'

He doesn't answer. Fear seizes my body. Childe Asher holds my hand. 'You didn't abandon her, Dad. You iced up. Shell-shock: the thousand-yard stare – it's still in your eyes.' I am crushed. My son – only five.

Again, I shout at Hrant. 'You said her spirit will make me a Dolphinero! Why didn't it?'

He faces me wearily. 'It can take time.'

'I needed to be one *today*!'

'You have her spirit. Hold onto it. Dolphineros are slain – that's often their fate. But when they leave their bodies, they become Leviathans. Look at me! Look at those arriving to welcome Belkis! We rise straightaway – not some thousand years later like a phoenix. We erupt from ashes, dust, water, sky, fire and carry on repairing humankind, the planet, the soil, the waterways, the thermal forces ... '

'The hackneyed mantra – death's a lie! Is that all you can say?'

'It's all that needs to be said. It's the Truth.'

'I don't believe it! I tried very hard! Now the Pilate in my heart asks: 'what *is* truth?' And the Saviours laugh. "Death is death," they say.'

Childe Asher interjects again. 'If you believe that, you wouldn't be here, Dad. You'd have disappeared.'

'If only I could.'

'But you won't!'

'Because I love you.'

Gently, he pulls me to sit with him. 'As a Leviathan said: "no heart is as whole as a broken heart." The breakage begets wisdom. Wisdom asks: is death a closure or the semicolon that brings the next existence? Is life really everlasting? You know the answer is yes. But you still doubt. That's why you've come back. You want to see mum and banish your doubts. Well, she won't be long. While waiting sing the lullaby your father sings in your dreams – it's another proof that life's everlasting.'

I can't sing. Instead I search the depths of Childe Asher's amber almond eyes. No signs of uncertainty in him – only extraordinary radiance. Before his birth, Hrant predicted that he'd be a prodigy. Impatient for a new human life like all Leviathans, he'd hastened his *Samsara* and reincarnated prematurely. Some of his predecessors,

Hrant related, composed heavenly music, painted sounds in dazzling colours, built magnificent edifices, prolonged life, correlated the stars' gravitations to the creation of galaxies. Childe Asher, he affirmed, will be a Solonian who'll attain Buddhahood, ingest the astral Akashi records and absorb the feelings of everything living and everything inanimate.

A sea-mist drifts in.

An albatross alights.

From under its wings, Belkis emerges. In blue chakra, she has the Leviathan look.

The albatross transmutes into a Leviathan. I remember the old belief that albatrosses are manifestations of ancestors and that when our sun loses hope, they cuddle it with their powerful wings.

Childe Asher runs to Belkis. They embrace. I watch them, my family.

Childe Asher brings Belkis over. 'Find each other again, you two! I'll help Hrant prepare the Agapé.'

Belkis explains shyly. 'Agapé is togetherness, the Leviathans' welcome.'

Hrant exapands, 'It is our ritual, since time immemorial.'

I rasp. 'I know what it is. You told us in the early days.'

The grotto has expanded.

The Leviathans' silhouettes stretch endlessly.

Belkis holds my hand lovingly.

Heavy with guilt, I don't know what to say.

I point at Childe Asher. 'So like you – the boy. Like earth welcoming the sun.'

'He's like you, too.'

'No, better. Infinitely better. Not craven. Not faithless. Not one to run away.'

Belkis caresses my face. 'Sometimes it's wise to run.'

'Not in my book.'

'You can only be who you are, Oric.'

'I thought I'd mastered fear.'

'You did – all this time you did.'

'Until the crunch.'

'There've been many crunches.'

'I could fend off Hidebehind those times. But this time you needed me – and I could do nothing. Hidebehind paralysed me.'

Gently she runs her fingers over my eyes. 'Look at me, Oric. They killed me. But I'm still with you. We'll continue. Proof that Death *is* a lie.'

I absorb her eyes, her face, her aura. I want to be embedded in her. Roam over that earthly body of untold delights. But now that she's a Leviathan, dare I breathe her perfume, hear her squeals, swim in her ultramarine eyes, cherish her sturdiness when she holds me tight? How do I become one with her as I did everytime we made love?

She feels my despair, presses my hands tightly. 'I'm not ectoplasm, Oric. Leviathans are flesh, too, when they reincarnate. I'll be with you forever.'

There's so much love in her eyes.

Led by Hrant and Childe Asher, the Leviathans start singing the *Ode to Joy*.

Belkis brightens. 'The Agapé is starting.'

I feel I shouldn't be here. Not yet.

I kiss her. 'Hrant believes I still have your spirit.'

'Hrant is always right.'

'Let's hope so.'

I dive into the pool before she can stop me.

SATURDAY 08.14

In the early days, as fresh Dolphineros, Belkis and I dreamed of perfection. Wanting to do something dolphinesque that would justify our distinction, we decided that the sea would be our Pegasus; that whenever possible we'd start our missions by swimming from our island. That's how we went to yesterday's demo.

Today I'm taking the ferry that serves the city's coastal hamlets. Swimming without Belkis would be another betrayal.

I'm going walkabout. A valedictory communion with my city to prime myself for tomorrow. I want to reabsorb people's hopes; inject my marrow with the fortitude that enables them to persevere while hunchbacked by oppression. I must bear witness to their plight. It is my understanding of the part I must play as the Dolphinero that I am.

Tomorrow's crowd should be larger than yesterday's.

I board the ferry. There are not many commuters. Hardly any work in the city for islanders.

For once I don't mind not swimming. The sea is a wonderful womb, but like all wombs it's a refuge. It diverts one from the horrors – and the miracles – happening outside.

It is time for me to achieve a miracle, to accept that existence has purposes, that life is meaningful because it has aspirations. Overthrowing Saviours is a cardinal one. That should be possible if we consider the Saviours' psychology as formulated by, of all people, my son, Childe Asher.

This is what he says: Saviours rise from embittered factions which postulate that there's no creator, no universal scheme, only the variable concepts of good and bad. To compensate for life's meaninglessness – and especially its loneliness – these factions exalt the nihilistic solipsism of an unquestionable reality. Besides precluding inquiry, this condition provides the Saviours with blank tablets on which they can engrave their rationales.

Numen, Childe Asher further theorises, is a variation of this archetype. He seeks to be the epitomic alpha-man, the wiliest statesman, the supreme juggler of power. But he knows that power, too, is subject to evolution, that a hyper-virulent species of Saviours has already incubated and that to ensure his survival he must emerge as the first Millennial. His choice of the turgid epithet *Numen* is indicative not only of this compulsion but also of his resolve to cauterise the insecurities haunting him.

I move to the fore deck. Moni, who uses ferries as squats, is asleep on a bench, curled up with his Shepherd dog, Phral. Phral gives me a quick glance, wags his tail, then resumes watching a Pinkie sitting nearby. In Numen's 'government that listens to the people', Pinkies, the eyes and ears of Homeland Security, are the only listeners. They've been watching Moni for ages but don't seem to have an inkling of his quicksilver persona. Belkis and I keep wondering whether he's a Leviathan. The Pinkie gives me a cursory look, ignores my 'good morning' and lights a cigarette.

Argus-eyed and omnipresent they may be, but Pinkies are mere ciphers of their precursors. True, they still burrow everywhere and still point their fingers at 'different drummers' – hence their name – but, increasingly dependent on state-of-the-art electronics, they lack the vulpine guile and the Daedalian ingenuity of past fingerers. They trawl for diabolical conspiracies even in vacuums. If the adage, 'where there's shit, there's flies,' needs proof, Pinkies provide it.

I watch the Pinkie. He's blowing smoke rings. He's not interested in me. Yet for some time now Belkis and I have featured in all the wanted lists. The fact that this Pinkie ignores me when my flight from Genovese Plaza yesterday should make me a priority target suggests that, in the main, Pinkies are a horde of opportunistic riffraff. That's partly true. Certainly, their ranks abound with mildewed men and women clinging on to the Security bandwagon, but not far behind them young and ravenous cadres are creeping up the ladders.

Belkis and I are adept at outsmarting them. Imperceptibility is the first skill Leviathans teach. Also, we have a retired French couturier who can make us look as dazzling as film stars or as down-and-out as men 'between jobs'.

Today my disguise is that of an oddjobber in splotched overalls and baseball cap, dragging tools in a tattered holdall after a boozy night.

The ferry departs.

The rising sun stipples the water with hues of Belkis's titian hair.

A wave, riding the headwind, breaks on my face.

Belkis and Childe Asher appear.

They're visible to me but invisible to the Pinkie. As a Leviathan Belkis can camouflage herself – or anyone she chooses – and render conversations inaudible. I want to hug her but hesitate. So does she, I think. We – or rather I – must get used to the fact that despite her changed status we're both still flesh and blood.

Childe Asher scrutinises my disguise. He looks impressed. 'We thought we'd just come by.'

I ruffle his ebony hair. 'To make sure I'm all right?'

He nods sombrely. 'Children are their parents' parents.'

Belkis holds my hand. 'About tomorrow, Oric. You don't have to demonstrate – not for me.'

'It's not for you. It's for me. And for Childe Asher.' I have to prove myself to my wife and son that I really am a Dolphinero. And things have to be said and done – repeatedly – until we repair the world. Maybe we're brainwashed, too – not unlike suicide-bombers. Maybe while they've been radicalised by death-worshippers we've been indoctrinated by the Leviathans.

'Oric, yesterday was my fault. I was impetuous. I moved before I should have.'

'Even so I should have backed you.'

'You are what you are, my love.'

21

'Then it's time to be what I should be.'

She kisses me. 'I can't convince you, can I?'

'No.'

Childe Asher hugs me. 'We'll be around, Dad.'

They vanish.

Pinkie lights a fresh cigarette.

I open my holdall. Take out a girlie magazine – another item in my disguise.

My journal's tucked inside. I brought it to strengthen my resolve.

Before I started writing my journal (around the time Childe Asher was born) I was supposedly in the throes of *Mal du siècle* – restless, sleeping badly, having nightmares. Then one night I had a good nightmare – the sort that makes melancholics happy. I was sitting by the sea sobbing like a hired weeper at a funeral when a toddler appeared (Childe Asher later admitted the boy was him).

'Why are you crying?' He asked.

'*Mal du siècle*,' I replied.

'You don't have *Mal du siècle*. You're an orphan – you suffer from *saudade*,' he said.

'What's that?' I asked.

'Portuguese term. Defines the bitter-sweet mood that possesses one when the memory of a time or a person is lost forever. *Saudade* – the yearning for the loss – provides some solace.'

'Is there a cure?' I asked.

'I doubt it. But jotting things down might help. Pessoa tried it,' he said and disappeared. And so I tried it too, on my son's advice, at first to assuage my own suffering but as time went on and the patterns of the crimes the Saviours inflicted on the people started to change, Hrant recognised the journal as an important aid for the Dolphineros and Immortals alike. It is a record of all that I have borne witness to as a Dolphinero. I have kept it ever since.

THE DOLPHIN CHILDREN

Belkis and I met when we were sixteen.

Numen prides himself as the architect of the country's 'robust' economy, a feat he achieves by laundering billions of dollars, via private banks, to help Iran and North Korea circumvent the international sanctions imposed on them – a service that reputedly also rewards him with tea chests of gold bars.

Numen stipulates that the destitute, the homeless, the unemployed, the LGBT, the disabled, the geriatrics – the asocials in fascistic parlance – must be swept under the proverbial carpet to preserve the country's lacquer of prosperity. Marooned in Termite Mounds – Social Services' euphemism for orphanages – Belkis and I fell into the asocial category.

There was one annual holiday, Salute the Saplings Day, decreed by Numen to seduce the new generation destined to extend the era he was tirelessly engineering. Orphans were included. These Youthfests, he declared, would not only soothe the youngsters' impatience as they journeyed to maturity, but also smith them as tomorrow's swashbucklers. The jamborees offered elaborate parades and sports meets for elite academies, and fairs for runt schools and orphanages. Show-piece events were televised, and focal points were decked with billboards bearing Numen's portrait above his proclamation that the blood in his veins is the true blood of patriarchal love.

While ultra-generous with huge tax exemptions to corporations that support him, Numen is a scrooge when it comes to welfare. He considers such charitable diversions as mobile clinics, soup-kitchens, old age homes and orphanages a burden on a country striving to become a superpower. To no one's surprise, he relegated the orphanages' fairs to humble venues. Our orphanages – albeit miles apart – were allocated a ramshackle eatery in the grounds of a defunct Carmelite monastery on Key Picayune, the smallest of the circlet of islands lying some six miles off the metropolis. According to a legend, Key Picayune owed its bantam size to a divine mishap: God, while creating the islands with His saliva, ended up with a dry mouth and could only manage a measly spit for the last one.

Belkis's orphanage, situated in an East Strand hamlet from where a dawn ferry transported the mainland's produce, was the first to arrive at the eatery. My orphanage came second. A third, from an even farther location, would delay breakfast and rosewater-time by another hour. Since orphanages are run like barracks – reveille at dawn followed by endless drudgery – the delay, allowing freedom to wander, was a boon. Key Picayune was blanketed by strawberries. I was impatient to have my fill. I made for the cliffs and gorged myself.

Accustomed to basic fare, how could I have known that gluttony hosts a thousand scorpions?

My stomach contorted. I buckled, writhing.

A voice, in the dulcet tones of a harp, rippled. 'All right?'

I looked up and saw ultramarine eyes like the Earth seen from space. 'Too many strawberries.'

She laughed. 'Stay!'

I watched as a titian dream gathered some lichens and rubbed them on my face. 'How's that?'

'Good.'

She handed me the lichens. 'Now rub these on your tummy.'

I did.

'Better?'

The spasms abated. 'Amazing! Just lichens?'

'Jasmin, our janitress, swears by them. Earth's cure-all, she says. I'm Belkis – like the Queen of Sheba …'

Her affability captivated me. 'Really?'

'So, named by the man who found me at a bus-stop.'

'Oh?'

'A Jewish tinker, I'm told. Named Vitali. Nothing known about him. I imagine the stars know … Anyway, I hope he's where all good souls are.'

'Does that make you Jewish?'

'Your guess. But somewhere between fair and dark, I must be cross-breed.'

'Do you care?'

'Not at all. I'm with outsiders. Strangers, others – the maligned, ostracised, persecuted. Makes them so wise.'

Somehow, I found the courage to free the voice I normally keep locked up. 'Whoever you are – you're heavenly!'

'Blatherer!'

I dared hold her hand. 'I mean it! Honest!'

She didn't withdraw her hand. 'What about you? Where're you from?'

'Some Balkan war zone. Maybe somewhere in Former Yugoslavia. All these years – they're still trying to trace the DPs. I imagine I'm from wherever gingerhairs come from.'

'The ginger hair is the sun shining in you. You got a name?'

'I've been given a list to choose from. I answer to all. To Wardens I'm Carrothead.'

'Ugh …'

'Sometimes I choose names for myself …'

'Like?'

'Oric. That's my favourite.'

'Very unusual.'

'It's from a fable. About an ancient tribe that hugged oaks to absorb their strength. One day a warlord attacked the tribe, killed the men and abducted the women. One youth, Oric, survived. He was in love with Semiramis, one of the abducted girls. He summoned the animals sacred to his tribe: bears, reindeer, lions, eagles, dolphins, whales; and searched the planet, shouting

Semiramis's name. Well, Semiramis had escaped from her captors and settled in Arkangelsk. There she became a dendrologist, studying the inner strengths of pines and spruces. She heard Oric. And they were united.'

'Grand story. Can I call you Oric?'

I beamed. 'I'd be delighted!'

She squeezed my hand. 'I believe in everything that's life-enhancing.'

I stared at her, confounded. 'I can't believe it. All this time Fate kept me in barbed shirts. Suddenly, she produces a miracle. She let us meet. Can She be kind?'

'We're destined for each other. She accepts that.'

'You really mean that?'

'I always mean what I say.'

'Then thank you, God!'

'Leave God out of it. Thank the Great Mother.'

'Same thing, isn't it?'

'God is vindictive. Forever angry! The Great Mother never! She's all love – like all creators. Women commune with Her – breast to breast. That's how I knew we'd meet.'

But for the arrival of the children from the third orphanage, we'd have stayed there all day.

I muttered gloomily. 'We need to get back. They'll start breakfast.'

Belkis snorted. 'Let's forget breakfast.'

'But –'

'No buts! Let's escape!'

'How?'

'Down to the sea. The sea loves runaways.'

How could I say no?

We cascaded down the cliff.

I surveyed the tiny beach wondering what to do next.

'Let's swim,' said Belkis.

I hesitated. 'We don't have bathing suits.'

She laughed and undressed. 'Nor do fish.'

'They'll be looking for us.'

'They'll never find us.'

We swam and danced like flying fish.

We encountered eddies and whirled with them.

We raced to a distant crag.

There, concealed by algae and thick moss, we discovered our grotto.

We slipped in.

A dreamcatcher's gem. Azure, large, beautiful, luminous. A pool purling gently. We became two souls in one, and she became my Paradise.

We watched the end of Salute the Saplings Day from twilit shadows.

Our custodians, infuriated by our truancy, called the police, provided them with our descriptions, then gathered their wards and left.

We hid until the police stopped searching for us.

We made the grotto our haven.

We lived on fish and on fruits and vegetables.

When winter honed gales into sabres, we sheltered in the ruins of the Carmelite monastery. Its thick walls feathered a cosy nest.

Hrant, our Leviathan, often praised us: 'You breathe the sea, soak the sun and avoid shadows – just like Diogenes.'

I put down the journal and doze.

SATURDAY 08.41

A yelp wakes me. It's Phral protesting that Moni hurt him as he turned over. Moni rouses instantly and cuddles Phral. 'Sorry, sorry …' Phral licks him forgivingly. Pinkie takes out his notepad and starts scribbling. I wonder what hogwash he'll fabricate.

Moni's a soothsayer. Blind, in the tradition of mythic seers, gargantuan in height and cocooned by a nimbus of mysteries, he looks eternal like a lion-headed Hittite deity. The Roma, able to tell people's ages as unerringly as those of horses, say there's no span of time engraved on his eyes. This happens, they add, when Fate tangles her strings as She weaves the future. Moni could be as young as a spermatozoon or as old as Big Bang.

Moni starts his day early and follows his nose to run-down neighbourhoods. In the evenings, he plies his vocation in waterfront restaurants. He shuns those who consider clairvoyance a fashionable pastime. He has the gift – as Phral does – of escape, even from unwanted conversations.

He never accepts payment. Grateful punters try to slip a bill into his pocket, but they always fail. The Roma, citing accounts from their own fortune-tellers (who in other circumstances would have regarded Moni as an unwelcome rival), interpret this altruism as the mark of a true diviner. Affirming that his portents are always unerring, they see him as an incarnation of the Theban prophet, Tiresias, who, they claim, was a Roma. That's worrying, they add, because Tiresias's avatars appear only at times of cataclysm.

For his auguries, Moni has five circular pebbles that, after years of use, have lost their sheen. Each pebble, he once explained, embodies a primary element: granite for earth; lava for fire;

moonstone for sky; coral for sea; a fig's fossil for evolution. Laying his hands on these pebbles, he shuts his dimmed eyes and delivers his good tidings. He only pronounces good tidings and waits for the bad ones to wreck each other as they eventually do. Most gratifyingly for me, it was Moni who foretold that my life will be forever graced by Belkis.

The Ferry Company, still run by big-hearted mariners, allows him to sleep in their boats and travel gratis. He doesn't have a family. But allusions to his real identity and the why, how and from where he suddenly appeared seven years ago – about the time Belkis and I met – abound.

Moni himself occasionally quips that he might be a descendant of the shoemaker whom people mistake for the Wandering Jew. More pertinently, he once confessed to Childe Asher that he'll never know who he is and where he came from because a soothsayer receives the gift only if he forfeits his own past.

He never has any money. The generous meals he and Phral enjoy are forced on them by chefs who elevate regional home-cooking to culinary heights. His clothes are tailored by Armenian seamstresses famous for their skills in copying exclusive creations.

Pinkie lights up another cigarette and continues scribbling.

Phral remains alert.

Phral is another mystery. A few years back, he was a stray playing hide-and-seek with the dogcatchers. One day, while slinking along a busy avenue, he saw Moni stranded on the opposite pavement. He dashed onto the road, brought the cars to a screeching stop and escorted Moni across. Thereafter he has never left Moni's side.

Phral is enchantingly affectionate to those who esteem Moni, but always wary of unfriendly dogs, suspicious strangers and Pinkies. It was the Roma who, impressed by his devotion to Moni, named him Phral which in Romanes means 'brother' and is the origin of our word 'pal'.

Moni, fully awake now, invites me to his bench. 'Not swimming today?'

'No.'

'Good to see you.'

Pinkie, spurred by Moni's amity towards me, is writing furiously. I can predict the baloney he's hatching: 'Subject meets scruffy bloke in ferry. When latter arrived, subject appeared to be sleeping. On waking up subject contacted bloke. Odd encounter. Recommend check bloke also.'

Moni senses my caution. 'Ignore him! Fancy good tidings?'

I know the good tidings I seek, but I'm curious to hear what Moni has to say. 'Sure.'

Moni casts his pebbles.

Phral has the ability to transmit Moni's vision. But he'll do so only when trusted souls stroke him.

I stroke the dog.

As Moni trawls the unknown, images appear in my mind's eye.

A long, wide river.

A hunched figure in a tub made of bulrushes …

'That's you, Oric. Sailing in your Moses basket.'

This is the ark in the Nile into which Jochebed placed her baby, Moses, to save him from the Pharaoh's decree that all new-born Jewish males must be killed. In Moni's esoteric stratum the basket is the uncertainty to which every mother entrusts her baby.

My Moses basket negotiates tributaries, weirs, rapids.

'Awesome, eh?'

Time moves on.

My Moses basket has another in tow.

Its occupant has moved into mine.

I ask: 'That other person – is it Belkis?'

'Yes. Your twin-soul.'

Time moves further on.

*Countless Moses baskets are destroyed; their occupants **are** massacred by swords, guns, cannons, missiles and nuclear clouds.*

My Moses basket is lurching.

Belkis is no longer in it.

'You again, Oric. A loving man who wants gracious tomorrows, who offers hope to the hopeless – yet desolate as if your Moses basket has become a prison.'

'Where's Belkis?'

Two other baskets appear nearby.

'In her own basket now. With Childe Asher's next to her.'

I'm talking to somebody …

'Who am I talking to?'

'To yourself. Not talking. Quarrelling.'

The baskets of Belkis and Childe Asher pull away.

'Belkis and Childe Asher – they're drifting away. Is it because I failed Belkis?'

'They're not drifting away. *You* are.'

'Me? Makes no sense! Without my Belkis? Without my twin-soul?'

'Do you wonder why?'

'I abandoned her!'

'You stopped navigating. You left her to navigate.'

'Because she's better than me.'

'That's weakness. You have to do your own navigation.'

My basket is still lurching.

'I'm lurching … To my end?'

'Souls don't have an end. Stop fearing. Fear causes panic.'

'I know fear. What's the good tiding?'

Moni collects his pebbles. 'You're still in your Moses basket. Still able to navigate. Still imbued with Belkis's spirit. That's the good tidings.'

He gets up, hands Phral his leash.

@

We've reached East Strand.

Pinkie has stopped scribbling. Muttering into his mobile, he follows Moni and Phral.

I watch Phral and Moni disembark, like an old couple still in love.

I realise how elementary happiness can be, how all it needs is Love and harmony. Sadly, many who've grasped it enjoy it mutely, fearfully. They know that Numen has identified happiness as a threatening force and is determined to root it out.

I should tell him: he won't succeed. One day happiness will bloom all over the planet. And our odyssey as Dolphineros will reach its destination.

I run after Moni. 'One more thing …'

'Yes?'

Pinkie photographs us with his mobile.

'Will I betray Belkis again?'

Moni's face oscillates like that of a yogi. 'I told you way back. You two are destined for each other. Destiny never changes.'

That alleviates my anguish.

Pinkie meets another Pinkie.

Pinkies must be like cabbies at taxi ranks waiting for fares.

The Pinkie from the ferry follows Moni.

The other lingers at the pier.

I think I know why Security is interested in Moni. His good tidings presage a repaired world. Such stuff terrifies Numen.

I'm at the café next to the pier. Earlier it was packed with commuters starting their day with hot drinks. Now there's only the Pinkie. He's at a nearby table, smoking while eating a doughnut and watching me.

The café owner and his wife are counting the morning's takings. They mutter dejectedly. Usual number of teas and coffees sold, but not enough snacks. They'll have to tighten their belts.

Yet even as they fret, they feel for the commuters. Young, middle-aged or old, most have humdrum jobs. Unable to afford the rents in the city, they've holed up in council estates. Their wages – plus the measly overtime they get on national holidays – barely cover the essentials; end of the month many will go cap in hand to moneylenders. Still they're lucky; they have jobs.

Everywhere there's fury over unemployment and great empathy for the unemployed. Yet no one blames Numen, condemns him for his personality cult or accuses him of funnelling the nation's wealth into Swiss banks, wall-to-wall safes, chests and shoe boxes. Why? It can't be just fear that afflicts people with herd behaviour. Belkis says that it's battle-fatigue. People no longer have the strength to break silence and tear off blindfolds.

Maybe it's more deep-rooted than that. A haunting sixth sense and the prescience that the horizon has drained away and that what's left is the unbearable weight of endless loneliness.

I order another tea and take out my journal. I realise that it is at once a love letter to my wife and son, and a testament to the secret work of the Dolphineros. Once the Leviathans have finished taking their own notes my journal, I hope it finds its way to Childe Asher. It's my apologia – I want him to hear *from me* that I tried very hard to be a true Dolphinero. But I surrendered to fear when I should have saved Belkis, whose love coloured my life miraculously. To save colours from grey matters one must shield them, as Newton did when he stacked them in a beam of light.

LEVIATHANS

We had just made love and were singing.

That's when our Leviathan, draped in sea-mist, wafted into the grotto.

Belkis saw the apparition first. 'Wow!'

A voice, like susurrations in a lavender field, answered. 'I hope I didn't alarm you.'

I gaped at the mist. It had alarmed me.

Belkis smiled, not at all confounded. 'Welcome, whoever you are!'

'A Leviathan.'

'Like the monsters in the Bible?'

The mist lifted to reveal a humanoid colossus with a congenial air. A blue corona – the blue of the Auric Field that illumines the soul's seat and which only great painters can create – girdled his body. 'Monsters only to Saviours.'

His reply beguiled Belkis. 'That's some introduction!'

He sat on the ledge. 'We've been watching you two.'

Belkis teased him. 'We? Royalty, are you?'

He laughed. 'My peers and I.'

'More Leviathans? Where are they?'

'Around.'

He looked like Hrant Dink.

Belkis was enjoying the encounter. 'Ask your peers to come in. The more of you, the merrier.'

'They don't want to crowd you.'

'Waiting for us to make love again, are they?'

He chuckled. 'We're discreet. On those occasions we snooze.'

'How come we didn't see you snoozing?'

'We can be invisible.'

'With your size?'

'We can also metamorphose. Turn into octopuses, horses, eagles. But we prefer our original human form.'

To prove his point, he shrank to average height.

That impressed her. 'Shape-shifters, too!'

'Just psychokinesis.'

Astounded, I said. 'How long have you been watching?'

'Since you were born.'

Belkis teased him again. 'In the orphanages, too?'

'Oh, yes.'

'Shuttling from Oric's to mine?'

'We can be in two places at the same time. Several, if need be.'

Mystified, I resorted to sarcasm. 'That couldn't have been fun – watching us moulder …'

'You two never mouldered. You embraced life when still in the womb. That's what caught our attention. As you matured, you perceived the wounds in people's hearts and minds. You read everything you could. Studied the past and the present and pondered about the future. Understood how people should love. You discovered that rocks will spout water if tenderly touched, but not if struck angrily.'

Belkis shook her head, overwhelmed. 'You saw all that?'

'We saw all that. We had to make sure that you really were Dolphin Children. You are, Belkis.'

Feeling excluded, I asked. 'What about me?'

Belkis held my hand reassuringly. 'Of course, you, too, Oric! You're more than a dolphin, you're a whale! Souls see into souls. He's seen yours. Right, Leviathan?'

'Yes.'

His response was cursory. Had he spotted my Hidebehind?

The Leviathan put an arm around my shoulders. He radiated the tenderness of the loving father who sings ballads in every orphan's dreams.

35

I wished he really was my father.

'In the orphanage, you kept running, Oric. Why do you think you did that?'

'To escape.'

'From what?'

'From everything.'

'You weren't escaping. You were searching. You'll never stop running. What I hope is that you'll run as a Dolphinero. You'll run to discover the many meanings that Life has.'

'Will Belkis and I stay together?'

Belkis embraced me. 'We certainly will. I'll make sure of that!'

The Leviathan looked pleased. 'I will, too. In any case Dolphin Children – we call them Dolphineros now – always work in tandem. You have Belkis's spirit and you'll keep breathing that as you run.'

I felt more confident. 'The Dolphineros – what do they do?'

'For now, let's just say Dolphineros are needed to repair the world.'

'Repair the world?'

'You'd think after countless genocides humankind would cry "Never again!" Not so. These days extermination has become the Saviours' primary strategy and threatens extinction. We aim to stop that. We shall – if we have help from Dolphineros.'

Belkis answered without hesitation: 'I agree!'

Confused as I was, I echoed her. 'Yes.'

Belkis held the Leviathan's hand: 'Now tell us – who are you really?'

'From now on, your mentor.'

My confusion made me officious. 'We should know who appointed you. Who your peers are.'

'Leviathans are not appointed. They've always been around, like the earth, wind, water, fire.'

'Some would say that's blasphemous,' I said.

He humoured me. 'Let's leave blasphemy to those who invent

hollow words. Our mission is to hold Life sacred. We contest the dictum that political power grows out of the barrel of a gun. We oppose violence. We toil for a future where killing will be a bygone pandemic. We expose the Saviours' worship of death in the name of a God or whatever ideology it is that they hold sacred. We send the Dolphineros as emissaries of peace, as life's voice.'

Belkis smiled. 'Great!' she said, and it was. Her views weren't different from mine. But I couldn't help feeling that we were setting out for a parallel world that does not exist.

The Leviathan became milder, almost sad. 'I must warn you: as life's voice, Saviours will try all the harder to destroy you. Even as we protect you from countless ambushes, one day, there will be one that will kill you.'

'And then do the Dolphineros die?' I asked.

'There's no end for Dolphineros. When they pass away – killed or not – they're transmuted into Leviathans. But they never tarry in their Samsara. They come straight back.'

Belkis gasped. 'As you did! Now I know who you are! Hrant Dink!'

That surprised the Leviathan.

Caught in Belkis's fervour, I affirmed. 'Yes! His spitting image! Struck me the moment I saw you!'

The Leviathan laughed dismissively. 'You flatter me.'

He clapped his hands.

Figures started to emerge.

The Leviathan introduced them. 'You asked me before about my peers …'

We stared at the figures. Faces familiar from portraits, sculptures, photographs. Some we could even name: Laozi, Rumi, Galileo, Goya, Neruda, Akhmatova …

@

I stop my history and watch the vendors across the road.

Five women; three men. Sooty and bent like burnt tree trunks. In tatters – probably their only clothes. Crumpled faces crisscrossed with the shame of peddling at street corners. Dimmed eyes sifting passers-by and hoping that one of them – two, if Fate turns compassionate – will buy something. They're farmers who, ejected from the soil by industrial raids, have migrated to urban jungles where, instead of finding streets paved with bread, they found scrawny rats. The only dignity they're left with is the dim memory of the grit their forebears had possessed.

The items they're trying to sell are few: a couple of copper plates, a bunch of wooden spoons, a few embroidered handkerchiefs, a patched jacket, two balaclavas, a threadbare sheepskin coat, a walking stick, a pair of worn-out clogs, a handful of medals …

Is that all they have? If they manage to sell those what will they get? Enough for a loaf? A handful of rice? Some firewood? And afterwards, how will they eat without the copper plates and wooden spoons? How will they keep warm without the jacket, the balaclavas, the sheepskin coat? How will they walk without clogs and stick? How will they wipe tears without their handkerchiefs? How, how will they survive the night?

Do Numen and his lackeys ever see these people?

I have some money. Not much. Leviathans provide Dolphineros with some cash in case of emergencies.

I hand a bill to the café owner and ask him to give the peddlers some snacks and drinks. He's not surprised. He'd do the same if he could spare a penny. People are born generous. If they can help, they will. It is a weakness of Saviours that they can't understand that.

Belkis and Childe Asher appear. My heart swells with happiness and longing.

As ever she has read my mind. 'Our parents must have been just as destitute. Maybe that's why they abandoned us.'

I bristle. 'Mine were taken. Killed.'

Pinkie lights another cigarette and starts messaging on his techset. He doesn't see Belkis and Childe Asher.

Childe Asher has read Pinkie's message and giggles. 'You gave food to the poor so you're a soft subject. He got a reply saying soft subjects are often the most subversive. I think you've got the Pinkie for the day, Dad.'

I snort. 'Like hell!'

Belkis interjects. 'We can whisk you away.'

'I should be able to handle him.'

She kisses me. 'I didn't mean to interfere. Not used to being a Leviathan yet. I get jittery. See you.'

She and Childe Asher vanish.

@

I pay the café owner and leave.

Pinkie follows me.

The vendors shout blessings at me.

I cross to the municipal building across the pier.

I flash my holdall at the doorman.

He waves me in without looking. Oddjobbers are nobodies. Pinkie loiters outside and talks into his mobile.

I make for the toilets and go into a cubicle.

I take out a carrier bag, a pair of weatherworn moccasins, fraying shirt, brown wig, shabby jacket and trousers.

I change my clothes. I sprinkle some sea-salt on the wig to make it look dandruffy and wear it.

I transfer my journal and the spare set of clothes to the backpack.

I stuff my overalls into the carrier bag and dump it into a wastebasket.

Donning the backpack, I leave.

I walk slightly hunched like someone with a bad back.

Pinkie is still outside.

I shuffle past him.

He ignores me. He's expecting an oddjobber.

His masters don't know it yet but tomorrow, from this seemingly torpid me, the real me will emerge.

SATURDAY 10.11

I've reached East Isthmus.

The sea invites.

Not many bathers about. Too early. On Saturdays the affluent indulge in the opportunity to sleep late into the morning.

But it's a good time for African youths. Two boys and two girls are beachcombing.

In Numen's caste system, blacks, as in many countries, are *Others*. Conditioned by history's hoary chestnut of 'purity of blood', they are shunned as humanoids of inferior races and faiths bent on depravity. They don't as yet face, as in some other countries, segregation, debarment from education, dispossession of property, summary imprisonment and extrajudicial executions, but those who can read Numen's mind believe that all those horrors are waiting in the wings.

I watch the youths.

They live in corrugated-iron shacks in the backwoods and trek here early to avoid the crowds. Like all *Others*, they're unwelcome in public places, especially on beaches where supposedly they lust after the bikinied women. Patrols – known as Rottweilers – prowl the city's leisure spots to stop and expel them – often forcefully.

The youths come to beachcomb for driftwood, algae, shells, coins, metals and, especially, odd-shaped or unusually coloured stones for their parents who craft these and sell them. Their artefacts, extolled by avant-garde galleries as 'pantheistic art', have become very trendy. During her pregnancy Belkis purchased three statuettes and lined them up in our grotto as talismans for the family we would become. In time, she mused, such curios might induce the cognoscenti to surmise that African artists might have preceded those of the European cave-dwellers. This is pure Belkis. For her every worthy endeavour is beautiful and timeless; the daily anomalies of Evil and ugliness are simply Saviours' aberrations.

@

I undress to my underpants and shove my clothes into my backpack.

I dive in and swim yearning for Belkis and our carefree pre-Dolphinero days.

I come out, even more impatient for tomorrow.

As I amble towards a spur to get dry, I stop by the African youths.

I offer them some stones I picked up from the sea floor. 'Any use to you?'

They inspect the stones and take three. 'Thanks!'

One of the boys taps my shoulder. 'You swim well.'

'Yes?'

'I'm Idris.' He introduces the others: 'Leila. Razak. Mimosa.'

'Oric.'

We shake hands.

Mimosa, one of the girls, asks. 'You're African, yeah?'

'No.'

'Sure?'

'Yes. Where're you from?'

Idris replies proudly. 'Leila and I from here. Mimosa and Razak are newcomers. From Somalia. And Eritrea.'

'Welcome.'

Razak smirks. 'You're sure you're not African? Only Africans welcome Africans.'

'I'm sure.'

Mimosa scrutinises me. 'Your skin – bronzy. And your hair … We have gingers, too … White father, African mother?'

'No.'

Razak insists. 'You have African blood. We can tell. Maybe in the past …'

Mimosa insists. 'And only Africans swim like you.'

Leila, a quiet type, mutters. 'Maybe you're related to Merman?'

That intrigues me. 'Merman?'

'Yeah …'

'Who's he?'

Idris explains. 'Before our time. Grannies speak of him. Appeared suddenly. No name and God knows where from. Lived on this beach. Water shortages in those days. He figured there was a spring on the seabed. Dived all day looking for it.'

I'm fascinated. 'Did he find it?'

Leila grins. 'No water shortages now.'

'What happened to him?'

Idris sighs. 'He drowned – or so they said. Grannies say, the King got scared of his popularity and had him killed. People forgot him. Only we remember him.'

Razak spits in disgust. 'No room for blacks in whitey heads!'

I sympathise. 'The sea will remember him. Water's like earth. It never forgets.'

Mimosa whoops delightedly. 'We say that, too!'

Razak, who's been keeping watch, tenses up. 'Company!'

I spot several Rottweilers sauntering towards us.

Idris bucks up. 'Got to scram!'

I nod.

They run off.

The Rottweilers, except for their Sergeant, chase them.

I note they'll never catch them. I'm pleased.

The Sergeant sizes me up. 'The jigaboos – friends, are they?'

I glare at him. 'Jigaboos?'

'Jungle bunnies …'

'You mean the kids?'

'They're not kids. They're Scum! Lepers!'

I remain passive. 'They were passing by. Friendly lot.'

'Trash always acts friendly. What did they want?'

'Nothing.'

'What's your business here?'

'Came for a swim.'

'Moocher, eh?'

'Hardly. Been working all night.'

'Doing what?'

'Book-keeping.'

'It's holiday – "History Unbound."'

'Some of us – like you – have to work on holidays.'

He doesn't dispute the point but remains suspicious. 'What did the coons want?'

I bristle. 'I told you – nothing.'

'They always want something …'

'I've nothing of value. Some coins …'

'That'll do.'

I face him angrily. 'They were showing me some stones …'

Rottweilers don't like commoners standing up to them. It insults their machismo. 'You're not street-wise, are you? They were distracting you. Pickpockets' oldest trick. Check your money.'

I show him my wallet. 'Nothing taken.'

He spits. 'You're lucky. We scared them off. Next time avoid them like syphilis!'

His men have given up chasing the youths.

Angrily, the Sergeant goes to join them.

I move to the spur to soak up the sun.

I think about the Merman. Surely a Leviathan …

I pick up my journal.

OPERATION PURSUIT OF HAPPINESS

A Dolphineros team is structured in units of two 'companions' who never abandon each other. That guaranteed that Belkis and I would always stay together.

The Leviathans extended our capabilities with intense courses.

Physical and mental fitness, of course, was imperative.

Since missions might take us anywhere, we had to be polyglots, too. Incredibly that proved easy. The Leviathans, asserting that the brain is the depository of every language, tapped deeply into our unconscious and released them.

History asserts that the oldest profession is slavery. When Hrant proposed that we should join an operation aiming to rescue some victims, we agreed immediately.

Code-named *Pursuit of Happiness* after that sublime phrase in America's Declaration of Independence, the operation was proposed by JJ, a prominent campaigner against racial, religious and gender discrimination in the USA.

While planning the operation, JJ secured funding not only from anti-slavery and human rights organisations, but also from a bevy of cosmopolitan billionaires eager to support humanitarian causes instead of indulging in châteaux, yachts and football clubs.

He also recruited a team of intelligence wizards – nicknamed *The Magi* – and installed them in London to provide logistical support.

Then he approached the Dolphineros in every country. Thousands volunteered. After months of scrupulous deliberations with *The Magi* and a large cadre of Leviathans, he formed a task-force which possessed physical and psychological stamina, special skills and familiarity with the targeted regions' geography, ethos and lifestyles.

JJ proved a master planner. He created a task force comprising 592 Dolphineros split into 296 teams from 88 countries and structured in units of two.

Every team was equipped with first-aid kits, satellite-phones, radios and tracking devices. Most teams were made up of male and female Dolphineros.

The task force's inordinate size was vital. Despite our concern for the thousands who needed to be rescued, we had to give precedence to those in imminent danger. *The Magi* compiled a priority list but forewarned us that we would rescue only a fraction of them. There were, of course, many contingency plans. But no plan guarantees success. We had to accept that there would be disasters.

Since the operation encompassed many countries, it was divided into six tranches. JJ code-named them after Raoul Wallenberg, the Swedish diplomat who saved many Jews during the Holocaust only to perish in a Soviet gulag.

I note below JJ's summary of the Wallenbergs:

Wallenbergs I was assigned to Africa and briefed to free: a) activists from Mauritania's oppressed black populations; b) girls abducted in Nigeria; c) Tuareg secessionists in Mali; d) youngsters from Cameroon and Chad sex trade; e) adults from Niger and Benin sold for organ transplants; f) imprisoned Eritrean journalists; g) Sudanese and Somalian boys for sale as child soldiers.

Many stages of this operation involved long and arduous treks through inhospitable desert routes known only to smugglers. Despite tips on acclimatisation given by Mauritanian and Malian Dolphineros, the Sahara's heat and sandstorms proved a bane to European teams.

In Mauritania where bribery is a traditional custom, envelopes of euros to notable 'white' officials secured the freedom of six political prisoners and fifteen young Fula and Soninké activists slaving in state-run agricultural compounds.

Bribery also enabled the Dolphineros to smuggle out five Eritrean editors arrested for daring to publish independent newspapers.

Four Tuareg leaders targeted by Ansar Dine, the Jihadist group that strove to impose a fundamentalist regime in Mali, were secreted into Senegal with the cooperation of activists. These men, prominent in the 2012 Tuareg rebellion for an independent state, *Azawad*, still campaigned to preserve their nomadic culture, a syncretism of Berber mythology and Islam.

Seventeen Nigerian school-girls kidnapped to breed future Jihadists were rescued after additional payments of danger money to facilitators.

Ransoms to human traffickers freed twenty-three men and women from Cameroon, Mali and Chad being groomed for prostitution in Europe, sixteen adults from Niger and Benin corralled for organ transplants and fifteen Sudanese and Somalian boys training under Al-Shabaab, the Somalian Jihadist group as soldiers-cum-suicide-bombers.

Three tragedies struck Wallenbergs I.

The first hit the Irish and Italian teams. While crossing the Sahara in Niger they were swept away by a freak sand drift. Mercifully the people they had rescued were picked up by another team using the same route.

The second occurred in Chad. A caravan of salt-traders coming across four teams and their charges mistook them for marauding nomads and opened fire. By the time they realised that the teams and their wards were unarmed, they had killed Khalil from Tunisia and severely injured Amina from Morocco.

The third transpired when an encounter in Sudan with an Al-Shabaab squad developed into a skirmish killing Somalia's Maxamed, and South Africa's Siyabonga. Only a reckless attack by the remaining Dolphineros and their wards forced Al-Shabaab to flee.

Eventually reaching Djibouti, the teams were flown to Paris where anti-slavery organisations took care of the rescued. The fact that 101 lives had been saved, offered scant consolation for the loss of seven Dolphineros and one paralysed for life.

Wallenbergs II were to free: a) women from Indo-China groomed for sex trade or enforced marriages; b) Malaysian youths on sale for organ transplants; c) Thai peasants in debt bondage; d) Filipino workers and domestics in slavery in Arab countries. e) Cambodian activists, writers, and intellectuals; f) Rohingyas in Myanmar facing ethnic cleansing; g) Uyghur human rights activists in China.

Poverty-stricken Laos, ruled by a communist military politburo, was rife with human rights abuses, extrajudicial killings, corruption and favouritism. Cambodia, an equally poor fledgling constitutional monarchy, was still recovering from Pol Pot's genocidal rule. In the prevailing disquiet, dollars deposited in Western banks proved effective sweeteners for officials.

In Laos, the teams were able to 'purchase' twenty-eight women ensnared for the European sex trade, eighteen men in debt bondage and twelve imprisoned dissenters and religious activists.

Equally successful in Cambodia, they bought twenty-two dissidents, journalists, writers and bloggers incarcerated in Social Rehabilitation Centres for criticising the regime and eleven evicted smallholders condemned to forced labour.

Myanmar proved a dangerous theatre. Ruled by military dictatorship for decades – abetted by owners of the jade mines in the north – its primary conflict involved the Rohingya, an indigenous Muslim minority in Rakhine State that the authorities refused Myanmar nationality. The Buddhist monks' organisation, Ma-Ba-Tha, alleging that the Muslims intended to devour them 'like cat-fish' became militant; so did the Arakan Rohingya Salvation Army (ARSA) that claimed to defend the Rohingyas.

Helped by pacifists from both factions, teams from Australia, New Zealand and South Korea hiked to a Rohingya community hiding in the sparsely populated Chin State's mountains. Dividing the people into manageable batches and trekking along craggy tracks, they transported all 115 Rohingya to the Irrawaddy Delta where they rendezvoused with an Indonesian junk hired by *The Magi* and sailed to Singapore.

The rescue proved providential for in August 2017, the government, using an ARSA attack as an excuse, descended on Rakhine Province and destroyed numerous villages and killed many of the inhabitants.

Other countries imposed dangerous situations, too.

Thailand was beleaguered by the Muslim Patani Liberation Front. Buddhist and Christian minorities in Malaysia, a federal constitutional monarchy that delegates to Sharia courts such religious matters as marriage, inheritance, divorce, apostasy and conversion, remained unsettled. Indonesia struggled with sectarian violence. Coup attempts, drug gangs, communist insurgents and overt hostilities from Muslim Moro separatists constantly plagued Democratic Philippines.

Nonetheless in Thailand, the Dolphineros freed sixty-two enslaved farmers, eleven youngsters sold for organ transplants, and nineteen young men and women trafficked for sex. In Malaysia, they rescued twelve young girls who were to be sold for marriages and three men who, choosing to convert to Catholicism, had been indicted for apostasy by Sharia Courts.

In Indonesia, they smuggled out eight male and seven female teenagers abducted for radicalisation. And in the Philippines, they bought thirty-six young women marketed as domestics to Saudi Arabia, and forty-eight men selected for slave labour in Kuwait, Bahrain, Qatar, United Arab Emirates and Oman.

They transported their charges, in yet more hired junks, to Singapore and thence by air to South Korea and Japan. Dismally, the mission to Xinjiang, China, failed. The teams, while able to liaise with each other, failed to establish links with Uyghur activists. The teams soon discovered that the Chinese government had built numerous detention camps all over Xinjiang with the objective of indoctrinating over a million Uyghurs into the joys of vocational education, Chinese nationalism and the Communist Party's humane laws. We had one satisfaction: we had alerted the world to the fact that many more internment camps were being built and gave the locations of those already in use.

Wallenbergs III were assigned to Asia to free: a) persecuted Christian priests, Buddhists, Ahmadiyya leaders and Iranian Bahá'í refugees; b) men in debt bondage; c) adults pressed into organ donation or domestic serfdom; d) Afghan youths being radicalised; e) Indian children sold for slave-labour.

The operation had a gratifying start. The teams sent to India, Bangladesh and Pakistan proved experts at bribery and bought out a total of 109 men, women and children from debt bondage.

Then we suffered two tragedies.

The first involved three teams transporting to Puducherry, in a hired bus, a community of forty-one Buddhists who, hounded by Pakistan's Jamaat-e-Islami activists, had had to shelter in the mountains.

According to a shepherd, the bus, driving through Odisha province on a pot-holed road made even more taxing by the monsoon, skidded into a ravine as it tried to avoid a cow. Noone survived.

The second tragedy struck the UK team of Torrance and Abigail who rendezvoused with six Iranian Bahá'í Teachers in Pakistan. The Teachers, accused of worshipping the false messiah, al-Masih ad-Dajjal, by obscurantist Pakistani Fundamentalists, had had to go into hiding.

Torrance and Abigail smuggled them into India and then,

renting a minivan, set out for Puducherry. Driving through the Sahyardi region they were ambushed by Maoist Naxalites. When these insurgents, mainly indigenous Adivasi, demanded cash and valuables, Torrance and Abigail gave them all they possessed. The Naxalites then turned to the Teachers, dragged them out of the minivan and shot them.

The other missions went according to plan.

Teams from Europe made their way to a ruined monastery on the outskirts of Lahore where thirteen Christian priests – 'a humble mirage of The Last Supper', as their elder Father Clement jested – had taken refuge. Furnishing them with false ID documents and acting as a group of hikers, they crossed into India at the Wagah border-post. Thereafter they proceeded to Amritsar and then by train to Puducherry.

Other teams rescued eighteen Afghan youths from the Taliban; freed ninety-two Indian, Pakistani and Sri Lankan bonded labourers in the Arabian Peninsula; and bought twenty-one Indian children slaving in cottage industries. They were all flown from Puducherry on various holiday charters to Norway, Sweden, Denmark, Germany, Italy and the UK.

Though the whole operation rescued hundreds of souls, it claimed the lives of many others.

Wallenbergs IV were assigned to Latin America and the Caribbean.

They were commissioned to free: a) journalists, writers, lawyers and security personnel targeted for assassination by drug lords; b) politicos hunted by death squads; c) foreigners forced into the drug trade; d) persecuted transgenders, gays and lesbians; e) kidnapped aid volunteers; f) indigenes held hostage by coca growers; g) campaigners for the conservation of the Amazon.

The eight Dolphineros of the four Mexican teams – Raul, Ines, Lautaro, Magdalena, Jerònimo, Carlos, Ricardo and Matteo – escorting to safe houses three journalists, six public prosecutors, two incorruptible police chiefs and eleven social workers, were all murdered in separate ambushes. The killings proved yet again that Mexico's Security Services were riddled with informers.

Medellin Cartel's hatchetmen also targeted the teams sent to rescue backpackers and campesinos coerced to deliver drugs to Haiti, Dominica, Belize and Honduras. As a result, five Dolphineros – Costa Rican Ciprina, Nicaraguan Xochitl, Cuban Silverio, Panamanian Ernesto and Guyanese Yannick – were killed and seven Dolphineros – three of them seriously – were injured. Those unscathed – carrying their wounded comrades – barely managed to reach the safety of Nicaragua's Little Corn Island. The grief of so many casualties and the failure to save a single person hit us very hard.

While teams from Brazil and Argentina succeeded in freeing thirteen politicos in Guatemala, yet another tragedy struck two American teams. Death-squads, liaising with the Guatemalan Clandestine Security Apparatus, managed to track the four Dolphineros – Dwight, Melanie, Leroy and Roberto – as they rendezvoused with six Mayan elders in the highlands and summarily executed them all.

Mercifully, the other missions ended satisfactorily. They rescued thirteen lesbians, gays and transgenders in Jamaica; six aid workers kidnapped for ransom in Haiti; five Ecuadorian journalists; the four lawyers defending them; and nine conservationists campaigning against the ecological devastation of the Amazon.

Twenty-one shepherds and nine indigene leaders used as slave labour by the coca growers were freed with the collaboration of both the Colombian Government and the FARC guerrillas.

Despite the fact that Wallenger IV suffered the loss of seventeen Dolphineros, and thirty victims they had failed to save, the teams had freed eighty-four people. This outcome was far below JJ's expectations, but it confirmed his conviction that the world needed Dolphineros more than ever.

Wallenbergs V were assigned to Islamic regions of the Former Soviet Union.

They were to rescue: a) dissident politicians and journalists; b) persecuted Russian priests; c) ethnic leaders; d) gay activists; e) people in bondage; f) a community of Jews; g) women facing sterilisation.

In Azerbaijan the teams, exploiting the country's raging corruption, freed six imprisoned journalists and four Armenian activists still campaigning for the disputed territory, Nagorno-Karabakh.

Kazakhstan's ethnic conflicts, economic troubles and the despotic Nursham's wily policies of divide and rule enabled the teams to manoeuvre with some ease. Bribing their way through officialdom, they smuggled out three editors and seven journalists; snatched nine Russian Orthodox priests and nine hieromonks under house arrest for practising religion outside state control; and liberated eight gay-rights activists and six minority elders. They led their charges via nomadic trails across steppes and taigas to the bordering Russian Republic, Altai.

The autocratic regimes of Tajikistan, Turkmenistan and Uzbekistan made the teams' manoeuvrability exacting. But the Dolphineros – all native activists and proficient in their countries' traditions – achieved appreciable success.

Hacking with precision through Tajikistan's tight control of the social media, they freed eight journalists. Then, trekking through the drug routes of the Pamir Mountains, they smuggled the journalists into Afghanistan and delivered them to Canadian Aid workers.

In Turkmenistan they freed seven broadcasters threatened with having 'their tongues shrivelled'; twelve Baluch activists campaigning for the restoration of their forbidden language and customs; thirteen Russian and nine Armenian priests; and eleven activists from the discriminated Kazakh, Tatar and Pashtun minorities. They were all smuggled into Russia in a cargo plane from Turkmenbashy International Airport.

The power struggle of members of Uzbekistan's Supreme Assembly allowed the teams to operate with relative freedom. As the dollar was stronger than God, hefty handouts liberated sixteen imprisoned dissidents; twenty-one men and women in bondage – a tiny portion of the four percent of the population living as slaves; thirty-two Jews from Samarkand; and fourteen women facing sterilisation. All these people, provided with forged passports, were flown from Bukhara to Russia on scheduled flights.

Wallenbergs VI, assigned to the Middle East, were to rescue: a) a conclave of progressive Sunni and Shia imams sought by both the Yemeni government and Houthi rebels; b) Yemeni children in war zones; c) Saudi women accused of adultery; d) Iranian converts to Christianity; e) homosexuals; f) enslaved Bangladeshi, Filipino and Indonesian domestics; g) Syrian democrats hunted by the Syrian Saviour Hakim.

Despite the region's numerous conflicts, most of these assignments went according to plan.

But we suffered a tragedy in Yemen.

Saudi Arabia, fearful that the new Houthi-Iran alliance threatened Sunni domination of the region, formed a coalition with Egypt, Kuwait, Morocco, Bahrain, Sudan and Qatar. With material and political support from the USA and the UK, the conflict escalated into an implacable Civil War.

The Dolphineros arrived at the height of this War.

Four teams rounded up eighty-four orphaned children and conveyed them to Mocha, the old coffee port on the Red Sea, from where they would sail across the Bab-el-Mandeb Strait to Djibouti. Their arrival coincided with Saudi bombardments of Houthi positions in Mocha. Though the teams managed to keep the children safe in the surrounding scrubland, their boat was destroyed and its captain and crew of three were killed.

Tonton promptly met the children and their Dolphineros

at a cove near Mocha and cramming them all into his *baghlah*, delivered them to Djibouti.

But Al Qaeda located the safehouse where the Imams were hiding and sent a couple of suicide-bombers. The eighteen Imams and the Dolphineros who were guarding them were killed.

Three Saudi teams liberated six 'adulterous' women sentenced by Sharia courts to decapitation. The indictments, the *Magi* had ascertained, had been fabricated in every case by the women's husbands who hoped to receive *diyya* – blood money – from the women's families. Since the women's families could not – or would not – pay the *diyya*, the teams readily paid out the demanded sums.

Other teams liberated seventeen Filipino, Bangladeshi and Indonesian domestics by offering compensation to the Saudis who 'owned' them. The negotiations went smoothly because the 'owners' were rapacious nouveau-riches who could easily purchase other domestics from the flourishing market.

Four Iranians accused of apostasy for having converted to Christianity with the intention of becoming missionaries – offences that carried the death penalty – had gone into hiding in the mountains near the Turkish border to evade Iran's notorious Guidance Patrol.

The Iranian team went to Urmia, the capital of Iran's West Azerbaijan Province, to find and rescue these men. Posing very convincingly as activists of a Christian Aid organisation, they discreetly questioned the registered worshippers of Urmia's historic Cathedral of St Mary the Mother of God. They found out that the men moved from place to place and only appeared at odd times by an old disused sheepcote to pick up provisions. The Dolphineros duly proceeded to the sheepcote and waited until the men appeared. Then, handing them forged papers, they rendezvoused with an Armenian itinerant tradesman who took them in his minivan to Turkey through the Sero border crossing.

The Syrian team smuggled out a pacifist politician facing

assassination for opposing Hakim's genocidal regime. The politician – and his family of six – were transported in a fishing boat to the RAF base in Cyprus and flown to England where they were granted asylum.

And so *Operation Pursuit of Happiness* ended. Though it had saved over a thousand lives, it had lost many others. We were left with the feeling that we had achieved only a Pyrrhic victory. Nonetheless, the number of people saved drove JJ to plan a second operation – one for which Belkis and I would certainly volunteer.

I look at the sea wistfully.

Belkis and Childe Asher are paddling. Hrant, too. My triad watching over me, but keeping their distance to leave me with my thoughts.

I remember how Belkis coaxed Hrant to agree to be called by a name. 'Leviathans prefer to be anonymous. But if you must have a name for me, pick one,' he said. And that's what she did.

He's proof that death is a lie. That doesn't mean Leviathans don't bleed. They bleed all the time.

SATURDAY 10.17

The sun is rising rapidly. Is it rushing me to tomorrow?

I'm passing through Shalimar, the garden suburb gilded with the cumulus of privilege.

Inflated Indian bureaucrats, carrying golf bags like trophies, are piling into chauffeur-driven cars. Their wives, stylish in haute-couture, are waving goodbye to fancy-dressed children as maids take them to History Unbound parties. On patios girls skip rope, play hopscotch and boys kick balls. Scents of freshly cut grass, chlorinated swimming pools and barbecues suffuse the air.

I could be inside a glossy brochure. The mansions are pseudo-Arcadian. But they look like off-the-peg strongholds which, even with heavy electronic gates, seem pregnable.

Ranged around kitschy shopping centres, they have been specially built for Numen's long train of yes-people who massage his megalomania in pecking order. The enclave has an undertone of impermanence. The voices are either mollusc-flat or affected falsettos. Hearty laughter sounds emphysemic. The residents know that their tenancy depends on Numen's idiosyncratic computations of their servility and that, therefore, the luxurious air they breathe is transitory.

Hrant often said this retinue, too, must yearn for a country where moral virtue displaces oppression. But if they do, then they must also wonder whether such a change, assuming it's possible, would be too Spartan. So they straitjacket their tongues, sew up their ears, blindfold their eyes and barter their souls in Faustian deals for a speculative existence of milk and honey.

I pity this menagerie of lackeys. I can detect Fear's yellow-green cloud hanging over their straw bastions.

I know Fear only too well.

He's a trickster that spreads disbelief. He has a favourite magician's hat: the word 'might'. A word which connotes 'power', 'impunity', 'persecution', 'weapons', 'violence'. From this hat he pulls out sharks that munch one's innards. For 'might' also disseminates the probability that a world cocooned by love was not necessarily tableted by the Creator, that all our aspirations to uphold Good and defeat Evil *might* just be vanity of vanities.

I know Belkis and Childe Asher are nearby. I murmur. 'You think I might run away again?'

No reply. I understand. It's a question only I can answer.

Which I will tomorrow.

Although I have Belkis's sprit implanted in me, I'm still afflicted with primal forebodings. When I'm haunted, I blame her for forcing me to become a Dolphinero. I know that's unjust. She didn't force me. I agreed – rashly – as those slow in mind do. I didn't want to expose my weakness. I deluded myself that I had the requisite qualities, that I could follow her example.

She worked hard to nurture me into a Dolphinero. Held me to her bosom unreservedly. Never revealed her qualms. She saw, very early on, I had phantoms; that Fear, in particular, stalked me. 'Touch your heart,' she said; 'Life needs Dolphineros. We *are* Dolphineros – that's the truth. All we need is fortitude. We have that. Because we know death is a lie,' she said …

As history has reminded us, 'fear of Fear' is the threat. We must confront it. Eyeball to eyeball. Know thine enemy etcetera. But that's bravado. Fear never stops attacking. How many souls can withstand that? I become catatonic. Conscientious thoughts fall comatose. My breath turns yellow-green with halitosis.

I should admit I portray my phantoms, too. Not as behemoths with blood-shot eyes and thousand-and-one tentacles flashing daggers. I don't have that sort of imagination. Whenever I try to conjure their physiognomies I come up with a blank mass. How can one face the faceless?

So, I cheat. I humanise my phantoms. Give them ordinary features like people I've come across and with whom I sometimes shared bread. In fact, I see them as victims, too, and try to befriend them. But they harangue me. 'Death is real,' they say, 'it's *not* a lie!'

Of course, I try to ignore them. But are those demons telling me something crucial about Death, something only they know?

I often see my mother. The mother I so briefly knew. I watch her beatific face as a midwife places me on her lap. I watch her suckling me. I watch her holding my frightened father's hand as soldiers approach. I see her triumphant as she hands me to a woman who hides with me in the woods and later hands me over to the Red Cross. I watch the soldiers chain my mother and my father to a rock in the badlands – fodder for wild animals like Prometheus. I watch her strangle my father with her chains to stop him suffering. And I watch her grapple with vultures until she and they tear each other apart.

My mother appeared again in a dream last night.

She held me and sighed. 'Poor Oric – bereft without his Belkis.'

I tried to comfort her. 'Not for long, Mother …'

She wailed. 'What do you know about Death? What *can* you know?' Then she drifted into a vast pit of twisted human remains.

What do I know about Death? I certainly don't know if it's real or a lie. But I know that if it's real it's brutal and humiliating. And I know if I don't share Belkis's fate I would become an unquiet spirit. Her name would be carved on my tomb, but my bones would never lie next to hers.

I go into a park, sit under a willow and pick up where I left in my journal.

RUSSIAN PUNCTUATION

Before we could be assigned to a Wallenberg, we embarked on a series of solo training missions. For our first we were sent to St Petersburg to collect a flash-drive that contained encodements of top-secret communiqués detailing Plutovich's plan to weaken Western democracies with cyberattacks and assassinations of world leaders likely to foil him. Briefing us, Hrant explained that transmitting intelligence of such importance electronically or by diplomatic bag – not as safe as it was purported to be – would be too risky. The flash-drive had to be collected in person.

The incriminating data had been compiled by a reputable historian, Yevgeny Ulyanov, who had hidden it in the manuscript of his explosive new book about the October Revolution. We were sent as excited publicity representatives of his European publisher. On arrival we phoned Yevgeny to arrange a rendezvous. Agreeing to see us the next day, he suggested that rather than meeting at his agent's stuffy office we should enjoy a leisurely lunch at Peterhof Grand Palace, a must-see marvel for tourists some fifty kilometres from St Petersburg on the Gulf of Finland's southern shore. The serenity of the place, he cryptically added, would salve our nerves.

We were indeed nervous – certainly because of mission-jitters, but also because of a niggling feeling that though while speaking on the phone Yevgeny had sounded eager to meet us – even boasted exuberantly about his book – his voice had betrayed flashes of dread. The odd clicks on the line suggested that his amiability had not been for our ears only. Obviously, his anti-authority blogs had spurred the VSH to keep him under surveillance, but had they now received intelligence about the encodements in the flash-drive? When he said 'salve our nerves', did he mean that VSH suspected our well-publicised meeting was not just a publicity appointment?

For our rendezvous, we took the hydrofoil from the Hermitage Museum's Embankment. The trip failed to calm our nerves.

Walking up from Peterhof's pier through the Lower Gardens to the Grand Palace, we remained alert, but we didn't spot anyone tailing us. As we approached the Grand Cascade, we saw Yevgeny standing by the main pool admiring Mikhail Kozlovsky's majestic 'Samson' sculpture. On the phone, he'd described how we'd recognise him. 'Writers fall into three categories,' he'd said: 'one: the outré, impeccably dressed, including bow ties and something in the buttonhole à la Oscar Wilde; two: Bohemian-like debauchees on a picnic in the woods; and three: shadowless shadows pickled in vodka like myself. You'll peg me straightaway.' With state-of-the-art unkempt hair and beard, a *muzhik*'s tunic, loose Turkic *shalwars*, flip-flops and a weathered satchel dangling from his shoulder, he looked like an understudy for Tolstoy.

He *was* under surveillance. Three couples seemingly awed by the Grand Cascade triangulated him. Young and fit, they were unmistakably VSH.

We strode over to him.

The three couples, maintaining their distances, edged closer.

One of the women, ostensibly videoing the surroundings with a camcorder, filmed us.

As we introduced ourselves Yevgeny kissed us the Russian way, several times on the cheek. 'You look just as I imagined. Book-kulaks. Right?'

We concurred.

'My English okay?'

'Excellent.'

'Self-taught. First Enid Blyton. Now on Classics. Shakespeare. Brontës. Dickens. Hardy. Can't go wrong, eh?'

'No.'

'Okay. Pleasure before business. I'll show you around. Okay?'

'Fine.'

'Palace first. Then lunch – and business. Then goodbye. Come!'

We followed him.

Yevgeny rambled on as we toured the Grand Palace. He explained that Peter the Great had ordered its construction to rival Versailles, the palace of his contemporary, Louis XIV of France.

The German occupation during World War Two destroyed many of the sixty-four fountains, ravaged the Palace and left one of the wings burning. Admittedly much has been restored since; nonetheless it would still take years to renovate the rest. Of the Palace's thirty-odd rooms two, the East and the West Chinese cabinets, had exquisite landscape paintings in yellow and black lacquer. The cynosure was the Chesma Hall where twelve great paintings by the German artist, Jacob Philipp Hackert, commemorated Russia's naval victory over the Ottomans at Chesma in the Aegean – an amazing feat given that the Russian fleet had deployed from the Baltic Sea to lure the Ottomans away from the Black Sea.

Then it was time for lunch. We had the choice of three restaurants. One was courtly, exorbitant even for 'tourists' like us. The second catered for guided tours and was always crowded and noisy. The third, the proletariat's café, served a selection of fast food.

Yevgeny pointed at the posh restaurant. 'We deserve that one.'

We went there.

As two pairs of agents stayed outside in case we tried to get away, the third couple found a table close to us. They placed their techset on the table; its tiny red light indicated that it was already on.

I noted that Yevgeny was also aware – had been aware – of being under surveillance. But he hadn't alerted us. Did he think we'd panic?

We had a lavish lunch. Yevgeny chose the most expensive items on the menu with a large dish of caviar as 'pièce de résistance' and two flagons of vodka to wash them down. The techset couple restricted themselves to a frugal vegetarian fare. Obviously, the agents' employers was miserly with expenses. I felt sorry for them.

Finally, dessert over, Yevgeny, sipping his second vintage cognac, opened his satchel. 'Business now!'

He handed us the flash drive. 'This is it! My book – it will make waves I'm sure.'

I noticed the flash drive's high capacity: 512 gigabytes. Obviously, masses of stuff in it. I pocketed it. 'Thanks.'

He smiled – probably for the video footage, I thought. 'No, it is *I* who must thank *you*. You're my midwives!'

He took out a thick manuscript from his satchel and opened it at a random page. 'This is my master print copy. Same version as what's on the drive. I've added some photos of me for your publicity. The book is important – it's my masterpiece. Now look carefully at the text. Examine the Cyrillic alphabet. There were minor differences in the past. Since 1990 we have modified most of them. So, I want you to instruct your editors to study my style, comb the text meticulously, make sure there are no anachronisms. Ditto the punctuation!'

Belkis nodded. 'I'm sure the translators would know what to do. They are the best in Europe. And I believe they already have your instructions.'

'Even so. Insist on these points!'

I reassured him. 'We will.'

Yevgeny turned prolix. 'I may sound paranoid but I'm a perfectionist. For me conjugations and punctuations are kleptomaniacs – like life. Some meanings always get pickpocketed. Translators must be detectives – find the gold; get rid of the mica around it. This is possible with words. But much more difficult with punctuation. Because even as principles remain the same, applications vary. Let them look at the text like at a map – language's map; my map. Tell them to explore the jungle of my mind and discover what I put consciously or unconsciously. Why did I use a full stop or a comma or a colon? Is there a double-entendre? Something left unsaid? A change of nuance? There are many banana skins in punctuation marks. Full stops and commas especially. They're like milestones. Full stops bring new thoughts, new departures, something insignificant that might or might not grow big or create change. So, let them pause, think, decide. Patiently – not once or twice but ten, twenty, as many times as necessary. Comma says: take breath, reflect. Any clarification needed? A signpost for what's to come? An aside revealing a secret? Again patience! Ten, twenty, breaths … I make these points because I know quick decisions can mislead or trick. Decisions are not clairvoyants. Right ones improve the translation. Wrong ones, the opposite …'

When he finished his speech, he looked drained.

I should admit Yevgeny's logorrhoea had engaged me. I thought it wasn't just bluster. There was, I felt, a pointer, a veiled instruction. When, later, I discussed his antics with Belkis, she remarked that she, too, had been mystified by it.

As I paid the enormous bill, Yevgeny chuckled. 'Make sure you hand in the receipt as expenses! No doubt they'll be furious at its size! Just tell them even workers must have a blowout now and again. That will be their punishment for being rich!'

I pocketed the receipt, imagining Hrant's shock when he converted the roubles into euros.

We said good-bye outside the Restaurant. Yevgeny was going to take the bus to Veliky Novgorod – or Novgorod as he insisted calling it by its pre-1999 name – where he lived and which he patriotically regarded as the place where Russia was really born.

After the long-drawn embraces, he dug into his satchel again and brought out two Matryoshka nesting dolls. Graciously, he handed them to us. 'Souvenir from Russia. Every visitor must have one! Particularly, new friends.'

As he walked away, two sets of the agents followed him. The techset couple stayed on and followed us into the hydrofoil.

When we disembarked at St Petersburg, four more VSH agents met the techset couple. Together, they arrested us on the suspicion that we were carrying contraband materials.

At the detention centre, they confiscated the flash-drive. We would remain in custody while their experts examined it.

They scanned and tested the Matryoshka nesting dolls and found nothing. We had verified that they were empty on the hydrofoil – but feared that they might plant some drugs to incriminate us.

We were then dragged into a cell in the middle of the night and – much to Belkis' horror and protestations – were strip searched and our whole bodies were sadistically investigated for 'alien matter'.

At some point during these proceedings, we asked about Yevgeny. They told us he was fine, celebrating his 'sudden prosperity' with a barrel of vodka.

We were released five days later with profuse apologies and all our belongings returned, including the flash-drive, the Matryoshka dolls and our receipt from the Peterhof restaurant. Then we were escorted to the Finland Station – famous for Lenin's return from his exile in Switzerland – and put on the train to Helsinki.

Two months later, Hrant reported that the contents of the flash-drive was hailed as one of the most daring whistleblowing coups of all time. Yevgeny had proved to be a tech wizard. He had hidden the communiqués in pixels inside various letters and punctuation marks – an ingenious development inspired by the old microdot system – that could only be opened as a file by using as passwords various combinations of the letters and numbers on my credit card receipt from the Peterhof restaurant. Since no other item in the world would have the same letters and numbers as the receipt no expert in the world – including Yevgeny himself – would have been able to decipher the passwords. This not only explained Yevgeny's tirade on punctuation, but also his insistence on safekeeping the receipt.

The exposure of Plutovich's strategic plans – vehemently denied by Russia as 'pure imaginative concoction' – stirred the Western governments to set up countermeasures.

When eventually Yevgeny's book was internationally published – even a samizdat edition appeared in Russia – it was hailed as the most illuminative chronicle of Bolshevik activities in the years leading to the Revolution.

But, alas, by that time, Yevgeny could not reap the accolades.

The VSH, outraged that it had been outwitted, countered in its traditional way. On a grey day, while waiting at a bus stop, Yevgeny suffered an anaphylactic attack. Breathless, his skin bursting with hives, he expired within minutes. The Russian media reported that he had been stung by a wasp – fatally allergic in his case – and praised him for his 'valuable contribution to history'. A photograph from cctv footage showing a bystander 'accidentally' scratching Yevgeny's ankle with her umbrella was quickly suppressed – but not before it went viral on the internet.

SATURDAY 11.05

I'm in Nestville, that motley of shanties which, erected overnight, shingle the Eastern hills. This is the district where flocks of landsmen winged over with their families and built their 'nests'. The 'ville' derives from a Swiss environmentalist's report.

Like the landsmen, they came seeking employment. Some did find work, mainly menial. Others, taking on casual jobs for pittances, toil day and night. The lucky few who've acquired a trade valiantly feign assimilation, but their eyes remain jaundiced with alienation.

In Numen's social categorisation, Nestvillians are squatters. Their petitions for the basic amenities of sewage, water, gas, electricity and refuse collection end up in shredders. Recently, however, in the way all activists are born from a necessity that others do not always see, they've demanded a council of their own in lieu of the tin-gods the municipality occasionally sends.

Today, vaulting like ibexes through mazes where shacks stand only by leaning against each other, they're on the move. Speculating that the celebration of the Union Made in Heaven would spotlight their demands, they've organised a demonstration to take place in Glorious Acre.

This is the lea where, in bygone days, the nation's armies drilled and paraded. A French historian awed by the expanse which enabled pikemen, archers, harquebusiers, grenadiers, cannoneers and cavalry to train together called it *Champ de Mars* after the Roman God of War. Later, as advances in weaponry raced away and warfare became an art, the Military relocated its Forces to grandiose garrisons. Thereafter the citizens reclaimed the lea, particularly the areas that quartered supply depots and camp followers.

The location, rapidly developing into an agglomeration of band stands, pleasure gardens, food-stalls and booths that sold everything from buns to saints' relics, soon gained popularity. For almost a century, it was extolled, in evocation of the lush grounds in Bunyan's *Pilgrim's Progress,* as Beulah Moor.

Today, imbued with nostalgia, people still wax lyrical about Beulah Moor. They remember the heady ambiance of shady trees, fragrant flowerbeds, raffish musicians, enticing booths and exotic eateries. This was not only the city's sole corner that belonged to everybody, but also the turf where they could dexterously hone their ingenuity. Here was the subversive melting pot where bachelors, spinsters, matchmakers, fortune-tellers, peasants, shepherds, coachmen, labourers, chisellers, artisans, hawkers, scribes and mendicants could haggle, laugh and squabble with the upper classes. This was the place, too, where the hungry found crusts, the plebs overspent on knick-knacks, the porcine gorged on confection and the parvenus regaled rare delicacies. Remarkably, they did so without forfeiting dignity or losing the illusion of freedom that permeated the minty air.

Today Glorious Acre is again a military showpiece. Numen trumpeted the appellation with the declaration that he was, at last, bestowing upon the country its long-merited apotheosised site – a site as evocative as Moscow's Red Square. 'Glory', he rhapsodised, is epitomised by the grandstand that overlooks the vast parade ground where the procession of his armaments warns the world that, like the shark, he has 'pearly white teeth'. 'Acre', he piously added, conjures 'God's acre', the graveyard where the dead await resurrection on Judgement Day. Latterly, in one of his oxymoronic statements, he declared that without his arsenal, without his lionhearted warriors, without the fertilisation of fallen heroes' sacred blood, he could not have become the fervent pacifist that he is.

Nestvillians are unmoved by such cant. Their concern is the

present. With that sudden vigour of turtle-paced, faceless folk that repeatedly surprises history, they're marching for a decent *now*!

@

Belkis and Childe Asher appear.

I tease them. 'Still watching over me?'

Belkis caresses my cheek. 'We've come to support the demo.'

They join the marchers.

I'm not here to march. I have my own protest tomorrow. But since they're here, I might as well follow …

@

The marchers approach Glorious Acre's iron gates.

Scythes in half-tracks have set up barriers.

Helicopters hover like kestrels.

Pinkies film the demonstrators.

Inside Glorious Acre, Numen's elite troops and the Grand Mufti's *Ghazis* are already parading in goose-steps. The rumble of tanks and missile carriers shake the earth.

The spectators – some hand-picked, the rest resigned to joining the silent majority in order to live untroubled lives – cheer and applaud. The sound system amplifies their clamour.

On the Grandstand it's time for speeches.

The Grand Mufti and Numen declare their visions of the future.

Were they not venomous, their ramblings would be farcical. But then history loves farce. Witness how it allows Saviours to duel with their cocks constantly.

The Grand Mufti affirms, through his interpreter, that he's ready for Armageddon, ready to emerge as *Al-Mahdi*, the twelfth Imam and Prophet's successor. Thereafter both he and Numen will syncretise their orthodoxies into the true religion humankind craves. To achieve this they will first extirpate the apostate creed, Judaism, that has poisoned humanity with its Mother of Big Lies – its claim to be the progenitor of both Christianity and Islam. For Numen the duumvirate will establish a devotion that immortalises rulers. The Grand Mufti, endorsing that fact, assures the world that as duumvirs they will at long last establish a final unalterable universal religion that will govern the emotions, social roles and standings of all the peoples. However, both Numen and the Grand Mufti give notice that to attain this objective they'll have to wait for Chaos to engulf the planet. Fortunately, there are indisputable indications that Chaos has already arrived. Which is good. Because it means that Chaos will soon be destroyed – if not by Saviours, then by the terror proxies the duumvirs unstintingly fund as advance units.

Disregarding the grandiose clichés, what is noteworthy is the duumvirs' tenor – a regression from the florid courtliness of yore to the pugnacious dictums of our brave new age.

The Grand Mufti has already been denounced by many *ulema* as *Al-Massih ad-Dajjal*, the false Messiah, the counterpart of anti-Christ and Armilus. But the crowds still flock to hear him speak.

I observe the Security Forces. Heavily armed and equipped with gas masks, they're in U-formation.

Platoons of Riot Gendarmerie are guarding Glorious Acre's gates. Other units in half-tracks are stationed at the edges of the throughway leaving the centre clear for the marchers.

Yet more Scythes down the road have closed ranks to block a retreat.

The Nestvillians, defying the encirclement, march on holding their banners aloft.

I look out for Belkis and Childe Asher.

I can't spot them.

I have a sense of déjà vu.

CHILDE ASHER'S LEGEND

We had just returned from a mission in Timor-Leste – a Portuguese colony since the sixteenth century which shared its island with Indonesia. In 1975 Indonesia invaded the eastern half and occupied it until 1999 when under the external mediation it relinquished control of the territory and ratified its independence.

We were to whisk into Australia Father Mateus Teixeira, a Jesuit priest in the Diocese of Baucau who had compiled a dossier on Indonesian war crimes during its brutal occupation. Most importantly, as a survivor of the 1991 massacre of some 250 demonstrators in Santa Cruz cemetery in the capital, Dili, he would be the principal witness against those who had ordered the carnage.

Tragically, we couldn't carry out the mission. Father Teixeira was assassinated before we could reach him.

It took all our guile – and arduous treks at night – to evade the assassins and regain our Australian support cutter at Tutuala, on the island's eastern tip.

All that time – and during the stormy voyage to Darwin – Hidebehind sat on my shoulder.

@

Belkis, always aware of my moods, whispered: 'Listen to the aether. It's decanting life's wonders.'

My breath soured. I started to shake. 'Saviours believe wonders are dangerous.'

Belkis held me. 'Trust your courage. It hasn't let you down.'

'If only courage could overcome Fear.'

'It can.'

'You're immune to fear! How would you know?'

'All I know is that we're driven by two emotions: love and fear. We embrace the first and defy the second. I defy it.'

'How?'

'There's a legend. About Childe Asher.'

'Tell me.'

'One day, Childe Asher asked a marabout. "Why is the planet in turmoil?"

The marabout explained. "Because while creating the Sun, God lost the ray of Tolerance – the ray that Life needs to keep alive. And He can't find it."

That prompted Childe Asher to petition God. "Let me find the lost ray."

God smirked. "Delusions of grandeur, lad?"

"It will benefit the people, sire."

"People might rather not have it. It's hard work – tolerance!"

"I can try."

God gibed. "You think you know better than me?"

"As Socrates says: I know that I know nothing."

"Cheeky runt! Go ahead – chase your tail! You'll never find the ray."

Childe Asher searched far and wide. Crossed rivers and oceans. Deserts and plains. Climbed onto the Earth's roofs. Burrowed into its bowels.

When forty times forty years old, he came upon a volcano in Oceania with a crater that shed a light never seen before. Convinced that only the lost ray could emit such a light, he went to the crater. At that moment, three colossal Sentinels – one black, one white and one rainbow-coloured – burst out of the stones. "What are you doing here?" they asked.

Childe Asher, surprised by their appearance, asked, "Who're you?"

The black Sentinel made the introductions. "We're the Trimurti. We guard Creation. Ensure evolution. I'm Brahma." He pointed at the white Sentinel. "Vishnu"; then at the rainbow-coloured Sentinel. "Shiva."

Childe Asher bowed. "Pleased to meet you, lords."

The Trimurti gave *namastes*.

Brahma asked amicably. "Now tell us what brings you here?"

"I've come for the light in the crater. My heart tells me it's the ray God lost."

Vishnu scrutinised him. "Your heart communes with you?"

"Yes."

"Very commendable! The ray is indeed the one God lost. But you can't take it. We protect it come what may."

"Protect it? From whom?"

Shiva grimaced. "From those who seek it to gain power."

"You mean the Saviours?"

"And their mentors, the Hydras. You see, although hidden, the ray still transmits enough light for some tolerance to prevail. That rankles with the Saviours. They won't feel safe until they possess it."

"Are you suggesting God didn't lose the ray but hid it to protect it from the Saviours?"

Childe Asher's naivety surprised Brahma. "Not God. His adversary. We're Her defenders."

"God doesn't have an adversary," retorted Childe Asher.

"So He pretends. Pachamama – Mother Earth – is His adversary."

"I don't understand."

Vishnu sighed. "Pachamama soon discovered that God loves chaos. He doesn't want a tolerant humankind. He wants them to run amok. That's why He favours Saviours who are psychotic to their nails. So He buried the ray beneath seven tectonic strata. Fortunately, Pachamama was watching Him. She dug it up and hid it here."

"Surely Pachamama would be happy if I exposed God's malevolence by delivering the ray."

"You wouldn't get the chance. God and the Saviours would destroy you. Pachamama wouldn't risk that."

"I can challenge God and the Saviours. I'll take the ray."

Shiva stroked Childe Asher's hair. "Be wise, son. God and the Saviours are too strong just now. When Pachamama finds a way to overwhelm them, She'll appoint a paladin to pick up the ray."

"What if I persuade God to change His ways? Would Pachamama consider that?"

Brahma held Childe Asher's hand. "She tried that. Tried very hard to make Him as God should be. Eventually she realised He'll never change. That's how it is with tyrants. Power broils their brains."

"I'll reform the tyrants when I claim the ray."

Vishnu held Childe Asher's other hand. "Brave Heart, only one soul can reclaim the ray. He is awaited. But nowhere in sight yet. Pachamama will know when he appears."

"I am he," retorted Childe Asher.

Shiva, much wiser for having many different bloods in his body, put his arm around Childe Asher's shoulders. "You're an exceptional soul. But not the awaited one."

"I believe I am. I'll fetch the ray now."

Agitated, the Sentinels clamoured. "You'll fail. And you'll die."

"Death is a lie," declared Childe Asher, and strode to the crater.

The Sentinels, expanding to even greater bulk, blocked his path.

Brahma agitated. "To claim the ray, you have to answer three questions. A wrong answer will force us to kill you."

Childe Asher beamed. "I like questions. Go ahead!"

"What is love?" asked Brahma.

"The essence of Tolerance," answered Childe Asher without hesitation.

"Correct!" shouted Brahma, pleased.

"What is hate?" asked Vishnu.

"The sickness that Tolerance will heal," replied Childe Asher, again without hesitation.

"Bravo!" hollered Vishnu, equally pleased.

Shiva spoke with trepidation. "Childe Asher, man of men, my question is the most difficult. Spare me asking it."

"Ask!" insisted Childe Asher.

Shiva lowered his head mournfully. "What is fear?"

That perplexed Childe Asher: "I need to think about that," he said.

The Sentinels consented. "Take your time …"

Childe Asher meditated for forty years.

The Sentinels waited patiently. They housed him and pampered him.

In the forty-first year, Childe Asher declared: "Fear is a blindfold."

"Wrong!" wailed Shiva.

Childe Asher bent his head stoically. "I'm sorry, I had to guess."

The Sentinels moaned. Again, they spoke in unison. "It was a good guess, but … We're heart broken, Childe Asher. We grew to love you. Yet we must kill you."

"I understand."

The Sentinels brought a chalice containing a warm liquid.

Shiva explained. "Hemlock. We sweetened it. It won't be too bitter."

Childe Asher took the chalice. "Before I drink this, please tell me what fear is. It's the one thing I don't know."

Brahma jumped up. "That's the answer!"

Vishnu jumped up, too. "Yes, that *is* the answer!"

Shiva kicked the chalice out of Childe Asher's hands. "The *only* answer!"

The Sentinels hugged Childe Asher. "You *are* the awaited one!"

They handed him the sun's ray and carried him to Pachamama.

Then Childe Asher and Pachamama forced God to put the ray into its rightful place. Thus, humankind shone with Love and Tolerance. And a dark nebula consumed the Saviours.'

Belkis embraced me. 'Still afraid of Fear?'

'I will cope.'

'Amorous …?'

'Oh, yes.'

And so, my mouth smelling of roses, we conceived Childe Asher and gave him our breath.

The Nestvillian's protestations drown the speeches in Glorious Acre.

'Respect our rights!'

'Equality now!'

'We're not scroungers!'

'We're not rats!

'We're human beings!'

Scythes tighten their encirclement.

I'm still looking for Belkis and Childe Asher.

A dog licks my hand.

Phral – with Moni in tow.

Concerned for his safety, I grab Moni. 'What're you doing here?'

'Came to sniff what History Unbound is all about.'

'Well, you've chosen a bad day!'

'So have you! You shouldn't be here!'

'On the contrary.'

'Your struggle is the greater struggle. Follow me!'

'I must find Belkis and Childe Asher.'

'They'll be fine.'

'I should be with them.'

'They'll be fine I tell you! Come on!'

I look around.

Scythes have encircled us.

Moni tugs Phral's lead. 'Phral will get us through. Come!'

Behind us guns start firing.

Phral sneaks us out of the encirclement.

'Where're we going?'

'Wherever Phral takes us.'

Phral leads us to the observation platform on the heights of Eastern Strand and barks gently.

Moni strokes him. 'He says we should rest.'

We sit on a bench.

I look out for Pinkies. None about. Phral can evade even Hidebehinds.

Below, the estuary stretches gloriously. Belkis and I swam there often. We frolicked where the waters mated and celebrated the oneness puritans profess doesn't exist. 'Whenever we make love, it's like we witness the first dawn,' she'd say.

Belkis's tongue is honeyed. Where I can string words together in my mind, they evaporate when they reach my mouth. Hrant says most people, especially Leviathans, are tortoise-paced with speech because, since the world continuously sprouts leaks, they have difficulty deciciding which leak to plug first.

Phral paws Moni's face.

Moni remarks. 'Phral says: this embrace of waters – so tender.'

I mutter sadly. '*Original immaculacy.*'

'*Original immaculacy*? Very evocative. Tell me more.'

'It's the potency that gives life to Life – as my mentor defines it. Look at the sea: if it's not inseminated by rivers and glaciers it would turn barren; it would not have breasts to nourish the globe. Saviours, threatened by such naturality, degrade the vigour of carnal kowledge. They tar and feather it as evil and replace it with its antipode, *original sin*. Flesh is carrion, they say; only when drained of fluids can the soul be free, they dogmatize. Hrant praised us for understanding that only love – flesh on flesh – gives life to Life. And when, one day, we liberate *original immaculacy* from the Saviours' claws, he avers, people will unfurl radiances unseen anywhere in the universe.'

'He's right.'

Phral woofs.

I laugh. 'One day … If it ever comes …'

'It will.'

'You really see that?'

'Most of us do. The rest choose not to see.'

'It's in our genes then – destruction …'

'No. It's in the venom with which the Saviours scrub the blindfolds they compel us to put on – a venom that makes destruction easy and immediate, even gratifying. Fortunately, there are some who refuse to be blindfolded. You're one of them.'

'A useless one.'

'I keep hearing despair, Oric! Is your Moses basket stuck in the marshes?'

'You tell me, you're the diviner.'

'I need my pebbles to divine. Still, some tidings hover in the aether and can be visible.'

'Like grief?'

'Waters know everything about the lie that death is. Even as you mourn Belkis they know she is deathless. It's your doubts that trouble them.'

'I abandoned her! No doubts about that.'

'We all abandon people – especially people we love. Often unknowingly.'

But sometimes knowingly, as I did. Because there's nowhere one can escape fear.'

'You're wrong! There are many ways.'

'Easy to say …'

78

'A lifeless life, a stone instead of a heart – is that what you want?'

'No.'

'Then defy fear! Any way you can. It's not invincible!'

Moni's empathy heartens me. I try again. 'When you dragged me here, you said my struggle is the greater struggle. What did you mean?'

'The greatest struggle is against one's Self – so Prophet Mohammad said. To beget the courage to journey through inner infernos. To root out hatred – particularly self-hatred. To enthrone love.'

'That's Belkis-talk.'

'Yours, too. She's your destiny. You have her spirit.'

'I keep hoping that ...'

Moni hoots. 'At last – you've mentioned hope!' He points at my journal. 'Phral and I would love to read it.'

'I'm thinking of leaving it to my son. To show him that somewhere there was a real me.'

'I'll borrow it from him.'

That pleases me. I love Moni. I'd want him to know I tried hard to be good.

Phral barks enthusiastically.

Moni strokes Phral. 'Phral says read something now. Lift our spirits with the real you.'

'You mean it? Really?'

'Yes.'

I read.

THE WEDDING

Belkis and I have just returned from a mission during which we exposed a gang of human traffickers selling illegal immigrants to companies that employed them without wages and kept them hidden with meagre food and dire living conditions in disused warehouses.

Waiting for us was an invitation from a dear friend, Haqqi Kadir, to his wedding in Ürümqi, the capital of China's north-western Xinjiang Uyghur Autonomous Region. Drained by the immigrants' ordeals, we welcomed the opportunity to participate in a life-enhancing event.

We had met Haqqi many years ago, when we had joined the International Relief corps in Indonesia's Mentawai islands which, following a huge earthquake on Sumatra's west coast, had been devastated by a three-metre high tsunami.

A tectonophysicist, Haqqi had been engaged by the Indonesian authorities to assess the earthquake's effects on the earth's crust and to infer the probable locations and magnitudes of future seisms. Haqqi helped our Relief corps whenever he could take time off from his work and particularly when bad weather hampered our efforts. As our friendship developed, he suggested that he and I became blood-brothers – an Uyghur tradition that bonds kindred souls for life.

We kept in touch and met here and there when our missions and his schedules permitted.

Haqqi picked us up from Ürümqi airport the day before his wedding.

We went to a bar to anoint our reunion. We would meet

his fiancée, Yuan Chengzi, that evening. A brilliant economic geologist – as he had proudly written to us – he had met her at a conference where their specialisations had dovetailed. Other conferences and discreet trysts matured into deep love. These days Yuan was on field duty in the Tarim Basin surveying for non-metallic resources around its rich petroleum and gas reserves. She was given only three days leave for her wedding.

Thrilled to be with my blood-brother, I didn't register the anxiety that lurked behind Haqqi's bonhomie.

But ever-intuitive Belkis did. 'Something's troubling you, Haqqi?'

Her insight surprised him. 'What makes you think that?'

'You haven't raised your glass as heartily as you normally do.'

He forced a laugh. 'I prefer drinking in the sight of you two.'

'You can talk to us. We have strong shoulders to lean on.'

Haqqi quipped awkwardly. 'Must be old bachelors' butterflies about getting hitched?'

'Feels more than that.'

Haqqi tried to remain light-hearted. 'Okay. But they're only quirky concerns. Like the age difference. I'm fifty-three. Yuan twenty-seven. Disregarding the innuendoes about our "surprising" decision to marry, I'm likely to straddle a cloud long before her. Is it right to condemn her to a young widowhood?'

Belkis scowled. 'Bullshit. You love each other.'

I backed Belkis. 'Surely that's what counts!'

Haqqi frowned. 'There are other matters. Where do we live? On the coast – in Lianyungang where my Institute is? It's well regarded internationally and I'm an important cog. Do I give that up and move inland to Lanzhou where Yuan's based? Or do we take lesser posts and move to a university here?'

Belkis dismissed the notion. 'No lesser posts for either of you. You told us Yuan's a gem. And you're a Colossus. Any Institution – certainly in the West – would welcome you both with open arms.'

Haqqi grimaced. 'That doesn't tempt us. We're Chinese. We love our country. We want to contribute to its development. But we're Muslim. I'm an aberration as a notable Uyghur. And Yuan, a Hui, deemed to be Chinese like most Huis, is mistrusted for condescending to marry a Turban Head from the Steppes.'

That fired up Belkis. 'That's the crux, isn't it? The political situation – that's what's worrying you!'

Haqqi grumbled. 'Do you know the political situation here?'

I retorted. 'We know quite a bit. We have read what is there for us to read.'

Haqqi got up. 'Come. Let me give you an idea about the troubles.'

As Haqqi drove, we summed up what we knew. He could have said more, but we had to stop at a checkpoint.

Haqqi explained. 'We're entering our "West Berlin" – the Hui neighbourhood.'

Four PSB – Public Security Bureau – officers came to inspect our papers. Dissatisfied by Haqqi's assurances that he was giving his overseas visitors a tour of the city, they contacted their superiors. After lengthy deliberations, they let us through.

Haqqi scoffed. 'We won't go walkabout. They'll keep stopping and searching us. Just have a look-see!'

Affluent suburb.

Bustling streets.

Fair amount of traffic.

Kids at school assembled for rollcall.

Fathers taking toddlers to mosques – despite the interdiction against teaching children religious tracts.

Cafés full of men: the elderly, mostly goateed, playing mah-jong. Others talking amicably.

Busy supermarkets and butchers with glaring halal signs.

Neatly dressed women shopping. Some in hijabs and khimars, but many in Western clothes – the 'fully assimilated' Haqqi called them.

Numerous armed PSB and plain-clothes MSS – Ministry of State Security – some patrolling, some guarding imposing buildings.

Some MSS photographing us.

The large police presence perturbed me. 'Is there an alert?'

'No need for alerts. Security is omnipresent. They protect the Hui. Checkpoint reported us as Uyghurs. They're vigilant in case we attack.'

'Are attacks frequent?'

'Occasional ones. Some from Uyghur separatists. Some from other Turkic minorities. Tajiks, Kazakhs, Uzbeks, Tatars have grievances, too. But they all look like Uyghurs and Uyghurs they are to MSS.'

From 'West Berlin' we drove to 'East Berlin,' the Uyghur neighbourhood.

Here, too, we passed through a checkpoint – named 'Checkpoint Charlie' in sanguine humour.

Haqqi stopped on the main road. 'Here we can walkabout. If I rant, forgive me.'

It was a walled ghetto sinking into its foundations. There were not many cars about, but a large contingent of armed PSB and MSS.

Haqqi gave a running commentary.

'The Security here is to control us – not to protect. Few people about, as you can see. So no noise pollution. Mosques almost empty. Some elderly attend, but MSS ignores them as fossils arranging their funerals. No calls from muezzins. Prayers curtailed. Religious classes proscribed. Most people stay at home in case they're marked as extremists.

'The cafés. Dormant. Just a few ancient patrons! Where are the workers taking tea-breaks? Or the unemployed? Keeping low. And men with long beards? Outlawed! Long beards mean "abnormal" religiosity.

'The women! Any hijabs, khimars, burqas? Not one. They're either in shabby Western clothes or Chinese *qipao*. Why? New regulation: they mustn't cover their faces and bodies in public. Particularly at airports and train stations where most work as cleaners.

'Those going to shops and markets hurry to be invisible. And the children they're dragging. To mosques? No! They'd be accused of "exaggerated religious fervour". Then why aren't they at school studying Chinese culture and ethnic unity as the law demands? Because they're not allowed to be taught in Uyghur. And the Mandarin they teach is elementary.

'The butchers – any halal signs? No. Religious signs undermine the "secular life". Those wanting halal will know which butcher to go to. And can you see the Turkic star-and-crescent anywhere? No. That would mark you a secessionist!

'The houses. Rundown. Who can afford repairs? The doors – all with photographs of inhabitants and Quick Response codes. Big Brother is watching.

'Hear the TVs? Very loud – right? The occupants are performing their civic duty by listening to patriotic broadcasts.

'The big house there – boarded up – was a centre for writers, musicians, painters, students. Now some are in jail under counter-terror laws. Actually, Uyghur artists aren't the only ones. Numerous Chinese writers and illuminati are imprisoned, too.'

Haqqi paused. 'I need a drink.'

I nod towards a couple of MSS that had been following us. 'They've been photographing.'

'And recording everything. Routine. Pity them – imagine the tedium of transcribing what people say ...'

We managed to laugh. Humour, the sapling that defies storms. Haqqi led us back to his car. 'Come, "*Serenity*" waits to welcome us.'

Serenity was Haqqi's parents' timeworn but spick-and-span home. On the way, he told us about them. His mother, Meryem, a midwife in her late seventies, was a Mother-Earth figure, always ready to help whomsoever, including many Hui women. Young wives in their first pregnancies with psychological problems regarded her as their guardian angel.

His father, Timur, almost ninety, was a venerated elder whose faith in an equitable society had vested him with the fortitude to survive. He had fought alongside Mao Tse-tung against Chiang Kai-shek; weathered the Great Leap Forward; and suffered the Red Guards' brutalities during the Cultural Revolution. Reduced to a paraplegic, he once confessed to Haqqi that his condition had proved to be a blessing in disguise, motivating him to heal the open wounds in people's minds by absorbing the teachings of both Western psychoanalytic theories and traditional Chinese medicine. His relative success had enabled him to send Haqqi, his only child, to a good university.

Both Meryem and Timur received us ardently. As Belkis remarked, we felt we had finally found the parents our unconscious had imagined. Honouring ancient practices of hospitality, Meryem served a lavish lunch.

She and Timur, humbly brushing aside our praises, contended that they owed their comforts and airy home – way above their needs – to Haqqi who constantly 'squandered' his earnings to provide them with a balmy old age.

Later Timur broached a subject that obviously had been badgering the family. 'Still no issues with your name, Haqqi?'

I, too, wanted to ask that question. Haqqi's birth name was Ziya, meaning 'light'. He had changed it to Haqqi, 'truthful', in protest against the incessant anti-Islamic laws.

Haqqi shook his head. 'None. Anyway, it's not in the forbidden list.'

I was intrigued. 'Forbidden list?'

Timur spoke ahead of Haqqi. 'The government's latest edict. Names with religious undertones like Asadullah – lion of Allah – or Abdulaziz – servant of Allah – are banned. Those with such names forfeit registration as citizens and are ineligible for social services.'

Haqqi interrupted Timur. 'Haqqi means "truthful". It's a common name. Hardly contentious ...'

Timur disagreed. '*Haqq* is one of Allah's ninety-nine names. While the National Congress proposes "a great wall of *iron*" against so-called "Uyghur terrorism", it can be interpreted as seditious.'

Haqqi responded passionately. 'What about our Human Rights? Should we renounce our faith, our ethnicity? Besides, terrorism is alien to Uyghurs. You know, I abandoned religion long ago. That makes me an apostate for many. They wait for Islam to reclaim its compassion. But I'm not that patient.'

Belkis pressed his hand. 'Hats off to you, Haqqi!'

I was moved, too. 'And that's why you insisted on a religious ceremony?'

'Yes. It wasn't easy to arrange. But I pulled a few strings. Promised it would be more folkloric than religious ...'

'How do you mean?'

'We'll hold it in a yurt. Like in the Steppes.'

I felt a premonition. 'Does Yuan agree?'

Haqqi chuckled. 'Heartily. She's a socialist. But her parents have disowned her.'

Belkis sympathised. 'She must be devastated!'

'Yes and no. Yes, because family is as sacrosanct to Huis as to Uyghurs. No, because she realised that her parents were, as she put it, puffed-up bourgeois with Hui superiority. Also, seeing the way the country is run, she lost faith in politics. She decided science was where she can find integrity and rationality.'

'Maybe her parents might change their mind and come to the wedding.'

'Not even if Allah interceded. Disownment is forever.'

'Won't any Hui attend?'

'Only those who esteem my parents.' Looking at his watch, he stood up. 'I should check that the yurt's sorted out. You two must be jet-lagged. Have a siesta. Be fresh when Yuan arrives.'

We stood up. 'Can you drop us at a hotel ...?'

Meryem objected sternly. 'No hotel! You stay here! You are family!'

Haqqi laughed. 'Try and say no to that!'

Meryem took us by the hand. 'This way ...'

Haqqi shouted as he left. 'Enjoy the mollycoddling!'

At the guest room – simple and sparkling – Meryem kissed us. 'Dream happy worlds.'

We woke up refreshed.

Yuan had arrived and was helping Meryem pile yet more food on the table.

Haqqi was uncorking bottles.

Timur urged us in. 'Come! Meet Yuan.'

Yuan rushed over and kissed us both. 'My Haqqi's brother and sister!'

We warmed to her instantly.

Haqqi, with Yuan clinging to his arm, served us. '*Museles*. Local wine. Delicious.'

We sat on the settee. Yuan held Belkis's hand and Haqqi mine.

Meryem and Timur watched us happily.

There's a saying: when happiness visits Uyghurs, the moon shines bright as the sun.

We spent hours talking, eating and drinking.

In the morning, still imbued with happiness, we attended the brief religious wedding.

Traditionally the ceremony is a private celebration conducted in the bride's abode with only an Imam, chosen witnesses, close relatives and friends present. But since Yuan's parents had disowned her, it had to be conducted at Haqqi's parents' home – a privation which saddened her deeply.

The Imam, affirming that the couple were dressed in plain Uyghur clothes – *ichigi* boots, *chapan* kaftans, *doppa* skullcaps – and thus possessed equal status to become each other's lifelines – asked whether they agreed to marry. When they replied positively, he directed Haqqi to kiss Yuan thrice on her cheeks and once on the forehead. Then the newly-weds shared salted bread, which symbolically guaranteed everlasting love.

The ritual should have ended with the groom's friends forcing their way into the bride's home with chants and music and urging her to bid farewell to her parents. But since this rite, too, could not be performed at the bride's family home, Yuan had to struggle with the bitterness of her disownment.

Then we rushed to the yurt.

Built in a corner of the Market Place, the yurt, with its classic simplicity, stood like a temple among the countless stalls selling everything imaginable. Constructed with a circular timber frame, it was covered with wool felts. Ornaments of sacred Uyghur images of geometric patterns, lions, tigers, dragons, the humanoid bird, *garuda*, and motifs of the universal elements, fire, water, earth, metal and wood, collectively symbolised strength and protection. Designed to be assembled and dismantled at speed – the factor that had sealed the municipality's permission for its erection during the night – it was big enough to accommodate a large congregation.

The premonition I had felt the previous day rebounded. 'What made you set the yurt in Market Square, Haqqi?'

'It's the perfect place. Customarily the reception must be

accessible to everybody – especially to strangers.'

'Market places have been attacked. They're soft targets.'

'There'll be security. Municipality knows we're good citizens. They accepted my view that a non-religious, non-political celebration featuring a "celebrity" – me – might defuse tensions.'

I lauded the custom but remained apprehensive.

We made our way through a throng of early comers queuing to get in.

The yurt's interior was like an ant colony. Streams of caterers brought huge containers of aromatic dishes and piled them on the trestle tables. Other caterers lugged crates of beverages. Bevies of waiters set up round tables – the mark of equality – around the circular dance floor. We calculated that since each table would seat six, some 300 guests were expected.

While on the bandstand the musicians tuned up, Haqqi checked the sound system. Uyghur weddings needed high decibels to reach the forebears' ears.

Timur – scurrying in his wheelchair – and Meryem and Yuan supervised the preparations and, most importantly, the placement of the wedding cake. The last, a recent addition to Uyghur confectionery, was to affirm that China was moving with the times and that even trouble-afflicted Ürümqi – once a hub of the Silk Road – was re-emerging as an important international centre.

As pampered guests, Belkis and I weren't allowed to exert ourselves. So we took our time laying out our wedding present – a circlet of statuettes depicting a large family by East Isthmus's African artists – on the centre tables reserved for the newly-weds, their parents, their close friends and the families of their immediate relatives.

@

Punctually at 3pm, Haqqi opened the yurt's door.

The musicians blasted away.

The guests stampeded in.

True to custom, men and women sat separately on opposite sides. Happy that Haqqi and Yuan cherished our gift – we settled together at the centre tables. The banquet started with sweeteners of tea, fruits, dried nuts and pastries. While some people helped themselves to food from the buffet, others took to the dance floor.

Men danced with men and women with women. Now and again, strangers walked in and more round tables were set up to welcome them. The poor, in particular, were pampered and encouraged to dance.

At about 5pm, the wedding cake was brought to our table. Yuan and Haqqi rose to cut it. Wild applause and the deafening music prevented us from hearing the sudden commotion. Seconds later, bullets rained.

Instinctively ignoring the horror that suddenly surrounded them, Yuan and Haqqi catapulted over to the children that had been running around and shielded them with their bodies. Belkis and I – also instinctively – rushed to Meryem and Timur. Too late. They had been shot in the head.

Belkis froze momentarily, then, grabbing a couple of children, hurled them onto the floor and covered them with her body. I flung myself on top of her. People screamed, wailed and ran towards the door. Many slumped over their tables or writhed on the floor.

We caught glimpses of the gunmen. Four of them. Heavily armed, masked and dressed in track-suits. They emptied their guns, then vanished. Moments later the Chinese security forces rushed in.

It took a while for the screams, groans and the pandemonium to abate. Methodically, the security forces, insensible to the prevailing hysteria, hauled us and the other survivors out of the yurt. As Belkis and I were pushed to a police van, we saw paramedics load Yuan's and Haqqi's blood-stained bodies into an ambulance.

The MSS informed us that an Uyghur separatist group claimed responsibility for the attack in retribution of what it considered was an ungodly wedding. The government regretting the heavy casualties – twenty-seven killed, fifty-three wounded – offered its condolences to the families and solemnly declared that the perpetrators of the atrocity would be caught and punished.

The state-controlled media proclaimed repeatedly China's commitment to protect the legal, cultural and religious rights not only of the Uyghurs but of all Chinese minorities. As an affirmation of this policy they published glowing obituaries of Haqqi and Yuan, honouring them as two of the most brilliant and valorous children of heroic China.

Three days later, after the funerals of Haqqi, Yuan, Timur and Meryem, Belkis and I, treated like VIPs, were repatriated in an 'official' plane. We had not been allowed to extend our stay and determine whether the attack had really been carried out by an Uyghur separatist group.

Moni had been listening attentively. 'So tragic. How brave you all were.'

'Belkis and I were bystanders. The brave were Haqqi and Yuan. They went for the children – and saved some.'

'When you protected Belkis where was Hidebehind?'

'Things happened fast. I didn't feel him …'

'Don't you wonder why?'

'I was sharing my friends' happiness. I'd had a premonition about the yurt but then I forgot it. Then the gunfire. Shielding Belkis. Whispering: "Keep still, soul of my soul! Keep still, my Queen of Sheba …" That's when Hidebehind pounced. When I froze. Belkis thought I'd been hit …'

'You blocked him before he could block you.'

'I must have.'

'How else?'

'I don't know ...'

Moni lectured me as if I were a child. 'I'll tell you how. It was your Ethical Self. You've heard of *Jhinjihar*, the Indian horseman. Emerged when violence threatened the oppressed. The despots beheaded him. Undaunted he put his head on his lap and galloped to liberate the people. What made him do that? His Ethical Self. Because that's what resides in our hearts. It's our fountain of love. Our birth-force that holds life sacred. *Original immaculacy* as your mentor called it. The potency that winnows Good from Bad and empowers legions of headless horsemen to defend souls ...'

I stare at him. 'That's Leviathan talk. Are you a Leviathan?'

Suddenly sirens blare in the distance.

I jump up. 'Ambulances – from Glorious Acre.'

My Dolphinero sinews scream. I must do something.

I shake Moni's hand and run.

SATURDAY 11.21

I reach the hospital.

Ambulances, queueing by the Emergency Wing, bode a heavy toll.

Agonised relatives and the throng of Nestvillians who came to support them are penned in the parking lot by Gendarmes.

Pinkies photograph the unruly.

Some Scythes, deployed to the Emergency Wing's forecourt, are hauling the wounded out of the ambulances and dumping them onto the forecourt.

Doctors and nurses clamour to minister to the injured.

The Scythes, brandishing truncheons, stop them.

Clinicians from other Departments, having rushed out to help their colleagues in the Emergency Wing, are blocked by Police units.

The families' outcry counterpoints the wails of the injured.

The Scythe Commander blares through a megaphone. 'The dead go to the morgue. They are enemies of the state and will be buried immediately. The injured will be held in custody and tried for sedition.'

I note that the waste disposal block at the back of the Emergency Wing has only a few policemen. Worried by signs of 'biohazardous materials', they're keeping watch from a distance.

I shuffle there and tell the Policemen, 'I'm a cleaner. It's my shift.' They give me cursory looks but don't intercept me. I slip into the block. I put on an overall from the cloakroom and run down the corridors to the main entrance. I join the orderlies waiting to assist the doctors at the forecourt. Belkis is already there. I'm not surprised. I know that she is pleased to see me. 'I knew you'd get here.'

'Childe Asher?'

'Outside with the families, trying to distract the kids.'

An official car, its siren at full blast, weaves through the Scythes' cordon and stops by the forecourt.

I recognise the driver: Professor Kjell Jensen. Hefty as a Sumo-wrestler and all the more striking with leonine white hair, he's famous for innovative procedures that saved several people deemed to have 'inoperable' brain tumours.

Enraged, Jensen confronts the Scythe Commander. 'Call off your men! Immediately!'

The Commander retorts haughtily. 'You've breached security, sir!'

'Bollocks to security! Disband your men!'

'I have my orders!'

'I'm countermanding your orders! I'm the Director here. I'm in charge. Now, move your men!'

The Commander maintains his officiousness. 'I know who you are, sir. But like I said this is Security matter.'

'We overrule security! We're doctors!'

'These people are public enemies, sir!'

Jensen fulminates. 'I don't give a damn what they are! We treat friend or foe! Rich or poor! Young or old! Here, everybody's equal. Now, fuck off with your men!'

'That's enough, Doctor! Or I'll have you arrested!'

Jensen ignores him and summons the staff assembled on the forecourt. They – and Belkis and I – rush to stand behind him. Jensen steps up to the Commander. 'We're taking in the casualties. You can try to stop us, but you'll have to kill me first.'

The Commander brings out his techset. 'We'll see about that, sir!'

Jensen grins. 'Ah, I should have thought of that.' He takes out his own techset. 'I'm calling Numen. I'm one of his doctors. He told me to contact him if ever I needed help …'

The Commander, confounded, stares at him.

Jensen speaks into his set. 'Good morning, Your Supremacy. Jensen … Yes …. I have a problem with a Security Commander. He's preventing me from seeing patients. Would you mind speaking to him? Thank you.' He hands his set to the Commander.

Flustered, the Commander takes the phone, steps back and talks very softly. Then, grudgingly, he hands the mobile back to Jensen and barks into his techset. 'All units! Back to barracks!

As the Scythes, the Gendarmes and the Police regroup, the medical staff galvanise into action. Some begin to attend to the injured; others race with defibrillators, bags of blood, saline, plasma, dressings.

Belkis and I, together with the orderlies, wheel out rolling beds. The Nestvillians rush towards Emergency. Jensen stops them. 'Stay back! We can't have you in there. Not yet. You'll only get in our way.'

His gravity subdues them. They wait outside restlessly on the forecourt.

Belkis and I exchange looks. Being together. Working together. Our destiny. I mustn't betray it.

SATURDAY 12.03

I'm scrutinising Belkis's orphanage, one of the Ottoman caravanseries that once dotted the Balkans. It's mouldering away but seems determined not to crumble just yet.

Belkis, always inclined to inject a congenial aspect to ugliness, called it 'Rapunzel's Tower', the bastille where maidens with long tresses dream of heroic princes.

I had to divert here after Glorious Acre's horrors. This is where Belkis broke through orphanhood's doleful fog and reclaimed the indomitable spirit she possessed even before her birth. The tinker who found her must have been dazzled by the Sheban lineage illumining her.

I must incorporate her spirit fully. It's the only way I'll cross the mortal-immortal divide that stands between us now. 'You are what you are,' she keeps saying. That's not good enough. To flow with her as one, I must be more than that.

Belkis is where my life began.

When we lived in each other's skins, we scoured Key Picayune for scraps and shared them with waifs and stray animals.

One night, after dishing out some slop to urchins who had heard about us from murmuring pavements, Belkis said: 'People profess childhood is idyllic. We know better. It seldom is. Demons interfere. Childhood within a loving family often ends in "if-only" requiems. Childhood in orphanages turns mites into dung beetles. A childhood where kids have never known their parents, can never remember their faces, is a vacuum. To fill up that emptiness, it questions graveyards. Why did my parents abandon me? Did they think I was a curse? Did they want to escape to a better reincarnation?

Were they too poor to feed me? Did they die naturally? Were they killed – because that's the culture of our times – as they tried to protect me? And the answers, sensible or irrational, breed other questions – questions that lie low in swamplands.'

It's the answers in the swamplands that haunt me.

Belkis hears my anxiety and appears.

'Don't worry about Childe Asher. He's already a Dolphinero.'

'He might be ripped apart, too.'

'We shed our mortal bodies quickly.'

'Not always. Remember Passang?'

'Souls rise before pain becomes unbearable.'

'You wish!'

'I know.'

'Where is he by the way?'

'Still keeping vigil with Nestvillians. He's their purveyor of hope.'

'I don't want him fatherless ...'

'He won't be. You're in his sinews.'

'Some Dolphineros don't become Leviathans. Especially the fear stricken. If I don't, I'll lose you – and Childe Asher.'

'Leviathan or not, you are and will be my love forever. And Childe Asher's father forever.'

She vanishes before I can argue.

A vision assaults me: Childe Asher crumpled up, blood seeping out of his mouth.

JEHAN

We had joined the relief organisations on the Greek island, Lesbos, where some 60,000 refugees had landed after sailing across the Mytilini Strait from Turkey. They were the lucky ones. Though the Strait is only about twenty kilometres wide, erratic winds and currents make it treacherous. Hundreds had perished during previous crossings. Many more were still queuing to come.

We sanitised the camps, cleaned the beaches, distributed food, clothes and bedding. Hrant, who had often witnessed the miseries of displacement, teamed up with us.

One day, a gas cylinder in the main camp exploded. In the ensuing fire, some three thousand people stampeded to safety.

Despite strong winds, firefighters and volunteers managed to put out the fire. But as the camp lost its living quarters and amenities, most of the refugees had to be sheltered in tents in open spaces.

We led a group to a park by the sea. Hrant tried to boost the refugees' morale with a positive perspective on deracination. Migrations, he maintained, whether undertaken by people fleeing from Saviours' tyrannical rule or uprooted by wars, droughts, famines and Nature's upheavals, punctuate history. While most governments, cynically cavilling national interests, disregard the migrants' tribulations and malign them as economic riffraff, the migrants bring changes that energise and enrich both themselves and their hosts.

That didn't appease Belkis. 'What about the endless tragedies, the despair that compels people to risk their lives? Are they ransoms paid to history?'

'Alas, yes. And always paid by innocents … That's another calamity that strengthens our determination to repair the world. I remember how you were affected after Jehan—'

That flustered Belkis. 'You know about Jehan?'

'I told you I've watched you both from the year dot. I often wondered how, given your intuitions, neither of you felt my presence.'

That jogged my memory. 'I think we did. We often spoke about sensing a force supporting us during our orphanage years. Was that you?'

'Yes.'

Belkis muttered. 'Were you there when Jehan …?'

Hrant nodded sadly. 'By your side.'

Belkis had told me about Jehan. In the months leading to the Arab Spring – now laid waste – when the refugee crisis in Europe was incubating, an American destroyer in the Mediterranean chanced upon an inflatable boat that had been adrift for five days. Carrying African asylum seekers far in excess of the number of people it could accommodate, the boat had set out from Libya, allegedly with 'Brotherly Leader' Gaddafi choosing to look the other way. Conditions while they drifted had killed most of those on board. The destroyer transferred the survivors to our Coast Guard.

Days later, the rescued were moved from hospitals to detention centres to await relocation when the politicking between our government and international welfare organisations yielded a decision.

One survivor, a Sudanese girl of ten, Jehan, emaciated and traumatised, was sent to Belkis's orphanage. There, spared the misery of an overcrowded camp, she would be under the care of a matronly Lebanese psychiatric social worker, Salwa, assigned by a UN agency.

Belkis, a year older than Jehan, immediately became Salwa's helper.

Their solicitude gradually soothed Jehan's trauma. Over the weeks, Belkis even invented a pidgin with which she and Jehan communicated with girlish enthusiasm. Since Salwa, like Jehan, spoke Arabic, she managed to piece together her story.

❦

The only child of a professional couple, Jehan had been chosen by Khartoum's pre-eminent matchmaker as the ideal new wife for General Zulfiqar. Sudan's High Command – reliant on Zulfiqar as the only commander who could control Janjaweed, the country's nomadic militia – declared the proposed marriage 'made in heaven'.

However, Jehan's mother, Ayesha, and father, Mohammad, declined the proposal. In a simple but adamant statement, they declared that although marriages of girls as young as ten were allowed in Sudan, they considered Jehan too emotionally undeveloped to be the consort of a warrior as legendary as Zulfiqar; and that, more pertinently, Jehan was mentally too frail to undergo the female circumcision that he demanded.

The refusal caused a furore. The *ulema* derided the parents as 'western secularists'. Ayesha was immediately dismissed from her post on the pretext that her perfidious disavowal of female genital mutilation would cause irreparable damage to her students' pure minds. Ayesha's apologia, courageously published by Mohammad, also stated that his wife still carried physical and psychological scars from her own genital mutilation – as did, no doubt, most of the eighty-eight percent of Sudanese women who had suffered the ritual.

Except for the castigations branding Ayesha and Mohammad as pretentious liberals, the matter should have ended there. But that would not have saved Zulfiqar's face.

Jehan's uncles and aunts – promised career opportunities by Zulfiqar – harangued Jehan's parents with admonitions to protect the family honour. They said that to prove their piety, the two parents must agree to the proposal.

This infuriated Mohammad. He stated that female genital mutilation was *not* an obligatory Islamic rite, that neither the Qur'an nor the Prophet's Hadiths had prescribed it, and that, most importantly, since Allah had forged women as intact and complete beings, the ritual was a crime against Creation. Then, urging that the practice should be abolished, he denounced it as a stratagem contrived by forefathers who aimed to enslave women by stifling their libido.

That liberalism cost Mohammad his life. He was killed on his way to Friday prayers by Zulfiqar's followers.

Instead of restraining Ayesha, Mohammad's assassination strengthened her resolve. Realising that unless she agreed she, too, would be killed, leaving the uncles and aunts to agree to the wedding, Ayesha determined to whisk Jehan to safety. Mindful that they wouldn't be allowed to leave Sudan, she approached Ishak, one of Mohammad's trusted contacts in a clandestine democratic group that smuggled out opponents of the regime.

Within days, three activists secreted Ayesha and Jehan out of Sudan. Their names were Ahmad, Hazem and Walid.

After weeks of arduous trekking through Chad and southern Libya, they reached Susah.

There they posed as tourists interested in Susah's Roman ruins and chartered a cabin-cruiser. On their way to the boat an armed gang, hired by Zulfiqar, tracked them down. Ahmad urged Hazem to flee with Ayesha and Jehan while he and Walid engaged the gang.

Hazem led Ayesha and Jehan to a distant cove where a crowd of Africans besieged human traffickers who smuggled migrants to Italy.

Hazem placed her and Jehan in an inflatable boat. Before leaving to meet his own uncertain fate, he gave Ayesha details of some exiled Sudanese in Europe who would help them start a new life.

In mid-sea the following morning, the boat ran out of fuel. As it drifted helplessly, weather conditions, sunstroke and lack of food and water took their toll. Many on board, including Ayesha, expired. The few, like Jehan, eventually rescued by the American destroyer, were found to be on their last faltering breaths.

@

Jehan's ordeal received world-wide coverage. But while Europe hesitated to offer her asylum, Zulfiqar's long arm reached the orphanage. The Warden broke the news. In a few days, Jehan's uncle Qasim would be arriving with his wife, Fatima, to take her home. The formalities appointing Qasim as Jehan's guardian had been processed by both the Sudanese authorities and our own. By then Jehan had appreciably recuperated; at least her heart-wrenching screams in her sleep had abated.

But the prospect of returning to Sudan with her uncle brought back her traumas. Only Salwa and Belkis could get near her when, seized by paroxysms of fear, she isolated herself in corners. At mealtimes, refusing to eat, she would run around begging everybody to save her from Qasim.

Salwa, frantic to help Jehan, contacted numerous organisations only to be told that their noninterventionist charters prevented them from interfering in a sovereign state's internal affairs. Her pleas to her employers, that Jehan was still too psychologically damaged to return to Sudan, failed. The UN agency proved sympathetic but declared that it could not mediate in cases that complied with International Law. But her last and desperate approach to a Scandinavian Human Rights Institute did offer hope. Presuming that somewhere in the labyrinthine statutes of 193 countries, they might find a loophole that could challenge Qasim's guardianship, the Institute agreed to send an official.

Qasim arrived, flamboyantly dressed in traditional *jalabiya* replete with sashes of merit and anointed with self-importance, and jubilantly declared this his long-awaited reunion with his niece. His wife, Fatima, and a retinue of lawyers and interpreters accompanied him. The Warden received him deferentially and conducted him to the welcome room on the top floor, where he could meet Jehan in private. As they walked up the stairs, the Warden introduced Sigrun Blom, a Norwegian Arabist and international lawyer, engaged by the Human Rights Institute to oversee the proceedings. Qasim, irked by what he called 'outrageous involvement of superfluous outsiders' – and further galled to have to deal with a woman – cast hostile glances at Blom.

Jehan's piercing screams greeted him as he haughtily stomped into the welcome room. Salwa and Belkis, standing by her side, tried to calm Jehan. Qasim reacted as if he were deeply hurt; then lost his composure and bellowed, 'Be quiet, girl!' Qasim's sudden dominance silenced Jehan. But when he walked towards her, she hid behind Salwa and Belkis. Fatima, realising that Qasim's temper would antagonise the gathering, pulled him back and led him to the table where his lawyers had laid out the relevant papers.

The lawyers show Blom documents that gave Qasim and Fatima incontestable rights to Jehan's guardianship. Qasim, reverting to affability, opened his arms to Jehan. 'My precious niece, taking you back into the fold makes this the happiest day of my life.' In response Jehan screamed even more stridently. At that point, Blom interjected. 'There's one vital document missing.'

Qasim glared at her. 'What document?'

'An affidavit guaranteeing that Jehan will inherit her parents' estate in totality.'

Qasim blustered. 'Her inheritance is immaterial. She'll remain a member of a noble household. That's confirmed by all the documents. I should remind you: I'm a diplomat. I uphold the law. The affidavit is unnecessary.'

This failed to intimidate Blom. 'On the contrary. It's essential. Without it I cannot ratify your guardianship.'

Qasim reacted furiously. 'I don't need your ratification! The papers are in order. Jehan comes with me. You can't stop me!'

That produced a hysterical rant from Jehan. Sobbing, she rattled incoherently that Qasim had come on General Zulfiqar's orders; that Qasim would have her circumcised before her marriage to Zulfiqar; and that Zulfiqar was a demon who murdered her father, forced her and her mother to flee, hired men to kill them in Libya and caused her mother's cruel death.

Then, emotionally drained, she collapsed into Salwa's arms. A shocked silence ensued.

When Jehan had started her tirade, Qasim had tried to silence her by outshouting her. But as Jehan kept raging like one possessed, he noted the heightened empathy in the room. That prompted him to flop onto a chair and shake as if maliciously wronged. Then, barely audibly, he muttered. 'These horrific lies ... Our lovely Jehan is sick ... Deluded ... She needs help ... Treatment ...'

Blom concurred. 'She certainly does.'

Qasim, as if summoning some vestiges of strength, rose to his full height. 'She will have treatment – immediately!' He turned to Jehan. 'Come, child ... Come now ... You'll have the best doctors in Khartoum ...'

Terrified, Jehan clung to Salwa and Belkis.

Blom intervened. 'Jehan can't leave – not until you provide the affidavit. In the meantime, she'll be cared for here.'

Qasim snarled. 'I can take her by force! I have diplomatic immunity!'

Blom remained impassive. 'Should you attempt to use force I'll call the police. It will cause quite a scandal, but ...'

Qasim turned menacing. 'You don't know who you're dealing with!'

Blom replied disdainfully. 'I certainly do.'

Once again, Fatima intervened. She urged her outraged husband to confer with the lawyers. After minutes of whispered deliberation, the lawyers, manning their techsets, left the room.

Qasim confronted Blom. 'My solicitors in Khartoum will notarise and send the affidavit within the hour to the Sudanese Chargé d'Affaires here. By this afternoon I'll have full authority to leave with Jehan.' Ignoring Blom's unimpressed face – Belkis thought she must have had another ploy in her head – he grinned triumphantly. 'Now, if you'll excuse me, I'll embrace my beloved niece.'

He strode towards Jehan. The moment he moved, Jehan, shaking her head hysterically, ran on to the balcony. And threw herself from it.

Salwa and Belkis rushed down to the courtyard. The others followed.

Jehan lay lifeless.

Belkis, weeping inconsolably, hugged Jehan's body.

Then, frenzied by the blood in her hands, she attacked Qasim, hitting him and smearing him with Jehan's blood. 'You killed her! You killed her! You killed her!'

Qasim raised a hand to slap Belkis.

Blom gripped his hand. 'Don't you dare!'

Qasim dropped his hand as if it had been soiled. Then he walked away muttering. 'Accursed women! Shaytan's whores!'

Blom stayed with Belkis for days and grieved with her.

Only later did Belkis discover that Blom was Hrant in one of his personas.

@

The orphans, dressed in institutional garb, come out into the courtyard.

Some sit on the grass for their lessons.

A few, who are watched by supervisors – 'Cerberuses' Belkis

called them – clear the rubbish on the pavements as part of their community work.

The rest weed the gardens.

An old woman, serene and smiling, supervises them. I wonder if she's Jasmin, the janitress who instructed Belkis on the remedial powers of lichens.

Horticulture – that was the orphanage's forte, Belkis used to avow proudly. The locals maintained that the girls owed their green fingers to the tears of former inmates which had soaked into the earth. Belkis cherished that notion. It had the truth of folks' wisdom, she said. Plus the transference of the girls' love for their unknown parents, she added.

I move on.

SATURDAY 13.50

I'm at the Forum. Inspired by Speakers' Corner and situated in a leafy park, this is where Numen pays lip service to freedom of speech which, he avows, 'is a right imbedded in his heart'. Here, people can assemble and dispute any subject. A police unit that protects the speakers embroiders the deceit. In effect, Homeland Security selects the orators – and most of the listeners – from its database of toothless strays.

For those still with teeth, classified as 'recusants' – dissidents, opposition politicians, lawyers, judges, journalists, artists, writers, academics who dare expose the iniquities of Numen's rule – Homeland Security clogs their platforms with rabble-rousers. But these stalwarts are as rare as four-leaf clovers. Most, if not all, are either in jail or under house arrest facing interminable trials on trumped-up charges.

There are few people about. I amble along.

I listen to a burly, thick-bearded Imam in a white caftan. Four women in black robes and hijabs stand behind him.

'Our sojourn on Earth is the test that determines who merits Eternal Life. Every millisecond of our existence is weighed on Piety's scales at the Last Judgement. Only the True Faithful enter *Jannah*, Paradise. Yet to those who constantly lapse, Allah, The Compassionate, gives one last chance to perform an act that glorifies Islam. Those who do so go to dwell with the green birds that nest by the Almighty's throne. Those who still fail find Heaven's Gates barricaded.

'Your Jihadist Imams – like me – are chosen to guide you through the Infidel's profane world. We are here to inform you that except for the Qur'an, Allah's sacred pronouncements that the angel Jibril revealed to Prophet Mohammad, the *Perfect Man*, Allah's blessings on him, and except for the Hadiths that reveal the words, actions and habits of the Prophet, the Cleaver of Backbones, everything Infidels assert is the blather of dogs, pigs and apes. Can those vile creatures know better than Allah?

'What Infidels call education suffocates Islam. Their so-called enlightenment is more dangerous than bombs. Our sacrosanct texts, the Qur'an and the Hadiths, provide all the knowledge we need.

'Politics and religion are not separate but *One* – like upper and lower jaws. The Qur'an has 500 verses on governance and justice – all inscribed in the Sharia. We are privy to the divination that peace will descend when Jihadism triumphs. We instruct you, as mankind's saviours, that Islam does not tolerate pluralism. You are obliged to convert the Kuffars or, failing that, to annihilate them. Even trees and rocks denounce the Infidels! "Oh, Servant of Allah, Oh *Ruby among stones*," they shout, "there are Jews and Kuffars hiding behind us! Come, kill them because religion belongs to Allah!"

'Hear me! I am revealing Allah's will! I am revealing the Truth!'

A mocking voice interrupts. 'Truth's a harlot who fucks whoever pays her!'

Two policemen bundle away the heckler.

The Imam continues. 'When you face the Last Judgement, you must be light as air and pure as *Zemzem*'s water, the holy spring Allah gushed forth to quench the thirst of Ismail, Patriarch Ibrahim's son. You will be commanded to cross *As-Sirāt*, the bridge above *Jahannam*'s fires, which is thinner than a strand of hair and sharper than Prophet Mohammad's sword, Allah's blessings on him. If you have honoured the Sharia, you will run across it like a child, laughing. But if you have slighted it or failed to perform a valedictory act that glorifies Jihadism, you will be cast into *Jahannam* where punishments in all its seven levels are inconceivable and everlasting.

'The Jihadist who attains *Jannah* will be welcomed by houris – seventy-two white-skinned, eternally young virgins with wide eyes like pearls, pomegranate breasts that never hang and translucent to their marrow. Childfree, non-menstruating, non-urinating and non-defecating, they will pleasure the martyr – who in *Jannah* will possess the strength of a hundred men – day and night with luscious vaginas with hymens unbroken by intercourse wherein the penis will never soften.'

Another man heckles. 'Will the women be rewarded, too? Will the martyrs pleasure them also?'

As he's carted away by the police, the Imam replies. 'Every woman will be provided with a husband who will satisfy her!'

Yet another man heckles. 'That's not what Islam is! You're betraying the Faith by letting your cocks guide you! You're enslaving our women! Getting erections only when you rape! Ejaculating only when you kill!'

He, too, is apprehended by the police.

The Imam's four women shrill in unison: 'Blasphemy! Our men have no equal! They honour our wombs!'

The Imam grins smugly. 'Hear my wives! They revere men's superiority! They understand they cannot be equal because they are constituted differently. Men rule, women bear children, motherhood is their function. The equality Kuffars grant women is unnatural. Even as mothers, women tend to forfeit their purity. They take pride in their seductive charms. They forget that only the immaculate will inhabit *Jannah*.

'But they can be rehabilitated – as I am doing with my wives. As you can see, they are self-effacing now, but in the past, they were harridans. Ignoring the Hadith that "a woman's Heaven lies under her husband's foot", they sought equality like one-breasted Amazons. They could have been stoned or beheaded for prurience or compassionately executed for being against nature and desiring other females. However, now that they have surrendered to Jihadism, I expect them to attain the purity to cross *As-Sirat*.'

THE FIG

Early in our tutelage, Hrant took us to visit a Theme Park in South America representing the Garden of Eden.

At its portals, an ornate billboard, embossed with the Star of David, the Cross and the Crescent, emphasised that every detail of this heavenly presentation had been meticulously replicated from certain divine revelations. A display of testimonies from saints who had had glimpses of Paradise substantiated the claim.

I was impressed. Watercourses radiating from a necklace of ponds reflected the light in kaleidoscopic colours. Flowers, plants, trees, many unfamiliar to my barnyard eyes, exuded exotic scents. But Hrant hooted scornfully. 'Pretentious hogwash! Typical of new Saviours. The old ones at least produced some mind-blowing art.'

On the way to the Garden, he had been comparing the New Generation Saviours – those with no brains and no hearts – with the old ones who lacked either one or the other. 'The difference,' he had summed up, 'is that even as old Saviours tolled bells of doom, terrorised and slaughtered mercilessly, ensnared masses with promises of earthly Edens, they didn't destroy the world. In fact, many loved the world – one reason why they lusted to possess it. Some even loved their subjects. Not so the New Generation. They love only themselves. They seek to be, onanistically as it were, Immaculate Conceptions. These days, they're almost unstoppable. Still "almost" is a favourable factor. Sisyphus rolled up the stone *almost* to the hill's crest; but he couldn't stop it rolling back. The same fate awaits the New Generation.'

We entered a rosy bower. Hrant brightened. 'Today is a good time to tell you about the fig. That's why I brought you here.

'Let's start conventionally from the beginning. The Bible says the Earth was empty. Poetic licence. There was Infinity – origin unknown; probably never to be known.

'Infinity teems with fundamental particles – quartzes, gluons, leptons – which perambulate, collide, bind and create atoms, thermal radiations, galaxies, supposedly even God.

'Now, the fig … A symbol, of course. Symbols compose allegories to reflect whatever they're symbolising. Allegories elicit interpretations of the symbolisms. In Aristotelian institutions these contemplations sought to fathom the vagaries that could be designated as truth.

'Let me offer my favourite narrative, which a school of Leviathans, taking the artless story in Genesis and adding smidgens of popular psychology, propose. Niels Bohr said: "everything we call real is made of things we cannot call real." A grand notion that suggests truths are elusive.

'A closer look at Infinity spotlights two major elements: Hydrogen, the Universe's kingpin, and the liberal Helium. Let's call them God and Pachamama.

'These two; moulding time, gravity, electromagnetic fields, radiation, dark matter, dark energy and roving elements, create flora, fauna and humankind.

'Let's assume they begat our primogenitors, Adam and Eve. My school of Leviathans, rejecting the myth of "Adam's rib" as another attempt at poetic licence, wonders whether the fertilised egg that begat them split partially and that, consequently, these first humans were born joined together like Siamese Twins.'

Hrant continued. 'And God and Pachamama surgically separated Adam and Eve. As these first humans grew up, they developed the gender traits of their parents. Adam became God's alter ego: strong, single-minded, combative. Eve absorbed Pachamama's rational, compassionate, inquisitive essence.

'Adam's pugnacity began to alarm God. He fretted that one day, wanting to live longer than the three-score-and-ten-years allocated to mortals, Adam might decide to overpower Him and become God himself – a feat he could achieve by eating the marrow of immortality contained in the fruit of the Tree of the Knowledge of Good and Evil. And He forbade the eating of that fruit. For good measure, he transplanted the Tree into a dank, sunless spot good only for compost.'

Belkis cheered. 'At last, we're getting there! The fruit is the fig! Right?'

'Not yet. The original Tree of the Knowledge of Good and Evil was not a fig tree but the Themis shrub which, like the Titan who cultivated it, held the cosmic forces that bind the universal laws.'

'Go on …'

'Pachamama refused to accept God's interdiction. Having embraced knowledge as a benediction, she constantly nourished herself – and Eve – with the Themis fruit. Undeterred by the shrub's harsh location, she continued to pick its fruit surreptitiously and share it with Eve.'

'What about Adam?'

'Of course, he resented the way Pachamama and Eve garnered knowledge, especially as this knowledge spurred Eve to defy his assumed superiority. But he felt confident that as an alpha male he was infallible. Besides, engrossed in matters far more engaging than arguments about Good and Evil, he preferred to forgo the Themis fruit and pursue his interests. In effect, obsessed with Universal forces, he was determined to find out their complex workings. How did they interact? Why did they avoid each other sometimes and merge at others? Did they bond for a purpose or by chance? Above all, could he harness these forces?

'As he unravelled the answers, he discovered that some combinations had great potentials as weapons. Exultantly he proceeded to invent weapon after weapon – each increasingly destructive.'

Belkis was outraged. 'Eve let him?'

'She tried to stop him. But he fended her off easily. That forced her to produce her own deterrents. Analysing Life's forces, she concentrated on the soul. How could one fathom its depths? Was the unconscious a source for healing? Was death real or a departure point for spirits travelling to other realms? Did humankind have the will to confront Evil? Was there an Ethical Self?

'The wisdom she gained as she sought answers enabled her to collaborate with Nature and devise strategies to sabotage Adam's inventions. Above all, she found ways to infuse Love – even to Adam.'

Belkis sneered. 'In vain, I expect.'

Hrant sighed. 'Sadly, yes. Sadder still, Eve's probity alienated Adam. He became estranged. Estrangement hatches narcissism. Narcissism demands witnesses. But since Eve, his only witness, abhorred his attitude, he turned paranoid ...'

I interrupted Hrant. 'Surely he had another witness: God! Certainly, God would have been proud of him.'

'God, true to his disposition, was indolent. Having transplanted the Themis shrub into the Garden's anus, He assumed His work was done. Leaving Adam to his devices, off He went following His nose. That galvanised Adam. God's absence, he decided, was his chance to be omnipotent; if he deposed God, he could rule over everything living and inert as The Almighty! Above all, he could overpower Eve and Pachamama!'

Belkis had been pondering. 'I suspect besides wanting to be the Almighty, Adam had another motive.'

Hrant beamed. 'What do you think that was?'

'Misogyny. The Themis fruit's knowledge could match Adam's power. Adam, like most men, couldn't suffer equality with a woman.'

'Quite. Add to that misogyny's corollary: offsprings and fathers' fear that their sons will regurgitate – as Adam did – patricidal thoughts. That classic syndrome drove Adam to destroy the Themis shrub.'

'Surely he couldn't …'

Hrant guffawed. 'He certainly did his best. Picking his time, he uprooted the Themis shrub and, forcing the horrified Pachamama and Eve to watch him, threw it into the ocean.'

'Wasn't God horrified, too?'

'Not really. He just rebuked Adam mildly. In fact, He was pleased. The annihilation of knowledge of Good and Evil guaranteed that nothing could challenge His omnipotence.'

'But the fruit survived. How?'

'Pachamama and Eve – no poltroons they – bided their time. When Adam triumphantly went on a bacchanal, they prevailed on the dolphins to search the ocean and find the shrub's seedpods.

'The dolphins obliged.

'Then Eve and Pachamama chose a humble gnarled tree – the fig tree. They grafted it with the shrub's seeds and replanted it. When Adam sobered up, he noticed the engrafted fig tree and realised that Eve had outwitted him. He went berserk. Later when he calmed down, Eve gracious as ever, offered him a fig. Depicting it as "outwardly a scrotum, inwardly a vagina teeming with worms," he refused to eat it.'

Belkis grimaced. 'Ugh!'

'Later still, the thought that Eve was now knowledgeable in all things brought back the fear of patricide. Reminding himself how he had seriously thought of destroying God, he fretted that she might produce an equally patricidal son.'

For fatherless me, the notion of patricide revolted me. 'Monstrous!'

Hrant concurred. 'And that explains why Adam's brood seek to control sex, censure its joys – even denounce it as *original* sin! Consider how artists were often compelled to cover the genitals of the men and women they painted or sculpted – and, irony of ironies, with fig leaves? Thus, for those who seek to maintain power indefinitely controlling our sexuality is an imperative. But since they need the procreation of generations to preserve their power, they'll allow coition, reluctantly, as a necessary evil.'

I broke in. 'Didn't Adam try to destroy the fig tree, too?'

'He thought of it constantly. But, aware of the fig's potency, he realised that brute force alone can't defeat knowledge. So, he resorted to concocting Big Lies. First, he portrayed Eve's gender as mindless, fickle and immoral. Then choosing a shapely tree – the apple tree – he pronounced it as the real Tree of the Knowledge of Good and Evil.'

We reached the oasis, the Theme Park's centrepiece.

An apple tree in full blossom bearing the caption '*The Tree of the Knowledge of Good and Evil*' stood in a parterre of flower beds. A life-size effigy of an anaconda twined on its branches.

Hrant chuckled. 'More kitsch! Apple and snake! Eden, if it did exist, would've had a Middle Eastern snake. Here, instead of oriental magnificence we get Hollywood! The snake – a healer in folkloric lore – would have been an Egyptian cobra, not an Amazonian anaconda! Besides, rather than being demonised for tempting Eve, it should have been lauded for offering humankind enlightenment!'

We moved on to a stony patch at the far end of the oasis.

Hrant pointed at a knotted tree amid basalt boulders. 'Lo! The real Tree of the Knowledge of Good and Evil! Laden with figs! Gnarled by weighty mysteries. It's fruit toxic to Saviours.'

Mediterranean fig trees were not exceptional to us, yet we stared at it as if we'd never seen one before.

'Hang on to the fig. There's no room for complacency. Particularly nowadays as Adam and his brood are working hard to devise the ultimate weapon.'

Belkis interjected. 'The ultimate weapon – that would be suicidal? It would kill the Saviours, too.'

'Most certainly. And they'd look at their demise as their last godly declaration – that obliteration is preferable to disempowerment.'

Suddenly I felt Hidebehind loitering somewhere.

Hrant concluded dramatically. 'Here endeth our allegory. Any comments? Resonances? Variable interpretations?'

Belkis mumbled. 'Lots to think about ...'

Unsettled by Hidebehind's presence, I kept quiet.

Hrant spurred us on. 'I repeat, hang on to your fig. Thanks to Eve it's in every woman's womb. That's where you started consuming it. And when, one day, you transmute into love the inhumanity Saviours dish out as ultimate morality, you'll eat cornucopias of figs just for their ambrosial taste.'

I pause by a middle-aged Rabbi dressed in a dark suit near the Imam. But for the crocheted kippa that barely covers the bald patch on his head, he could pass for a businessman.

He, too, has a female escort: a woman about his age and two teenage girls, presumably his wife and daughters. Primly dressed as if attending a function, they sit demurely by his side.

'I'm a shepherd to my flock, but I'm also a firebrand. I globetrot as the harbinger of the Messiah, the Teacher of Righteousness. Of Essene descent, I have the gift of revelation! When Titus devastated Judea, my ancestors' exhortations were ignored. But *you* won't ignore my exhortation because Truths are no longer veiled.

'Either of two cataclysms will hasten the Messiah's arrival.

'One: when He ascertains that Jews, having truly attained righteousness, will follow Him to free the world from oppression.

'Two: should Jews, constantly scapegoated by heinous factions, face extermination, He'll storm in to save them so that they can continue to be a light unto nations.

'However, it's not only Jews who are threatened with extermination today. Today anybody can be scapegoated as a "Jew". Genocide is the morality play of our times. Terror is staged as extravaganza. People are as expendable as ammunition.

Religious and nationalist factions produce the special effects. Demagogues are adept at hocus-pocus. They can put Truths into top hats and produce griffins heralding a new and better civilisation.

'But you – and many of my fellow-Jews – fail to see all that! You prefer silence to defending morality!

'Yet the Messiah's advent is imminent.

'So is Armageddon, the long-predicted war between the Children of Light and the Children of Darkness.

'You might ask: who *are* the Children of Light?'

A heckler shouts contemptuously. 'Yeah, who *are* they?'

As the Police pounce on the heckler, the Rabbi addresses him directly. 'We are! We who gave birth to The One God; we, who gave breast to Christianity and Islam; we, Messianic Jews, are!

'And when, led by the Teacher of Rightousness, we defeat the Children of Darkness, Peace will bloom! Religions, nations, races will stop committing serial massacres and serial reprisals! We'll inaugurate the Messianic Age! The Lord our God, has pledged that!'

His wife and daughters declaim: 'Hear, O People! The Messianic Age is nigh!'

I move on.

I stop by a choir carolling and clapping hands. Its few congregants are from a fringe white supremacist sect that had dribbled here from America.

A Caucasian Preacher addresses the gathering. He's tall, chunky, groomed in a gold-lamé robe. The breeze ripples his blonde hair.

'Oyez! Oyez! *Jubilation* is here! Yeah, brothers and sisters, sons and daughters, papas and mamas, we're in *Jubilation* time! Rush over! Fasten your seat belts! We're taking off! Believe me!

'We're no longer wallowing in sin! No longer obeying the Devil's whisperings slithering around us. We've crushed the Devil's head. Now it crawls on its belly. It will eat dust to the end of its days. We've strait-jacketed the whore of Babylon! Stopped flashing our nudity shamelessly! We've tarred the black dragon, God's opponent! We've feathered its vassals, the yellow beast from "out of the sea" and the red beast from "out of the earth"! Fire and brimstone consume all three! And, not least, we've shackled in hell's deepest holes the antichrists who deny The Lord Jesus Christ!

'Thus, we're ready for The Lord Jesus Christ! He's with us! Violent and humiliating death is no longer the ticket to Paradise! When we touch The Lord Jesus Christ, we'll be reborn! That's the *Jubilation* awaiting us! Trust me! Believe me!'

The Preacher's evangelism is combustible. He is mimicking the postures, pauses and pouts of the Italian Saviour, governed during the second age of War.

'Fasten your seat belts, brothers and sisters! Hurry to our launch-pad! We're ready to take off! You are your own spaceship! Your destination – Paradise! A one-way trip! Hurry! Fasten your seat belts! It's *Jubilation* time! Time to be reborn! The Lord Jesus Christ is waiting for you in mid-space! Believe me! Trust me!

'Yeah! We're skedaddling from the Great Tribulation! Leaving the sinners behind! Soon you'll be in *Jubilation*! The Lord Jesus Christ will catch you in mid-air and personally accompany you to Paradise! Too bad for the unbelievers! Endless tribulation awaits them because they won't be reborn!

'Yeah, brothers and sisters, The Lord Jesus Christ will brush off your sins like dandruff on your lapels! He'll vest you with immortality! So, prepare to rocket to The Lord Jesus Christ! Fasten your seat belts, papas and mamas! It's *Jubilation* time! Believe me! Trust me! Believe me!'

I move away. The obsession with eternal life, spreading like bushfire, is shunting us back to the Middle Ages. Revivalist hysteria offers hope instead of enlightenment. Ignorance – not reason – swaddles comfort.

When will people cry out that Paradise must be created on

Earth before they can dream of it in a hereafter?

I move to the Recusants' corner. A man swaying unsteadily tries to step onto a soapbox. A couple of Pinkies manhandle him. 'You've got something to say, have you, methhead? There's no one's here interested in you! So piss off!'

No police to protect him. Recusants aren't entitled to protection.

The man protests. 'I'm … not … drunk …'

One of the Pinkies hits him. 'Is that a new dance you're doing then – staggering?'

'My balance … They … smashed my balls … In prison …'

The other Pinkie kicks him. 'Didn't do a good job, did they?'

The man starts weeping.

I intervene. 'Can I help?'

The Pinkies turn to me. 'Who're you?'

The man looks at me and mumbles. 'Ah, a Samaritan!'

The Pinkies are puzzled. They don't know what 'Samaritan' means. 'Who?'

I retort quickly. 'From his village.'

The man wails. 'I'm Amador …'

The first Pinkie spits at him. 'That's a shit-name for a start …'

'Means "Lover" …'

The second Pinkie smirks. 'Yuk! Amazing what some mothers come up with …'

'I'm … a poet …'

The first Pinkie makes a retching sound. 'Scum poets are. Like Jews! Perverts! Arse-bandits!'

The second Pinkie concurs. 'And Gyppos! Muslims! Jungle bunnies!'

Amador faces them defiantly. 'I try to follow … the footsteps of … Lorca, Hikmet, Neruda, Adonis …'

I'm elated to meet Amador; but appalled by the state he's in. He's not only a god of poetry but also a guiding light of love and life. Much as the devastations of our times have eroded his optimism, he clings to a multicultural world sans frontier, sans states, sans religious tyranny, sans racism, sans chauvinism, sans xenophobia and sans Saviours. This vision, having inspired multitudes of artists, scientists and humanitarians of many nations – and, in defiance of Numen's war against enlightenment, most of our own illuminati – garlanded the poet with prestigious international prizes. It also honoured him with the epithet 'Amador' which, on his publishers' insistence, he agreed to use as his pseudonym.

He's barely middle-aged but looks geriatric. I hold him. 'Come, Uncle. I'll take you home.'

He resists. 'I've come ... to read ... my latest poem ...'

The Pinkies stop me. 'He's our charge!'

I badger them. 'He's sick! On his last legs! Do you want a famous poet die in your custody?'

The Pinkies look at each other, then release Amador.

The first one waves his notebook at me. 'We'll report this. Your name – Sam something ...?'

'Samaritan.'

'Foreign?'

'From the outback.'

'No such thing as outback. Immigrant or minority ...'

The second Pinkie spits again. 'Both, I bet. The sort that's bleeding us dry!'

The one with the notebook rasps. 'Spell your name!'

I spell 'Samaritan' for him.

'Surname?'

Irritated, I remember Odysseus's answer to the Cyclops Polyphemus. 'I am No-man.'

'A joker, are you?'

'No-man – with an "o". Not Numen with a "u"!'

'You're on thin ice with that name. Not many would see the difference. Better change it.'

I put my arms around Amador. 'Come, Uncle, come ...'

Leaning on me, he allows me to drag him away. But keeps

mumbling. 'My poem ... says things ... about clement times ... love for life ...'

I go with Amador to a nearby tavern.

I remind him that true to his pseudonym he loves the world, its people and all that lives, that he imparts this love even to Saviours, that his voice, constantly stifled, is treasured by millions.

He is cadaverous. I ordered a healthy meal, but his broken body can only manage a thin soup.

I want to acquire his steel. Learn how he confronts fear. Osmose the fortitude that kept him sane during indescribable tortures. Understand what preserved his love for humanity when all his jailers – human beings – competed to be inhuman.

I also want to talk to him about children. He has two: a fifteen-year-old son whom he called Rudolph after the boy's childhood icon, the red-nosed reindeer whose shiny nostrils lit up Santa Claus's sleigh; and a nine-year-old daughter, Sonya, named after Dostoyevsky's heroine in *Crime and Punishment*.

But he doesn't want to talk. He wants to write another poem. 'Poets must poetise,' he says.

That's what he's doing now, scribbling on a napkin. Frustrated that his squiggles aren't getting through the swamps in his head, he has already scrunched several serviettes.

He crumples yet another then bangs his head with pulped knuckles. I try to encourage him. 'Be patient. You'll write many more. Give yourself time.'

He can't finish his soup.

He manages to get up.

He attempts to hug me. His head, too heavy for him, drops on my shoulder. 'Look after yourself, Samaritan.'

I get up, too. 'Where do you live? I'll take you.'

'No ... no need ...'

I take his arm anyway. 'I'd like to …'

A gleam passes through his fading eyes. 'I'll find a hillside … meet ancestors … I can still walk …'

'Hardly …'

'If you're really a Samaritan … you'll let me go … I beg you …'

I hesitate. I don't want to hurt his pride.

He extricates himself with a simper. 'Bless you.'

Forlorn, I watch him limp out.

Then I hear a thud.

I run out.

He's sprawled on the pavement.

Vomiting his soup.

And blood.

He mumbles faintly. 'My poem … my …' His voice fades.

A waiter calls for an ambulance.

An old man rushes over. Gently he takes Amador's pulse. 'I'm – was – a carer … He's …'

I seethe. 'A broken urn … A precious timeless urn …'

'He's been tortured …'

'Canonical in our country for a poet …'

Colour drains from Amador's face.

The old man feels Amador's throat. 'His soul's leaving the body.'

I smell graveyards. Maggots gnaw my tongue. A scream, inaudible, howls inside my guts: his children – orphans now.

The old man starts murmuring a prayer.

The ambulance arrives. Paramedics push through.

A crowd gathers.

The old man and I stand like skulls with empty sockets which once housed eyes.

Belkis and Childe Asher appear.

They hold my hands.

SATURDAY 14.19

I want to run to the sea, back to the womb. Instead I drift into the red-light district that bordered our old orphanage. The timeless profession is legal in our country.

The locale is a chirpy street with arched entryways at both ends. People have named it 'the confessional', an allusion to its clients – the politicians, top brass, bankers, fat cats, media-bods, judges, ecclesiastics and celebrities who stream through incognito and confide countless secrets to perfumed loins.

If the pillow talk of the incognitos was to be weighed on Doomsday's scales, it would prove heavier than all the tea in China. While most of these confidences do eventually leak out, they only serve to enhance reputations. The hoary dodderers especially are lauded as golden-agers still capable of quickening their gonads.

Before I met Belkis, I used to sneak here whenever I could save enough pennies from odd jobs. However, burdened by the orphanage's homilies on the pitfalls of carnality, my escapades always felt like slinking into vipers' nests. Only the relief of surviving without fang marks mitigated shame's heavy yoke.

The place bustles. The French-windowed brothels rub shoulders with cafés and bars. Vendors hawk barbecues, pastries and ice-cream. Romani matriarchs sell posies to men hoping to allay their partners' suspicions. There's the usual Police presence, but, judging by their badinage with prostitutes recharging batteries in bars, they seem benign.

Men dart from one brothel to another. Some encounter acquaintances and banter. Those who have just 'flicked their ash' are easily spotted by their jaunty strides. Equally noticeable are those flustered by their indecision about which woman to choose.

The most conspicuous are the poor. They skulk from door to door and masturbate furtively. These rolling stones, so desperate for love, sadden me. The sex-starved are downtrodden, too. They must wonder when, or if, a lover will ever yearn for their touch. Are there lands of milk and honey for down-and-outs? For anybody?

I don't know what made me drift here.

I don't want a woman. Belkis is my woman. I never desired another.

I sit at a café and order a coffee.

A dog licks my hand: Phral, leading Moni.

Moni chuckles. 'Phral purrs so happily when he sees you. Good to meet again, Oric – here of all places.'

I bridle. 'It's not what you think.'

He pulls out a chair. 'Not thinking anything. Just happy to bump into you.'

Several waiters rush with coffees. They kiss Moni's hands. Serve him snacks. Also, some for Phral. And some for me.

I offer to pay but they protest. 'No, no, no. You're Moni's guest. His guests are our guests.'

Moni shrugs apologetically. 'It's so embarrassing ...'

'They love you. Everybody does. You give them good tidings.'

'I try.'

I attempt to sip my coffee, but my hand shakes.

Moni takes my hand and steadies it. 'Grief is very heavy. Sometimes the heart needs to let it out.'

'A short while ago I was with Amador, the poet. He passed away in front of me.'

Moni pours some coffee onto the ground in libation. 'May his earth be plentiful, and may his soul live in light forever.'

'He has children. A daughter, Sonya. Only nine. A son, Rudolph, fifteen. And a wife, Rosalind – for whom he wrote amazing poems. Mostly from prison. Ballads bursting with love. He called her Rosalind-Selene, after the moon goddess.'

Moni sighs. 'I just passed the undertakers. She was there with the children. Organising his funeral, Phral said.'

'What will become of the children?'

'They – and Rosalind – will celebrate his spirit. They'll fight the evils we see and the evils to come. Like Amador they'll denounce inhumanity.'

I mutter. 'That's good news. I sound glib. But I mean it.'

Moni holds my hand again. 'You're thinking of Childe Asher.'

'And Belkis!'

'Belkis is a step ahead of you.'

'But can I catch up with that step?'

'There's someone here – Aurora.'

I protest. 'I'm not here for that!'

'I know. You're here to find your Moses basket.'

I look up thinking he's joking. 'What?'

'We spoke about it this morning. The Moses basket that brought you this far. The one that's taking you to your destiny.'

'Don't I still have it?'

'You do. But you're not sure whether it'll survive the rapids ahead.'

'Might it … Might it not get me to Belkis?'

'Belkis is your destiny – written on your forehead. As I told you.'

'I have fears.'

'Everybody has.'

'Not like mine.'

'Fear is fear. You can't pigeonhole it.'

'You don't understand. I've got Hidebehind chasing me!'

He pats my shoulder. 'Go to Aurora.'

I screech. 'I don't want a woman!'

'She'll help. She wipes the sweat from tortured heads.' He points vaguely at the brothels. 'She works there. Go to her.'

I stare at Moni. 'Now?'

'Now's always better than later. Phral will take you.'

Phral wags his tail.

I follow Phral.

We stop at the door of a brothel.

I hesitate.

Phral barks softly to urge me on.

I go in.

Several women, most of them semi-naked, look at me expectantly. One of them – bare-breasted – comes across.

I stammer. 'I've come to see Aurora.'

The woman smiles. 'That's me. Just saw Phral. Did Moni send you?'

'Yes.'

She takes my hand. 'Welcome.'

She leads me into her room.

I look around, mesmerised. I had expected it to be Spartan – like the cubicles I remember. But this one, an extravaganza in hues of indigo and violet, could only belong to an astral imagination. Everything – not just the carpet, the walls and the ceiling, but also the huge bed, the armchair, the tablecloth, even the bowl, pitcher, urinal and soap in the toilet alcove – glitter in shades shamans attribute to blue moons.

My amazement pleases Aurora. 'Nice?'

'Stunning.'

'I'm saying goodbye to the Piscean Age and welcoming the Aquarian. The Piscean has been ruling us with dictatorial energy for 2,000 years. That's the span of every Age. The Aquarian will rule the next 2,000 with *agape*, brotherhood, sanity and integrity. The indigo chakra – the spiritual power – emits our sensitivities. The violet chakra is earthy, visionary, rational, magical, hence the wisest and most receptive. It affirms the soul's love for all life.'

Belkis would understand her, but I'm bemused.

She strokes my cheek then takes off her panties. 'Undress.'

'Completely?'

She lies on the bed. 'Completely.'

126

I strip off clumsily and look for a place to hang my clothes.

She laughs. 'Drop them anywhere. Births don't need decorum.'

I put my clothes on the armchair. Naked, I feel unbearably shy.

She pats the bed. 'Over here.'

I sit on the bed uncertainly.

She pulls me down. 'Lie down.'

I do, but at a distance from her.

'Close to me.'

I move until our bodies touch.

'Look at my face.'

It's the first time I've dared to look at her closely.

She's not as beautiful as my Belkis. But her eyes, infinitely deep, radiate the same tenderness. Her face glows. She looks ageless. She could be … 'Pachamama!'

She laughs. 'Very kind of you to say so. Now look at my body.'

Again, I dare.

She emanates – like Belkis – the poise of a woman proud of her body.

'Still like Pachamama?'

'Yes.'

'Good man! Time for birth.'

I yield to her softness.

'Souls need several births to evolve. Seven is the standard. There can be more. Do you remember your first?'

'Who can?'

'Some do. I'll tell you yours. It was joyous. Your Mum and Dad were ecstatic. They had waited a long time to have you. Seeing them so happy, you floated on air.'

My mind opens. I feel that happiness. Tears of joy swell up. 'It's so blissful.'

'What about the second birth? That's also usually associated with one's parents.'

'They were taken away. Killed. I was still an infant.'

'You remember it happening?'

'In nightmares and daymares. Whenever I'm afraid. One of Hidebehind's grand guignols ...'

'That's your second birth. Onto the third! That's normally an event that accelerates the Self's evolution.'

'I'd say meeting my Belkis. I loved her instantly. She gave me life.'

'She is your fourth birth. There must have been one before that – one that primed you for her.'

'I can't think ...'

'A transitional event. A rite of passage.'

I freeze. 'Oh.'

'Tell me.'

'I can't.'

'Why not?'

'It tears my guts out. I managed to mention it to Belkis ... also my mentor, Hrant, knows it. Now I keep it locked up.'

She wipes the sweat from my brow and wraps her legs around my body. 'I'll read it off your skin. Shut your eyes. Breathe slowly. Shallow breathing helps births.'

FUGUE SYNDROME

Kosovo, after the turn of the millenium. Yugoslavia had fragmented. Independent states were rising from the wreckage.

The UN Refugee Agency was delivering me to the Serbian Orthodox Patriarchate in Peé.

I was twelve.

At the time, Kosovo was being ruled by the UN. Demographically it still comprised a large Albanian majority with significant Serbian, Roma, Bosnian, Montenegrin, Macedonian and Turkish minorities. The predominant religion was Islam - a conversion dating back to Ottoman rule from the fifteenth to the twentieth centuries.

The Refugee Agency had arranged to return some orphaned and displaced children to relatives who had found refuge in various European countries. The Patriarchate agreed to serve as the reception centre for the reunions.

An elderly seamstress of mixed Albanian and Roma blood, Vlora Yusufi, who was now living in Slovenia with her second husband, a civil servant, claimed that I was the son of her son from her first marriage. She would come to Peé to collect me.

I wasn't the Agency's only ward. There were other teenage boys and girls.

One Albanian boy, Xherdan Kukeli, who had lost both his legs to a bomb in Mitrovìca, was from my orphanage, placed there by the Red Cross. A cousin who had settled in Germany before the troubles would be coming to pick him up. As Xherdan, a few years older than me, was an amputee who barely participated in outdoor activities, our paths had not crossed often. On this trip we became close friends.

Under the custody of Giacomo Manonne, a jolly, lanky, polyglot Swiss-Italian official blessed with the magnetism of a Pied Piper, we assembled in Bari, Italy, took the ferry across the Adriatic to Bar, Montenegro – then still part of the Federal Republic of Serbia – and there transferred to a coach for Kosovo. The journey invigorated me. For the first time in my life, I felt free. No peers mocking my red hair or bullying me to join their gangs. No tedious rules. No wardens to slap me if they deemed my behaviour unsatisfactory or when I sat hunched up or gobbled my food. No Punishment Number 2 that launched punches and kicks for waking up with an erection. (As I hadn't yet reached puberty and didn't soil my sheets with seminal emissions, I was spared Punishment Number 1 of cold baths, dunce caps and days without meals.) Above all, no dreaded Zero Tolerance for wetting the bed. That incurred a bastinado.

But I was also apprehensive. Institutionalised, I didn't have a compass for the outside world. How would I fare in a new life with my unknown grandmother?

As we crossed into Kosovo, the weather broke. The twisting road to Peé through the Rugova Mountains greeted us with a torrential downpour.

Giacomo, whose custodianship included driving the coach, proved to be a good tenor and defied the elements with his favourite arias. Excited by the hazardous weather, we cheered every time he negotiated sharp bends, muddy patches, loose rocks and branches torn by the storm.

Then, in Rugova Gorge, disaster struck. A sudden landslide hit the coach and pushed it to the edge of the road. Only Giacomo's skilful driving prevented us from nosediving into a precipice. We had survived but we were not safe; the rear of the coach stood suspended over the bluff.

Giacomo appeared unperturbed. 'Okay. We have a problem but no problem. We'll be okay providing we keep the front heavy.

Grab your coats, water bottles, snacks and come forward. Slowly!'

Fearfully we did as he urged.

'We'll get out one by one. I'll get some rocks for ballast. Stay calm!'

He alighted gingerly. Impervious to the storm, he lined up some boulders by the coach's door. 'First out, the handicapped!'

We started to disembark. To compensate the weight loss, Giacomo put a boulder inside the coach. His strength amazed us.

When we were all out, he whooped.

We whooped back, relieved.

Giacomo consulted his map. 'We're quite far from Peé. We can't carry the disabled – so walking's not an option. We'll wait for someone to come along. It could be a long wait. There might be more landslides. So, find somewhere sheltered. Avoid trees! They attract lightning.'

Xherdan interrupted him. '*You* can go to Peé, sir, to get help. We'll be all right waiting.'

'And abandon you? What do you think I am?'

'The Great Stork, sir – delivering children.'

Giacomo rebuked him affectionately. 'Cheeky toad!'

'But a stork that can save the kids by going for help, sir.'

'Shut up!'

That's when I volunteered. 'I could go, sir! I can run to Peé.'

'Don't you go nutty, too, boy!'

'I'm a good runner, sir. Gym teacher says I can race Zephyrs. I've got fugue syndrome.'

'What?'

'Fugue syndrome, sir. The compulsion to escape. From the past. Or the present. Something like that.'

'Your Gym teacher says that?'

'The psychiatrist, sir.'

Giacomo scrutinised me. 'You're seeing a psychiatrist?'

'I saw him in the orphanage.'

'What's the treatment?'

'There's no treatment, sir. It's for life. Running, swimming, any sport – they help.'

'How often do you see this psychiatrist?'

'I saw him once, sir. Since I have this for life, he didn't think I needed to see him again.'

Giacomo shook his head in disbelief.

'Anyway, sir, I'm a good runner.'

Xherdan interceded. 'He is a *great* runner, sir. I give you my word. He's always running. Even on the ferry – you might have seen him.'

'I caught a glimpse.'

That heartened me. 'I'll go straightaway, sir.'

'Like hell you will!'

I surprised myself with my boldness. 'You can't stop me.'

'I certainly can. I'm a good runner, too. A Boreas who catches Zephyrs.'

'You wouldn't abandon your wards, sir.'

Giacomo growled. 'Another cheeky toad!'

Xherdan urged him. 'Let him go, sir. For our sakes. We could be here for days. Cold, hungry, hypothermic …'

I insisted. 'Trust me, sir.'

My appeal touched him. He faced me. 'I trust you, lad. But it's not right.'

'I won't let you down, sir. I'll be careful.'

Giacomo gave in. 'I have your word?'

'Yes, sir.'

Keeping out of the rain under the coach's door, he scribbled a note in both Albanian and Serbo-Croat. 'Find a garage with a tow-truck. Hand them this note. With luck, we'll save the coach too.'

I pocketed the note and started running.

@

I ran for about three hours. With the rain still pouring, the wind at full blast and the road spattered with mudslides, it was hard going.

But I felt elated. I was helping the helpless. I was shedding the old skin from my senses, dumping the detritus that had immobilised me. Looking back, I think that was when I began to fantasise that I could have a place in life like most people.

Not far from Peé I came upon a homestead.

Its elderly farmer, Sadiku Mehmedi, intercepted me with typical Albanian benevolence.

I showed him Giacomo's note.

He read it and immediately summoned his wife, Fetije. Knowing a few foreign words, she improved on our sign language and soon understood the severity of my group's plight.

Assuring me that normally he would take me to Peé himself, Sadiku insisted that these days the trip would be extremely dangerous. Serbian xenophobia had flared up again and despite KFOR's vigilance, some clashes had occurred in the vicinity. Therefore, he declared with a grin, it would be an honour for him and his wife to help. They had a tractor, old like him but strong enough.

Hastily we took the road back to the Gorge. We got there late in the afternoon. Giacomo, commending my efforts with a hearty hug, immediately attended to the coach with Sadiku.

While they tied a towrope onto it, Fetije – definitely a Pachamama – fortified us with the cakes and yogurt she had brought along.

Sadiku's tractor, despite its age, was sturdy, wellmaintained and endowed with gutsy horsepower. Guided by Giacomo, he skilfully pulled the coach away from the precipice.

To our cheers, the two celebrated with long swigs of Sadiku's home-made *rakiya* – a permanent item in his tractor.

Then, cautioned again that travelling to Peé during the present troubles would be dangerous, Giacomo accepted Sadiku's generous offer that we should spend the night at his farm.

He would contact KFOR in the morning and urge them to give us safe passage to Peé.

As Sadiku put it, the evening 'embroidered a *bajram*', a holy day.

Somehow Fetije laid on a banquet. Xherdan, spellbound by her, pirouetted on his crutches as her sous-chef.

Fetije let it slip that, in his youth, Sadiku had been a champion arm-wrestler. This led Sadiku to invite Giacomo for a contest. Giacomo accepted the challenge as etiquette demanded. But when he let Sadiku win, the old farmer admonished him. Declaring that arm wrestling celebrates equality – not prowess – because by giving their all the contestants prove they are of the same mettle, he challenged Giacomo again.

When on that occasion Giacomo won, Sadiku embraced him. 'You have the Tengrist spirit, my friend. Will you accept to be my blood-brother?'

Humbly, Giacomo kissed Sadiku's hand. 'I would be honoured.'

They solemnised their blood-brotherhood by consuming a big pitcher of *rakiya*. As they drank, Sadiku told us about Tengrism, a pre-Islamic religion from Turkic Central Asia that spread as far as Hungary. Xherdan translated for us.

Tengrism, explained the farmer, protects those who worship the spirits of sky and earth for begetting life and beneficence. Tengrist worshippers settle wherever plants can be grown, and animals can be fed, and Tengrism conveys to them spiritually the Earth's secrets. In this way, people learn about Nature's nature. When the environment changes, as it often does, they detect the effects of the shift and unravel truths that they hadn't known before.

Later, as if by magic, Fetije spread out rugs, cushions, blankets and quilts for everybody and we went to sleep.

Then in the middle of the night – for me the best night I had had in all my twelve years – Sadiku, Fetije and Giacomo woke us.

Some houses on the outskirts of Peé were on fire. We could see the smoke in the distance and hear echoes of gunfire and mortars. Taking advantage of KFOR's deployment in Peé, Serb gangs were attacking outlying homesteads.

Sadiku was categorical: we could not go to Peé now; nor could we stay in his homestead as it, too, might be targeted. We had to leave immediately and drive back to Montenegro.

Giacomo urged Sadiku. 'You must come with us. You are in danger here.'

Sadiku held Fetije's hand and shook his head. 'We are rooted here. Generations of our families lived here. We stay.'

Giacomo insisted. 'You can come back.'

'Don't waste time. I have two spare cans of petrol. You might need them. Now go. Please!'

Giacomo, deeply saddened, beckoned us.

We started collecting our things.

Xherdan hobbled over to Sadiku and Fetije. 'I'm staying!'

Giacomo, taken aback, turned to him. 'What?'

'This is home for me.'

'You have a cousin – you'll have a home with him!'

'Sadiku and Fetije have become my home. It's as if Allah suddenly gifted me parents. My cousin will understand.'

'You're my charge!'

'I'm sixteen. An adult. Free to decide for myself.'

Giacomo pleaded with Sadiku. 'Sadiku, please tell him.'

Fetije started crying.

Sadiku was tearful, too. 'Look at his eyes, Giacomo. They reflect Allah's will. How can we ignore that?'

Xherdan hugged Giacomo. 'Thank you for being you. For all you did for us. For all you still will do for my friends. Tell the Agency I found my home.'

Sadiku had the final say. 'I give you my word of honour, my brother. Xherdan will be our son as long as we live. Even should he decide to join his cousin.'

Giacomo, much moved, ushered us out.

And we left, tearful and heavyhearted.

◉

KFOR intercepted us on the road and we did get to Peé.

Giacomo's wards were reunited with their relatives.

But not me. The Agency informed me that my grandmother, overcome by the excitement of meeting me, had died of a heart attack as she was about to leave for Peé.

I was sent back to my orphanage.

◉

Two weeks later, I received a message from Giacomo informing me that Sadiku's homestead was attacked before KFOR could get there and that Sadiku, Fetije and Xherdan had been killed.

I never stopped thinking of Xherdan hopping around on crutches, never stopped grieving for him.

I should mention: it was when we left Sadiku's farm that Hidebehind appeared for the first time.

I should also mention: in the Rugova Gorge we saw many birds of prey; one in particular, an osprey, seemed to follow us all the time. Years later, when I spoke to Hrant about Xherdan, he confessed that he was the osprey and that the trip to Peé was one of the occasions when he was assessing me.

◉

I've been weeping.

Aurora disengages. 'That was good.'

'I'm drained.'

She rose from the bed and redressed. 'Perfect!'

'That's it?'

'The third birth. Yes.'

I get up, too, and put on my clothes. 'What about the fourth?'

'You know already that was when you met Belkis.'

'Shouldn't there be one when my son was born?'

'That was your fifth.'

'Is there a sixth?'

'You've had that, too.'

'When? Yesterday? When they gunned down Belkis?'

She strokes my cheek. 'Yes.'

'The seventh … My death?'

She holds my hand and leads me out of her room. 'Death is a lie.'

'That's what Leviathans say.'

'They're right.'

We reach the front door. 'When I go, will I find Belkis?'

'Navigate your Moses basket bravely.'

She kisses my brow. 'Time you left.'

'I … I haven't paid.'

Gently she opens the door. 'Moni's people don't pay. Farewell.'

SATURDAY 15.08

City planners are all men, a feminist once quipped. She was referring to the peculiarity that adjoins the red-light district with the esplanade of gourmet restaurants – an epicurean haven for *bon viveurs* where they're pampered by both courtesans and Michelin star masterchefs.

I saunter along the esplanade and ponder over my births. My mind, unlike Belkis's, doesn't manoeuvre nimbly around esotery and prefers precise concepts. But the question remains. Will I navigate my Moses basket bravely and fulfil my destiny?

'Did you enjoy your third birth?'

It's Belkis and Childe Asher.

'You heard?'

'I saw.'

'You *saw*?'

'Couldn't resist the temptation.'

Embarrassed, I look at Childe Asher. 'Did you, too?'

He demurs as if accused of indiscretion. 'I was having an ice-cream with Moni and Phral.'

Belkis grins mischievously. 'So how was it?'

'Cathartic.'

'Like most births.'

'You … weren't jealous?'

'A little.'

'You've no cause.'

'I know. I was just being human.'

A demonstration, led by two floats, enters the esplanade.

On the first, festooned with flowers and wreaths, a group of prominent actors, writers and artists are reciting Amador's poems.

On the second, chart-topping popstars are singing songs composed from some of the odes Amador wrote for his wife and children.

I turn to Belkis. 'What's going on?'

'They'll hold a wake for Amador. In Elysian Fields.'

Elysian Fields is the famous cemetery for our 'greats'.

'They're burying him already?'

'No. Nor is he allowed to be buried there. Numen just pronounced Amador "a scatological balladmonger whose remains would desecrate the cemetery".'

I scrutinise the crowd. Everybody's wearing a Tshirt imprinted with Amador's portrait and the caption, "I am Amador!"

I'm heartened that such an impressive gathering has assembled in a matter of hours. 'Well done the people! Do his wife and children know?'

'They're at the head of the floats.'

'Do you like my new shirt, Dad?'

Childe Asher, wearing an 'I am Amador' shirt, is pulling at my sleeve. Why didn't I notice him wearing it? And unforgivably, why didn't I gather him in my arms when he appeared? 'It's great!'

'Want one?'

'Sure.'

'Won't be a sec.'

He runs off and a moment later returns with a shirt. 'Might be tight on you. You're too big.'

I put on the shirt. It's tight indeed. 'A bit of a straitjacket …'

Childe Asher giggles as he scrutinises me critically. 'But makes you charismatic. You could be taken for King Arthur trying on Percival's armour.'

I hug him. A mere tot, yet so extraordinary. But then he's from Belkis's womb. He has the fig.

As usual Belkis reads my mind. 'He's you and me, my Oric. A blessing. Yet … Remember when we …?'

Childe Asher pulls her. 'We don't have time to waste.'
Belkis nods. 'Right.'
And they vanish.
I yell after them. 'Of course I remember. How can I forget?'

SINJAR

Autumn. Sinjar Mountains, Northern Iraq.

The Middle East was in turmoil. The Black Standard had declared itself a Caliphate. Its holy duty, it proclaimed, was to fulfil Allah's will and convert the world to Sunni Jihadism. In the process it would cleanse the Faith not only of Infidels but also of the heretical sects.

Indoctrinated with the belief that only terror would institute its rule, the Black Standard had overrun large stretches of Syria and Iraq with unconscionable savagery.

Belkis and I had rushed to Iraq's Sinjar province to help out the Yezidis, a people indigenous to the region, specifically targeted by the Black Standard for practising 'a satanic faith'.

As the Black Standard overran Northern Iraq, it gave the Yezidis two options: conversion to Jihadist Islam or death. When the Yezidis refused to renounce their faith, the Black Standard wreaked a genocidal orgy massacring over 5,000 men and abducting some 7,000 women and children. Most of the women – including prepubertal girls – became 'spoils of war'. With the exception of those deemed too old and unmarketable, they were either sold as slaves or given to Black Standard combatants as 'brides'. Many, rendered worthless by tortures and rapes, were executed; children and infants met unknown fates.

These atrocities prompted the President to intervene with airstrikes. Some 40,000 Yezidis flocked to the Sinjar Mountains – according to local legend the landing place of Noah's ark.

Thereafter, teams from various international relief organisations provided succour with food and medical airdrops.

That was when we joined the aid teams.

I should confess: Sinjar came close to breaking our spirits.

Videos of the Black Standard's executions of groups of men in orange garments, the ritualised beheadings, the burnings in iron cages, the live burials of journalists, aid workers and other enemies, scorched our minds. We wondered how the future could be repaired when insatiable Molochs kept running amok.

We worked indefatigably.

We saved those we could – alas not nearly enough.

We buried many children.

And many young girls.

Some of the latter, adhering to Yezidis' strict tenets on purity and convinced that, eternally defiled by rape, they could never pilgrimage to Lalish, never be illumined by Tawûsê Melek's radiance, had sought redemption by throwing themselves – sometimes in twos or threes – from Mount Sinjar's summit.

Unable to shield our eyes from these horrors, Belkis and I hardly spoke during the three months of our stay.

When it was time to leave, we felt we were defecting and condemning the teams replacing us to Sisyphean torment.

As Peshmerga drove us to a military airport, we kept hoping that the desert's arid air would cauterise the field-hospital's gangrenous stench. But the miasma of killing fields never disperses. The cuneiforms of dried blood, seared eyeballs, scorched hair, hacked bodies, crumbled bones forever susurrate threnodies. Burnt waters, unearthly earths, dimmed suns, tubercular winds, fire-eating fires confirm that the present has been assassinated, that the future is in melt-down, that mercy had emigrated to another planet.

To discharge our anguish, we bellowed like animals in stockyards.

Eventually Belkis murmured. 'I've something to tell you, Oric.'

'Yes, my love?'

'All the children we buried had their hands crossed. They looked like they were relieved to have been killed.'

'Crossed hands are a Yezidi custom. It means the children became angels.'

'But the grief … The parents' grief …'

'Bleeds until their hearts burst.'

'Then … How can we have children, Oric …?'

The question had haunted me, too.

'Do we have the right? To create life – only to see it killed in abominable ways?'

'I don't know, my Belkis. I keep trying to keep strong. Believing one day we'll stop the killings. But I despair and despair. I even think *let's desert, let's hide in our little island, live on fish and algae.*'

'If only we could.'

'Haven't we done our bit?'

'There's no end to bits. We can never give up. Remember that boy – redhead like you?'

'Jangir.'

'Loved the way you played your harmonica.'

'And the way you played the flute.'

'Fascinated by our prayer wheels.'

'Yes … He promised he'd go to Tibet to see the big ones when he got well.'

'He was so proud of his name. Jangir Agha is Yezidis' national hero; defended Armenians from genocidal Turks.'

I grunted. We had attended to Jangir days on end, but we could not save him.

'He always smiled, Oric – even when in agony.'

'Yes.'

'We loved him as if he were our own.'

'Yes.'

'We must preserve his memory; prove we'll always believe in love.'

'If only that were enough.'

She dropped her head on my shoulder. 'Nothing else is …'

I clasped her.

She whispered. 'I'm pregnant, Oric.'

I stared at her. Shocked. Happy. Troubled. 'You … You're … sure?' Tearfully, I embraced her. 'My Belkis.'

She clung to me. 'We'll protect our child … Won't we?'

'Yes.'

I can understand why Belkis and Childe Asher didn't dally. They're concerned about my seventh birth. My last birth. Belkis is in two minds. She wants me to join her. But also, doesn't want me to get killed. Both want to keep me as I am. I can imagine them saying: 'If Hidebehind appears, run! Step back to jump better. We'll always love you. There'll be another day to defeat Hidebehind!'

Yes, she and Childe Asher won't think less of me if I fail tomorrow.

But *I* will.

I decide to attend Amador's wake. I'm still a Dolphinero.

SATURDAY 15.30

Embowered in cypresses and cossetted by breezes, Elysian Fields overlooks the sea from a plateau on the city's highest hill.

Marble mausoleums house the remains of the 'greats' – generals, politicians, aristocrats, clergy and tycoons.

The real 'greats' – our artists, writers, philosophers, humanists, doctors, scientists, explorers and philanthropists – are interred in humbler tombs in a separate sector. That's where the people have gathered for Amador's wake.

As usual, Pinkies abound. Since shadowing every gathering is standard Scythes duty, armed units stand by the monumental vaults. Hoplites guarding silver-spooned skeletons – what can be kitschier?

What's surprising is that Numen hasn't ordered the Scythes to rout the wake. Those with ears to the ground attribute this volte-face to Numen's fears of blanket condemnation from Western democracies. Rosalind, Amador's wife, launches the wake. 'Athena, the goddess of wisdom, is also the goddess of the arts. Though her pleas to her fellow gods to protect artists from tyrants have fallen on deaf ears, she still passionately supports those who give life to Life with their works.

'During Numen's war against freedom of expression, she stood by Amador whenever they dragged him into torture chambers. Wearing Osip Mandelstam's Gulag rags, she took Amador to her bosom to soothe his agonies. Recently, distraught by his shrivelled state, she borrowed the Sun's chariot to whisk him away. Amador, wanting to finish the last poem he was composing, begged her for another snippet of time. Athena granted him that snippet. When

Amador delivered the poem, she winged him to Eternity, that realm where artists live in the hearts of generations.

'Right now, he is imbibing nectar with the Immortals.

'So, by way of replenishing their chalices, we – his family – will read that last poem.'

'It's called *Tomorrow*:

> *Yesterday, the poet, al-Ma'ari, told us*
> *there were two kinds of leaders:*
> *those with brains and no religion;*
> *and those with religion and no brains.*
> *Yet many people somehow survived*
> *there were still*
> *the skies*
> *the sun*
> *the sea*
> *mountains and forests*
> *love of life and wisdom to create*
> *and myths and prophecies*
> *that promised clement times ...'*

I freeze. I realise it's the poem Amador wanted to read in Recusants Corner.

Sonya, Amador's daughter, takes over.

> *'Today, unquiet souls warn us,*
> *leaders have congealed into one kind:*
> *those with no religion and no brains.*
> *Yet the people strive to survive*
> *and*
> *the skies*
> *the sun*
> *the sea*
> *mountains and forests*

> *love of life and wisdom to create*
> *are still here*
> *defiant,*
> *and myths and prophecies*
> *of clement times*
> *are still remembered …'*

Rudolph, Amador's son, concludes:

> *'Tomorrow, the unborn will say:*
> *there are*
> *no skies*
> *no sun*
> *no sea*
> *no mountains and forests*
> *no love of life and no wisdom to create*
> *and myths and prophecies*
> *of clement times*
> *have been effaced*
> *because*
> *there are no people left.'*

I am not surprised that the poem expressed Hrant's views on Saviours. As he once quoted Freud: wherever we go, we find a poet has been there before us.

Rosalind suggests an intermission for people who wish to commune privately with Amador's spirit.

I should go and commiserate with Rosalind. Tell her and the children that I was with Amador when he passed away. But how would that help so soon after Belkis's murder and Nestville's eight killed, twenty-three injured and eleven disappeared?

I withdraw to the parapet and gaze at the city.

Many travel books claim that the most majestic panorama is the view of its seven hills lined up as sentinels. True, but it's a truth that's eroding fast. Corporation skyscrapers compete for height like trees chasing the sun. Villas creak with the weight of wealth. Apartments silent with tongueless bourgeois. Colourful tenements with castrated plebs. And defoliated warrens of those who have lost everything.

The promenades braiding the sea with acacias are full of people. So are the boardwalks by the river's banks. A family rummages the dustbins. Some men sit on the grass and stare into emptiness searching for the future Numen keeps promising.

Here and there people entrust bottled messages to the estuary in the ancient belief that rivers are the quickest conduits to deities. If asked what gives them faith that the messages will reach their destination, they laugh and say mysteries are mysteries.

I believe that.

THE MOSES BASKET

When we told Hrant we were expecting a baby, he said he'd known since Belkis had started walking, eyes peeled for danger, like a lioness carrying a cub in her mouth. We were in our grotto preparing lunch – a role that delighted him as he cooked yet another of his delectable Armenian dishes. But that day although he seemed happy for us, he looked subdued.

Belkis tried to hearten him. 'We've chosen the baby's name.'

'Yes?'

'Childe Asher.'

'After your mythical hero?'

'He'll be the real one.'

'What if it's a girl?'

'The same: Childe Asher.'

Belkis faced Hrant. 'But you're sad. Why?'

Hrant feigned surprise. 'Am I?'

She took his hand. 'Is it because we're Dolphineros? Targets for Saviours? Are you wondering what will happen to Childe Asher if we're killed?'

'The thought crossed my mind.'

'When we're killed we become Leviathans – right?'

'Yes.'

'Then we'll still be able to look after him – or her. Like you've been looking after us.'

'If you're sent somewhere far away?'

'We'll rush back and forth.'

'No qualms then?'

I frowned. 'Plenty. But we don't have a choice, do we?'

'None. But remember time's not always on Dolphineros' side. And Saviours are unpredictable …'

'Being a father. Tending to Childe Asher. I can't think beyond that.'

Belkis backed me. 'We are what we are, Hrant. Right now, we're thrilled that we'll be parents! And you, our beloved Leviathan, are what you are. I can't see you abandoning Childe Asher if for any reason we can't.'

'That's for sure.'

'That's that then.'

Hrant nodded, then moved to a corner of the ledge and brought out a cradle. 'Childe Asher's birthday present. His Moses basket.'

We stared at the basket. It was beautiful. 'You made that?'

Hrant grinned, pleased by our reaction. 'I'm not just grey matter, you know. I'm handy, too.' He showed us the mattress, blanket and pillow. 'The bedding comes with it. Belonged to a Leviathan who had all the pre-Platonic gifts – a prodigy every time he incarnated as a new life. He's in the souls' departure lounge waiting to come again.'

I was intrigued. 'A prodigy, you say.'

'Yes. During his many lives he built reservoirs to trap rainwater for irrigation. Befriended albatrosses and learned to navigate by the stars. Discoursed with plants, discovered their medicinal qualities, taught them how to seduce bees so that they could pollinate plants. Fathomed the psychologies of all living matter. He loved this bedding. So, I'm hoping he'll decide to be Childe Asher. Maybe while he sojourns on Earth, he'll discover what dark matter and dark energy are, whether these forces mutate or not, whether the Universe will expand until it implodes, how humankind will evolve into different creatures as it tries to understand the inexplicable ways machines and robots teach themselves to perform overwhelmingly complex tasks.'

The wake is in full swing.

The gathering, disdaining the Scythes, clink glasses, utter sighs of sad cheer, libate ceremonial beverages, smoke peace pipes, banish bad karma by rotating prayer wheels and sing Amador's paeans. The polyphonous harmony rises like a concert from a parallel world.

Childe Asher's waving hand catches my eyes.

He's sitting with Rosalind, Sonya and Rudolph and pointing at a windmill in the sky.

I look up.

On the windmill's sails, Amador and Belkis are waltzing the Dance of Life.

I leave invigorated.

SATURDAY 16.06

This afternoon, at the Folly on Copernicus Peak, undergraduates from the Faculty of Humanities will present a *commedia dell'arte*, *The Marriage of Mustachio and Beatricia*. I learned this from people at the wake with a good connection to the *Bush Telegraph*.

Copernicus Peak is our observatory. It's situated at the crest of the same hill as Elysian Fields. The Folly – so-named for its ostentatious imitation of Le Corbusier's Zurich Centre – is the loggia that houses shops, restaurants and an open-air recreational area with mini theatre.

Since a play with such a provocative title will no doubt lampoon Numen, the venture is reckless. Have the undergraduates forgotten that Homeland Security monitors the *Bush Telegraph*? Didn't they hear about the carnage in Glorious Acre? Doesn't it occur to them that Scythes can speedily divert from Amador's wake to Copernicus Peak?

The public address system spouts Numen's latest mantra: 'The long-awaited utopia cometh! That's Numen's promise and Numen always keeps his promise!'

Our Saviour's personality cult is a daily liturgy in public places. But the proclamations aren't for citizens only; they also aim to remind the international media that he is a beacon for all nations and the architect of a new world order. Endless repetition can convert Big Lies into Truths.

@

I reach the theatre at the Folly.

I keep my eyes open.

As yet only Pinkies around.

Actors and musicians have erected a crude set.

A recording announces that the play is about to start.

Day-trippers and tourists gather around.

A woman, dressed in a Grecian tunic and wearing a tragedienne's mask, enters and bows to the audience. 'Welcome, ladies and gentlemen … I'm Cassandra, the prophetess who foresees calamities but whom no one believes.'

A damsel, dressed in a ragged but clean frock and wearing a beautiful maiden's mask, follows her and demurely moves to stage right.

A man in a ballooned jumpsuit and wearing a satanic mask with a bushy, toothbrush moustache stomps haughtily to stage left.

Cassandra takes centre stage. 'We have come to hold a mirror to our times. You will note Harlequin, Scaramouche and Colombina are absent. They would have appeared, but they've been jailed. However, our protagonists are here. Let me introduce them …'

Cassandra points at the damsel. 'Beatricia: a lady as beautiful as our country. She has the fragrance of flowers. She's a blessing to humankind. That makes her a target for ravagers. But she doesn't notice them. Her soul is pure. Filled with the irrepressible love of life, she has no perception of evil. Devoted to Goodness, she labours day and night to dispense help and happiness not only to those around her, but also to strangers and undesirable others. She has just finished mopping the blood from the latest massacre thinking that someone had inadvertently spilled red paint. Give her the ovation she deserves!'

The audience applauds Beatricia.

I spot a squad of plainclothed Dragon's Teeth edging stealthily towards the Folly.

Cassandra resumes. 'On my left is Mustachio, instantly recognisable by his fuzz! Isn't it grotesque that these days the noble moustache has become the emblem of ogres who declare themselves Saviours?'

Some in the audience hiss.

'You might wonder: why are these fiends obsessed with moustaches? The answer is banal: because the hours they spend trimming their bristles gives them time to plan ever more brutal ways to rule.'

A few in the audience laugh.

Cassandra continues. 'Alert eyes should espy enmeshed in his well-barbered tash the crumbs of the innocents he insatiably eats. Now look at his elephantine jumpsuit. The lining has many pockets. See how each pocket is stuffed with shoe-boxes.'

Mustachio takes out numerous boxes from inside his jumpsuit.

Cassandra points at their contents. 'Look – wads of dollars, pounds, euros, roubles, pesos, yens and yuan – all pilfered from the Treasury!'

As yet no one has noticed the Dragon's Teeth's silent incursion.

Cassandra sighs bitterly. 'By rights in a sane world, this evil-personified Mustachio should disdain the pure-spiried Beatricia. But no! He wants to marry her. Why?

'Is it because he loves her? But how can he love lacking as he does a single loving neuron! No, he wants to marry her because he wants to destroy all the Goodness she represents. He wants a world cloned in his image –'

Suddenly the Dragon's Teeth rush onto the stage.

Some bludgeon the actors.

Others smash the set and arrest members of the audience.

INTERROGATION

It was the last day of the Autumn Semester.

Undergraduates were spilling onto the campus. With three weeks of intemperance to look foward to, they were ebullient. Some were horseplaying or kicking balls, others organising revelries and a group, gathered around a guitar-player, were singing ribald songs.

Belkis and I were distributing printouts of a batch of Amador's poems smuggled out of prison.

Hrant had assigned this lightweight task in consideration of Belkis's pregnancy.

The undergraduates were grabbing the printouts.

We reached the group of singers and lingered.

The guitar-player picked a couple of poems, read them eagerly and beamed. 'They're great! They'd be perfect lyrics. This one here – *every breath I take is your breath* – begs a *Cante Grande*! It's Doleful. Passionate! Hits the soul!'

That drew my interest. '*Cante grande?* As in Flamenco?'

'Yes. If integrated, it would give pop a terrific new dimension.'

'Ever thought of trying it?'

'That's what my Mum urges me to do! A Jew with Andalusian blood, a salamander from the Inquisition's autos-da-fé – she says I should be oozing *Cante Grande*.'

Belkis encouraged him. 'Mums know. Go for it!"

'I might. If I can convince myself my songs aren't run-of-the-mill.'

'Anything of yours we might have heard?'

'I doubt it. I cut two CDs. They got lost in the Milky Way.'

'We'll look out for them. What's your name?'

'Cuenca, Daniel.'

Suddenly Black Marias teeming with Riot Gendarmerie roared in.

The campus rocked with panic.

Daniel hollered. 'Run! They must be after the printouts!'

We ran but were soon caught.

They nabbed Daniel, too.

As he tried to resist, they hit him and smashed his guitar.

Rounded up with a dozen or so undergraduates, we were whisked to Homeland Security's Headquarters, a flashy skyscraper in the administrative complex dominated by a large statue of Numen.

As they frogmarched us, an undergraduate shouted. 'Welcome to Lubyanka, comrades!' Coshed mercilessly, he was dragged away.

@

We were hauled into a bare, freezing hall. We squatted where we could. Daniel, battered and distraught, slumped against a wall.

We counted eight interrogation rooms. According to those who had been lucky enough to see daylight again, inside each room there was a back door that led to another hall named the limbo. Every so often an interrogator in civvies emerged from one of the rooms and summoned a detainee. Often, he re-emerged minus the detainee.

Daniel, addressed as 'Jew-boy', was among the first summoned. Soon after, his examiner came out without him.

We waited some three hours. Finally, an elderly interrogator came over and pointed at Belkis. I stood up with her. He waved a scornful hand.

'Her first! You later!'

'We're together, sir. Always. A couple …'

Belkis squeezed my hand. 'I'll be all right.'

I ignored her and pleaded desperately. 'Please, sir … Please, don't separate us.'

The interrogator, beguiled, scrutinised Belkis's stomach. She wasn't really showing much but his half-smile implied that he had guessed she was pregnant.

That encouraged me. I reasoned that the interrogator must have a family. And inscrutable as he was, he seemed distracted rather than insensitive. More promisingly, there were convivial cobwebs around his eyes. Can someone who looked benign be cruel?

He relented. 'Very well. Both of you!' We followed him into a warm office. He sat behind a desk and directed us to sit opposite him. Belkis held my hand to quell my fear. I noted some of our printouts on his desk.

He lit a cigarette and spoke softly. 'I'm Inspector Willis.' I nodded respectfully. Wearily, he asked: 'What induced you to distribute this junk?' Belkis answered heatedly.

'It's not junk, sir. Amador's poems are life-enhancing masterpieces. You'll see, sir, if you read them.'

'I have.'

'Then you must agree they're inspirational!'

'They're banned.'

'They shouldn't be.'

Suddenly he barked. 'Saboteurs, are you?'

Belkis faced him. 'How can we be saboteurs, sir? We love all that's beautiful.'

The Inspector hissed. 'Missionaries? Preachers?'

I answered before Belkis could. 'No, sir.'

As ever Belkis had to be precise. 'We believe in the Great Mother, sir.'

That surprised the Inspector. He rasped menacingly. 'Some radical outfit? Communists? Fascists? Jews? Supremacists? Ultra-nationalists? Environmentalists? Animal Rights? Some such? Maybe all those?'

Belkis shook her head. 'Hardly, sir!"

The Inspector stubbed out his cigarette and lit a fresh one. 'Terrorists then?'

Belkis' voice turned icy. 'We're against all violence, Inspector.'

I backed her up pompously. 'We believe in the sanctity of life, Inspector. We uphold the commandment thou shalt not kill. And its corollary, thou shalt not hate.'

The Inspector guffawed. 'Yet it's those who uphold those commandments that kill the most – on the pretext of saving souls! Are you different?'

Belkis laughed, too, but softly.

The Inspector turned to her sharply. 'What's funny?'

Belkis shook her head. 'Your distorted vision of us. How can we advocate violence, killings, brutal conversions to crazed faiths, wars, when put simply, we are Dolphin children.'

Her defiance and honesty dismayed me.

The Inspector stood up. 'Dolphin children, you said? Who are they? Who are their leaders?'

'The Leviathans.'

The Inspector poured himself a large drink, leaned against his desk and sniggered. 'You mean whales? Based where – in the oceans?'

Belkis ignored the sarcasm. 'Everywhere. They're immortals. They're the men and women who envisioned a better world and are now guiding us.'

The Inspector chuckled. 'We live and learn. Even from fantasists!'

Belkis bridled. I coughed to stop her arguing. The Inspector gulped down his drink then poured another one. Again, he scrutinised Belkis. 'Pregnant, aren't you?' That surprised Belkis.

'I didn't realise it showed yet.'

'I told my daughter she was pregnant a month before she knew it. Strangely enough you remind me of her.'

Belkis smiled. 'Really?'

'She's older than you. But stupid. A stupid girl. Still hankers for an imaginary world.'

'I think you're proud of her.'

'Proud? Hardly! She fell in love with a Dane. Lives in Copenhagen now. Wants me to visit once she has given birth.'

Belkis touched his hand. 'You must! She'd be so happy to have you there.'

The Inspector picked up one of the printouts. 'This poem... *Earth never forgets her children; Earth will give them restorative soil: thick and sweet and plentiful* ... Poignant stuff ...'

We affirmed spiritedly. 'Yes, sir.' He took another drink then opened the door.

'You can go.'

We jumped out of our chairs.

Before we went out, he stopped me. 'A lesson for you, boy. Thou shalt not kill never meant anything. Bombs and bullets are raining all over the Earth. Death is a hairbreadth away. Remember that.'

Belkis protested. 'Death is a lie, sir.'

The Inspector turned to her. 'Stop talking rubbish, Girl.'

Belkis retorted gently. 'I hope your daughter gives birth to a healthy child. Go to her. Celebrate life.'

For a moment the Inspector looked wistful, then he wagged his finger. 'Get wise, you two. Give up your illusions of Dolphin children and Leviathans. You're on the wrong planet. Find a cranny. Hide! Keep your child safe. Now fuck off.'

Belkis was about to argue with him. I dragged her away. As we left, we spotted Hrant. Clad in a cleaner's dungarees, he was mopping the floor.

As the Dragon's Teeth run riot, I pull a frantic tourist into a gift shop.

We wait until the arrested are whisked away in police vans.

Mary, an American, screeches. 'What was all that about?'

'A quotidian event in our country.'

'But this is a democratic country!'

'It is – with a gargantuan *lèse majesté.*'

'Meaning?'

'Gods' rights. One mustn't criticise Numen – let alone insult him.'

'Can't you fight back?'

'We do.'

'With mummeries?'

'We have the Word – mightier than the sword, as they say.'

'That's proven wrong – every time!'

'Maybe. The imperative is to believe it. Otherwise we'll be sucked into a quagmire. We'll fade away lamenting that we could have saved the world had we but kept believing in the Word.'

Mary looked unconvinced but declined to debate further. She wanted to reach the safety of her cruise ship without delay. I agreed to escort her to the city docks.

I linger on a bench by an Admiral's statue.

The plethora of memorials in adulation of military bigshots is another baleful aspect of the Saviours' addiction to wars.

I'm surprised – and comforted – that the scent of the sea can still override the pungency of fuel, not least those of the Grand Mufti's aircraft carrier anchored close-by.

I vent my feelings to Hrant. Wherever he is, he hears me.

'The only newness the New Generation have brought is a higher coefficient of hatred for Life. Hardly an original observation, you'll say, and list countless despots who also tried to launch a millennial rule. Yes, but they didn't have Inter Continental Ballistic Missiles! They didn't have chemical and biological vapours that discolour minds. They hadn't yet developed the deceitful enterprise of alchemising Truths into fake-news and Big Lies. The loss of Truth is humanity's greatest loss because it destroys the Self and facilitates his downfall and enslavement. Today, history's evergreen ills – fanatical religion, chauvinism garbed as patriotism, xenophobia, relentless exploitation of hatred and demonisation – are laurelled as sacred commandments. Apologies, Hrant. I'm regurgitating your teachings, ranting because I'm still haunted by my betrayal. But my cowardice didn't surprise *you*, did it? You've known all along that I'm caught in Hidebehind's cobwebs.'

I feel hands on my hands.

Belkis and Childe Asher.

Belkis kisses me. 'There can't be betrayal between us, Oric.'

'You keep saying that! Say something that offers hope.'

'Very well. Guilt is fine, but it has to stop eventually. Something more important, hope, chases it away.'

I shake my head. 'Hope? That's a daydream.'

'Think again! You believe your Moses basket lost its rudder. That your compass is broken and you've sprung leaks. That life faces defeat, if it hasn't been defeated already.'

'Yes.'

'And you can't believe that somehow you're still plugging up the leaks. You won't credit the way we Dolphineros regenerate and find a way to navigate by the stars. You refuse to see we still confound the Saviours, still affirm that Pachamama wants Life to be sane and vigorous. You distrust the fig we still have!'

'*You* have the fig, Belkis. I don't.'

'That's how you try to absolve guilt! Yet you have the fig, too. Despite Hidebehind you give your best – always and bravely. Always will.'

Childe Asher whispers. 'And your next best will be the best.'

I stare at him. Then at Belkis. Dare I believe them?

Belkis kisses me again. 'Listen to our son. He's always right.'

They vanish.

SEVEN BIRTHS

It was nativity time.

Belkis's waters had broken.

Hrant, who had once assisted Hippocrates, appointed himself midwife.

During her contractions Belkis had been exercising, walking to and fro on orchid petals we had strewn around. Orchids, Hrant had informed us, have been an essential birthing aid in China for some two thousand years. Its oil – which I had amply rubbed on Belkis – facilitates delivery by dilating the cervix.

Bringing the orchids had been fun. Swimming to the grotto, Hrant and I had dog-paddled with one arm to keep the flowers aloft. We thought our aquarobics would impress Belkis. Instead, she admonished us for the amount of water we'd swallowed.

As Belkis's contractions became regular, I lit the aromatic candles that legends say Eileithya, Greek goddess of birth, prescribed. The perfumes of lavender, neroli, jasmine and myrrh suffused the grotto.

Hrant increased his sound system's volume. He had prepared a medley: Verdi, Theodorakis, Schubert, Beethoven, Khachaturian, Beatles, Livanelli, Dylan, Cohen.

Then he helped Belkis into the pool.

He had planned the delivery meticulously. It would be at dusk when the crepuscular light would reflect the placenta's ambiance, and the water, having absorbed the day's heat, would be tepid enough to spare the neonate the shock of coming into this world.

Hrant also knew the baby's gender. This perception, he once

explained, is innate in humans, but wanes when people abandon musky soil for polluted urbanism. He himself would have lost it had he not befriended the Leviathan, Robert Gordon, the seventeenth-century Aberdonian philanthropist, who extolled the happy times he had spent in local cattle-breeders' farms. The perception develops through constant observation of the treads and smears a pregnant cow leaves as she walks and sits during her gestation.

Belkis and I didn't have that gift. But then we didn't want to know our baby's gender. Boy or girl it would be a blessing.

Belkis was easing her contractions by doing breaststroke.

I became nervous. 'Should she be swimming, Hrant?'

'She's a dolphin, isn't she?'

Belkis, breathing shallowly, shouted. 'You two – stop behaving like anxious fathers! I'm fine! I feel *I'm* the one in my womb instead of my baby.'

Hrant shouted back. 'You're releasing endorphins.'

That unnerved me. 'What are they?'

'Peptides – amino acids. They suppress pain. Produce good feelings.'

Assuaged, I joked. 'I'm releasing endorphins, too!'

Belkis stopped swimming and trod water.

Hrant moved to the ledge. 'Ready?'

Belkis nodded. 'Ready!'

I stammered. 'Is it … happening?'

Hrant eased himself into the pool. 'Yes. Don't faint! Get in here!'

I slid into the pool and held Belkis's hand. 'I'm here. Hold on to me.'

Hrant instructed Belkis. 'Take a deep breath and hold it!'

Belkis did.

'Now, exhale and push! Keep doing that!'

I started quivering. Was it joy? Was it concern?

Belkis laboured for what felt like an eternity.

Hrant dived under the water then came up instantly. 'Emerging now!'

Belkis managed a murmur; I shouted. 'What is it? Boy or girl?'

Hrant shouted back. 'Big bonny boy!'

Belkis panicked. 'Pull him out! Before he drowns!'

'Don't worry! Water is his element – evolution and all that … Keep pushing!'

I became even more agitated. 'What can I do?'

'Keep holding her!'

Belkis screamed.

Hrant shouted. 'She's done it!'

He dived in again and brought up our baby.

Gently, he slapped my son's buttocks.

Childe Asher howled.

Hrant handed him to me.

I held Childe Asher's face against mine and wept and laughed deliriously. I realised then that nothing in the world can excel the ecstasy of parenthood.

Hrant jumped onto the ledge. 'You can come out now, Belkis! Time to cut the umbilical cord. Oric, give me the baby.'

I handed him Childe Asher, helped Belkis onto the ledge, then climbed out and hugged her. 'It's a boy, my love, a boy – just as you wished.'

For once Belkis was tongue-tied. She laid her head on my shoulder and started weeping, too.

Hrant, holding Childe Asher on his knees, picked up a pair of sterilised scissors and cut the umbilical cord. Then he clamped both navels.

Childe Asher had stopped howling. In fact, he had hardly cried. Instead he was scrutinising us with his amber almond eyes. Was he wondering whether we were the right parents for him? He was so like his mother. Not a hint of yellow-green on his mouth. Hidebehind would have no dominion over him.

Hrant laid Belkis down. 'Now rest, dear girl. Oric, let her have Childe Asher. Belkis, hold him close. Flesh to flesh. Best way to bond.'

Then he dived again and came up with the placenta.

Childe Asher found Belkis's breast and started feeding happily. Hrant chuckled. 'Knows what's good, eh?'

I watched mesmerised while my son darted his eyes here and there as if to imprint onto his mind every detail of the grotto. Is that how prodigies suckle? Will he really be as Hrant believes he will be?

When he appeared satiated Hrant and I washed him.

Then I placed him in the Moses basket Hrant had made for him.

Hrant, humming triumphantly, brought out an Etruscan *bucchero* jug and three glasses. 'Special *usquebaugh*. Pure nectar. Recommended by Robbie Burns.'

He filled our glasses to the brim. 'Welcome Childe Asher, dearest Dolphinero!'

We repeated his toast and drank the *usquebaugh*.

Hrant sprinkled some of his drink into the pool then picked up the placenta and the umbilical cord. 'I'll leave you two for a while. Finish the bottle. Pour a portion into the water as an offering.'

Later as Childe Asher slept in his Moses basket and Belkis and I nested in the Carmelite monastery, Hrant cremated the placenta. He let the air winnow the ashes. The winds, he assured us, would scatter the fig seeds in Belkis's womb all over the globe. And humankind will have a new generation of Dolphineros.

@

A dog nudges me: Phral and Moni.

Moni ruffles my hair. 'We meet again.'

'Always a joy, Moni. Is this one of your turfs?'

'Coffee break.' Moni points at three anglers by the pier. 'I always join those retired Tritons.'

Lost in thought, I hadn't noticed the fishermen. Oldsters. In faded Greenpeace overalls. Against the backdrop of cruise-liners, they look like Lowry figures. 'Anything worth catching?'

'Let's ask them.'

We join them.

Moni introduces us. 'Lads – Oric. Oric – Paddy. André. Joe.'

The men greet me affably, bring out thermos flasks, mugs, and serve coffee.

Phral gets some biscuits which he gobbles up.

Moni banters. 'Oric wonders if you catch anything.'

'I was thinking about the pollution. Our beautiful sea – defiled by ships' effluence, plastic rubbish, you name it!'

Joe replies wryly. 'We've got a pact with Nature. She cleans the waters. We make sure we don't overfish.'

Paddy casts his line. 'It's also a spiritual journey. For us, anyway.'

'Spiritual?'

André doesn't have a rod – just a container teeming with bait. He throws a handful into the sea. 'Like how the sea was before, how will it be at the end.'

Joe has caught a mullet and drops it in a bucket. 'The end being the beginning of another cycle.'

I'm intrigued. 'Go on.'

André, throwing some more bait into the sea, appeals to Moni. 'Tell him, sunshine. You're better with words.'

Moni's voice goes into his good-tidings mode. 'Their pact with Nature. They know Evil has no place in Nature's designs. She wants to feed the living. To do so She serves her species as food for other species. But that's to prevent their extinction – something that humankind chooses to disregard. Because even as She offers her species as food, She provides them with the miracle to beget enough of themselves to ensure their survival. You'll find there are only a few rogue species – like humankind – that kill for the sake of killing. That's a mystery no one has yet been able to explain.

'These lads admire that about Nature. They take only what they need. Paddy has a large family, so he fishes a lot – but no more than what they require. Joe has only his wife to look after. So, he fishes enough for two. André is single and vegetarian. He never catches any. Instead he feeds the fish – you saw the way he does that.'

I'm enthralled. Belkis – and the Leviathans – would approve.

Moni chuckles. 'I should mention André's fare is *haute cuisine*. The fish love it.'

I laugh. 'Like strawberries and cream?'

André chortles. 'Curried prawns – that's the *piéce de résistance*.'

Phral barks gently.

Moni pats Phral. 'Phral reminds me. When Paddy and Joe get their catch they ask the fish to forgive them. They explain: the law that keeps Life alive by feeding it other lives cannot be transgressed. So, in return, they promise to be food for the fish.'

Paddy clarifies: 'We will cast our remains into the sea.'

I envy the clarity of their philosophy. Hidebehinds banished. End of doubts.

Phral paws me gently to say 'yes'.

SATURDAY 16.49

Late afternoon.

Jujube Palace beckons. Named by Numen after his favourite lozenge, the edifice is a compound of dormitories, refectories, recreation centres and pharmacies – a dead-end where pasts and presents are mummified, and all the maps of the future are illegible.

Originally a cloistered tenth-century Romanesque Abbey, it was taken over by the Secular Franciscan Order for those who wished to observe Saint Francis's 'Gospel of Lord Jesus'.

The Order soon attracted itinerant visionaries. Within a century, the tombs of nine of these ethereal men spiralled into shrines and the Abbey, expanding ramblingly, became an anchorage for pilgrims, wayfarers, outcasts and seekers of miraculous cures. Frequently pillaged and razed while Europe ladled out endless wars, it eventually lost its historical and pastoral importance.

The Abbey was given a new life after World War Two when an audacious entrepreneur converted it into a modish hostelry by restoring its ruins, adding another storey in its original style and installing open-air kitchens on the lawns.

Numen, affronted by the Franciscan fiat on the Abbey's portal, '*Pax et bonum*', and paranoid that the supplication for peace and goodness might embolden pacifist opponents, confiscated the edifice and transformed it into a gingerbread version of the old Saviours' psychiatric hospitals for insubordinates. To gull the Western democracies, he now flaunts the place as a showpiece sanitorium where his compassion for ill-starred citizens leaves every leader in the shade.

Effectively, Jujube Palace is a narcotic Shangri-la. Nicknamed

'*The Waste Land*' by the literati, it dispenses, in addition to such favourite drugs as cannabis, heroin and cocaine, sundry chemical concoctions produced as new panaceas by Numen's shrouded laboratories.

The denizens are divided into four categories.

The first comprises the 'stinging nettles', the politicians who tried to sabotage Numen's dominance by campaigning for democratic rule. Numen would have preferred to liquidate these 'Brutuses' but, needing to curry favour with the EU, he had reluctantly abolished capital punishment. Nevertheless, bearing in mind Nelson Mandela's extraordinary odyssey from prisoner to president – a reminder that leaders can surface even from remote jails – he incarcerated them in this overheated conservatory that guarantees early graves. At the very least, he surmised, Jujube Palace would scare vacillating supporters to unreserved fealty.

The politicos are complemented by numerous civil servants, military and security officers who, classified as 'schizophrenic cosmopolitans', fell from grace for their lapses.

The second category consists of servicemen wrecked in Numen's punitive wars. Categorised as 'dross', these veterans lie on hallucinogenic cloudlands that whisk them to firmaments where they can disown their fragmented bodies. This category includes the families that refuse to abandon their men.

Aware that these isolated people would feel forgotten, Belkis and I regularly visited them. Belkis devoted herself to sprucing up the veterans' female relatives with cosmetics and colourful dresses. I, for my part, goaded by memories of my own Empty Quarters, mingled with the children and tried to instil into them that, beyond the bleak spacewalks they resorted to, there's one mysterious force – hope – which rescues forsaken children. As examples I related how Hope had guided shepherds to baby Oedipus abandoned on a mountainside; how it had also sent a she-wolf to suckle the twins, Romulus and Remus.

It is rumoured that initially this group was designated to

accommodate additionally those soldiers gassed by friendly fire. But Numen, alarmed that the existence of these poisoned men might reach the world's ears and thus expose his criminal use of internationally prohibited chemical weapons, not only vetoed the proposal, but also decreed their immediate demise as 'heroes with unknown tombs'.

The third, nicknamed 'Cloud-Cuckoos', consists of the artists, writers, journalists, scientists, students, academics, judiciaries, unionists, enlightened military and Security personnel who turned quisling by condemning the human rights abuses Numen's social engineering had let loose. Spared long terms in dungeons by the grace of international appeals, these stalwarts of yesterday bandage their mental wounds by courting amnesia. Families of these illuminati are also included in this category.

The fourth category – derided as 'Damselflies' – is composed of drop-outs from notable families who, having travelled from hippiedom to yuppiedom, embraced nihilism in confirmation that life, devoid of any intrinsic value, is purposeless. Ineligible for free narcotics, they're admitted as outpatients on two conditions. One: that they consume their drugs on the premises – a measure that at least saves them from the claws of dealers – and two: that they buttress Jujube Palace's philanthropic work with hefty donations.

A fifth off-the-record category comprises people of different sexual orientations, who come out publicly to campaign for their rights. Tagged as 'Chameleons', Numen discriminates against them as brutally as the ultra-puritan communities where they're treated as mutants. Those who warrant special attention and thus cross the arbitrary red lines are arrested at unearthly hours and rushed to Jujube Palace where they're injected with lethal panaceas. Within twenty-four hours their remains are returned to their families with harsh homilies against the perversions that killed them. It is said Numen considers this procedure to be far more civilised than the 'act of mercy' whereby the victim is hurled from a rooftop.

I go in and sign the guest book in an antechamber where visitors used to leave their weapons before entering the Abbey. The residents' privilege to receive guests and socialise is an integral part of their rehabilitation.

There are some Pinkies sitting on chairs here and there like museum guards. But since, except for painful groans, frustrated shouts, muted arguments and the occasional hysterical outburst, nothing of Security interest happens in Jujube Palace, the Pinkies have been reduced to showpieces. Indeed, the observant eye might note that they're quite lethargic – caused either by narcotic fumes or by the moonshine they surreptitiously gulp down.

The bars, the cafés in the cloisters and the eateries on the lawns are packed with many familiar faces: senators, judges, writers, journalists, artists …

The first-floor quarters the war veterans and their families.

The second provides dovecotes for single incumbents. Five for men; three for women.

On the first-floor balcony, clusters of women chat, smoke, drink. Presumably their men cannot leave their beds.

I spot someone familiar at the bar: Willis, the Inspector who interrogated me and Belkis when we were caught distributing Amador's poems.

I approach him. 'Inspector…'

If a face can be slurred, his definitely is. 'Willis … Just Willis …'

'I'm sorry to see you here.'

He stares at me with eyes that have few embers left. 'Who're you?'

'Oric. You interrogated me. And my partner, Belkis.'

'I've interrogated thousands.'

'You have a daughter – in Denmark. She was pregnant. Belkis urged you to be there for the birth.'

The embers in his eyes flicker. 'Belkis, you say?' He points to the war veterans' floor. 'You mean *her*?'

I look. I hadn't noticed Belkis. But there she is helping the women try on new dresses.

I wave to catch her eye.

She sees me and waves back.

Willis titters. 'She's preparing a fashion show.'

'Naturally.'

Willis smirks. 'I was too lenient with her. With you both.'

'You were kind.'

'Fat lot of good!'

'Did you go to your daughter?'

'Stupidly.'

'What did she have – boy or girl?'

'Twins. One of each.'

'Great!'

Willis takes a pill and swallows it with a swig of brandy. 'Great for them. But my undoing. Didn't want to come back. When I did, couldn't get going.'

'You should've gone back to your daughter.'

'A schizophrenic cosmopolitan? On travel-ban? Perfect candidate for Jujube.'

I touch his shoulder in sympathy.

He offers me his pills punnet. 'Have some. They work wonders.'

'I'm a visitor.'

'We're eyeless in Gaza here. True there are Pinkies about. But they're in somewhere else, too. If they see anything they'd probably think it's a mirage. Go on, pick a pill.'

'I won't. Thank you.'

'To celebrate.'

'Celebrate?'

'Rumours percolate. Your Belkis – she was gunned down, someone said. Yet here she is – alive!'

'Only her earthly body was gunned down. She still lives.'

Willis snorts. 'Ah, your mantra. Death is a lie … I remember.'

'There's the proof. Here she is with us.'

He watches Belkis. He looks inconsolable. 'My daughter. And

the twins. They're with me, too. But not here … Where? In my dreams? In my prayers …?'

'In your heart?'

He sneers. 'You're full of shit!' Then he nudges me. 'Go on, have some poison! Free – even to visitors I never get …'

I catch sight of Childe Asher. On the greens. Surrounded by elders. 'What's *he* doing here?'

He turns to look. 'Childe Asher? He visits regularly.'

'On his own?'

'Yeah.'

'What for?'

'Teaches the kids. Discourses with eggheads – like boy Jesus at the Temple.' He points at a flyer on the counter. 'He's having a debate. You should hear him.'

I read the flyer: *What's the difference between the readiness to kill for a cause and the readiness to sacrifice yourself for a cause? What use is reason when irrationality governs us?*

I know Childe Asher is already a Dolphinero, but I didn't expect him to be active so soon.

I wave at him.

He blows a kiss and beckons me to join him.

I should, but I linger. The subject is not one I need today.

Willis senses my ambivalence. 'Come on, have a pill!'

I vent my frustration. 'How about this, Willis? There'll be a protest tomorrow. Against Numen. Come along. You might feel better than being cooped up in this latrine.'

Willis takes another pill. As if it's cleared his head, he speaks lucidly. 'Does it ever occur to you Saviours might be right? That they really save us from the worst?'

I growl. 'There's nothing worse than Saviours!'

'You're a fool, man! Sure there's worse. More to the point: there's us: the *ultimate* worst! You and me: humanity. The Evil within us, timeless, invincible, determined to destroy the planet, which we will. Maybe it's thanks to Saviours we haven't yet.'

Then, wearily he shuts his eyes.

Childe Asher has started his debate: 'Whether in pursuit of a cause or in defence of one, killings are always glorified. Why?'

ANWAR

We were in Dagestan, the mountainous Republic of the Russian Federation in the Caucasus. Our mission was too dangerous to bring Childe Asher, so we had left him in the care of a trusted nursemaid.

We were sent there, on Hrant's recommendation, by a global organisation that researches the collateral ravages of conflicts.

Dagestan's predominantly Muslim population prides itself on resisting the Russification policies of the former Soviet Union of which it was a member state. After the Union's dissolution in 1991 it became an arena for ethnic, nationalist-separatist and Islamic movements.

Our brief – surprisingly initiated by Russian authorities who normally conduct their investigations behind closed doors – was to provide an independent report on the mass suicide of sixty-five young males in Kaspiysk, a city twenty kilometres south of Makhaschkala.

The grisly event had occurred a week ago in the vast refectory of a derelict wharf that had been part of Russia's Caspian naval base before it was moved to a more spacious location.

Numerous hypodermic needle marks on the corpses' arms and a large stock of heroin suggested that the youths had overdosed ritually.

The calamity was discovered when a truck-driver had managed to avoid hitting a delirious youngster who had rushed at his vehicle on the main road. Taken to hospital, the youth, Anwar Sahin, barely seventeen, had gabbled that he was the only survivor of sixty-six boys, that since the death he was meant to share with them had eluded him, he had tried to throw himself under a car.

A security team from Moscow escorted us to the wharf. As if to prove that Russia, unlike the Soviet Union times, was now an ultra-efficient superpower, the 'crime' scene had been set exactly as it had been found – including, macabrely, mannequins representing the youths set around a large heroin-laden table.

We were given carte blanche to question Anwar.

Repeating his previous statements, Anwar related that the youths – none older than twenty – had been kidnapped from cities and villages up and down Dagestan by four three-man teams of the Black Standard officers. The operation, spread over several weeks, had been conducted with exemplary professionalism. Surprisingly, these seasoned Jihadists had not been circumspect. They had divulged how they had contracted reliable mobsters – always ready to associate with well-funded radicals – to keep the wharf 'out of bounds' both from the authorities and the locals. They had also boasted about their cause, their *brutalities*, even how they rose from the ranks. Hence Anwar disclosed not only the noms-de-guerre of the twelve Black Standard bearers, but also that six were from Syria, three from Europe and three from Dagestan itself.

Following incarceration in various safe houses, the youths had been brought to the disused wharf, a few at a time, six weeks ago.

Anwar clarified that the purpose of the abductions had been to convert the youths – Sufis all – as fresh recruits for Black Standard's Caliphate. Since Sufis profaned Islam as grieviously as Jews and Christians with their pursuit of cosmopolitanism, converting their youths into ruthless warriors would have the cachet of divine punishment.

The decision to kidnap sixty-six youths was inspired by Abjad numerology in which each Arabic letter has a numeric value. Since Allah's four-lettered Name, bearing the values 1+30+30+5, amounted to sixty-six, the conversion of the same number of kuffars would please the Almighty especially.

The Black Standard had sound-proofed the wharf. Again, dealing with mobsters, they had purchased sleeping bags, septic tanks, bottled water, toiletries, detergents and ample supplies of food, alcohol and drugs. Lastly, they had summoned a Black Standard Imam proficient in mass hypnotism.

The refectory served as a madrasa. From dawn to sundown the youths watched and listened to incessant recitations of the Qur'an on laptops and large screens. To 'hone' their souls this phase was periodically bolstered with cocaine-spiked sherbets. Any resistance incurred immediate confinement in the wharf's rat-infested boiler room. In the evenings they were encouraged to help prepare lavish meals as preludes to the banquets waiting for them in Paradise. The feasts were followed by communal mainlining and screenings of pornographic films that evoked the houris' 'rapturous skills'. Lastly, to induce 'the sleep of angels', the hypnotist Imam, flashing stroboscopic lights, indoctrinated them with Jihadism's resolve to conquer the world.

Initially, the Jihadists either mainlined their captives forcibly or supervised them while they did so themselves. After three weeks, when most of the youths had become addicts, the supervision slackened.

The relentless programme caused havoc in the youngsters' minds. Most of them verged on insensibility. Many stopped disdaining the indoctrination. But a few – five in all – inspired by Rustam Khabib, a staunch wayfarer on Sufism's spiritual path and at twenty the oldest of the captives, managed to remain relatively lucid. (Months later these youths, acclaimed as *Hamsa* – meaning 'five' in Arabic – were compared to the open-palmed amulet against the evil eye.)

On the fifth week, the captors decided that the youths were ready to be sent to Syria. Once there and wrapped up in the black flag, their conversion would be immutable.

Thereupon, leaving behind the three Dagestani Jihadists as

guards, the nine Black Standard bearers and the hypnotist Imam left for Turkey to arrange the youths' transportation.

At that juncture, the *Hamsa* seized their chance. After the evening banquet, they waited for the guards to indulge in their routine of drooling over the porn, chain-smoking cannabis and getting drunk. As intoxicants are forbidden to the Faithful, the guards should have eschewed arak. But for front-line men stimulants had become standard issue.

Eventually, when the guards started gushing patriotic songs, the *Hamsa*, frantically fighting withdrawal symptoms, attacked the guards and disarmed them. Then, leaving them with a liberal supply of drugs, arak, water and food, they locked them in the boiler room.

While the guards pounded the boiler room's metal door and threatened to kill the youths unless they were released immediately, the *Hamsa* arranged the refectory trestles into a large round table.

Onto this they piled jugs of water, hypodermic needles, citric acid, cotton wool, spoons, Bunsen burners, matches, tourniquets, bags of heroin, laptops and camcorders.

Rustam invited the youths to sit facing each other.

Below is the transcript of the video recorded by the laptops.

Rustam: 'We are seemingly free now. Let's not fool ourselves. We've been defiled – reduced to carrion – by a creed that is not a religion but an evil ideology that sanctifies killing, conquest and spoils. An ideology that instead of purifying souls for Allah kills both Allah and souls.

'Were we just innocent bystanders? Or were we being tested to see if in our hearts we covet extremist Islam, harbour thoughts of power, glorification, material goods and the savagery of beheadings, burnings, stonings, live burials; do we harbour fantasies of bedding houris instead of attaining union with the Beloved?

'Were we being punished for our weaknesses when the only

punishment we fear is abandonment by the Beloved?

'We'll never know. They've broiled our minds.

'So, where do we go now? How do we shed our putrified souls?'

Rustam pauses as his fellow-captives exclaim. 'If only we could …'

Rustam pacifies them. 'I think we can!'

Some youths beseech him. 'How? Tell us!'

The pounding on the boiler room door and the guards' threats get louder.

Rustam takes a deep breath. 'We have two options. One: since we, Sufis, keep our doors open to everybody, we can crawl back to our communities hoping they can cleanse us.'

The youths groan.

Rustam continues. 'Two: Although we're irreparably wounded, "the wound", as Rumi says: "is the place where the light enters". If we can look at our plight in that light, we can see a solution. We can kill our polluted selves and come back from the dust to try again to become people of faith!'

The youths protest loudly.

Rustam outshouts them. 'Returning to our communities in our present selves would be unconscionable – it would be like spitting on their souls. Very likely we'd contaminate them. But the second option – suicide – is transgressive!'

The youths, in two minds, argue incoherently.

In the background the tumult from the boiler room continues.

Rustam raises his hands to silence the youths. 'I'm as addled as you are. Islam forbids suicide. Yet most of its doctrines have been open to interpretation. The Ayatollah, the Hamads deployed suicide-bombers – "poor man's atom bombs", they called them. They justified that those who blow themselves up not only serve Islam but also attain martyrdom. Today the Black Standard and Jihadists of its ilk are using the same polemic for their suicide-bombers.

'Our objective would be different, the very opposite in fact.

179

We would commit suicide not for warfare but to save our souls. We'd do so knowing that unless we sacrifice the Self – kill its demands and cleanse its impurities – we can never ascend the Seven Heavens.'

He pauses.

A silence, disturbed only by the pounding on the boilerroom door, ensues as the youths ponder the implications of Rustam's reasoning.

Rustam resumes: 'Should you, like me, choose to end your lives here, there's more than enough heroin for a fatal overdose. Anybody who considers this the wrong option is free to leave.'

Again, a long silence as the youths deliberate.

Finally, some youths shout: 'You have lit the way, Rustam.'

The rest clamour in support: 'We'll "*seek the unseen and see beauty appear!*"'

Chanting the Beloved's many names, the youths begin to heat the heroin.

Laughter, hugs and kisses harmonise their farewells.

@

Later the guards break down the boiler room's door.

Bewildered and disoriented by their captives' suicide, they grab their guns and run off.

Much later Anwar, having regained consciousness and distraught that he is still alive, frenziedly staggers out of the refectory.

@

Russian Security summed up the aftermath. Helped by Anwar's descriptions, they cornered the guards on the outskirts of Khasavyurt near the Chechen border and killed them.

Identikit pictures of the Black Standard officers and the

hypnotist Imam, again based on Anwar's descriptions, were circulated to many foreign Security Services. Seven of the nine and the hypnotist Imam were located in Iraq and arrested by American forces.

We went to say goodbye to Anwar before we left.

Belkis: 'The case is closed. They'll let you go now. You should start thinking about the future, Anwar.'

Anwar: 'I have. I'll join my friends.'

Belkis: 'You have a beautiful religion. You can guide your people.'

Anwar: 'Not as carrion.'

Oric: 'That's not what Rumi says:

"Come; come, whoever you are,
Wanderer, idolater, worshipper of fire,
Come even though you have broken your
Vows a thousand times,
Come and come yet again,
Ours is not a caravan of despair."'

Anwar: 'There is another view:
"Till you reach Nothingness you cannot see
The Life you long for in eternity."'

That night Anwar slipped out, leaving behind this note: *'I'm swimming to Kazakhstan. It's about 400 kilometres. That should purify me.'*

His body was found the next morning.

The post-mortem reported that far from being bloated his body was translucent.

I should admit I felt I had come of age in Dagestan. I had come to understand, as true Dolphineros always understood, that questions always produced many different answers and that often truth and untruth are indistinguishable.

Belkis, ever judicious, thought Hrant had an ulterior reason for involving us in the mission. 'Perhaps he wanted to prepare us for our end. To let us see – as proof that death is a lie – the luminosity a soul leaves behind when it departs for its next existence.'

I asked her. 'Do suicides become Leviathans?'

'There's a more important question: What's the difference between those who kill people who don't believe in a cause as zealously as they do and those who kill themselves equally zealously for their beliefs? Particularly when in both cases the killings are oblations to a Divinity?'

'I want to say there's no difference. But I don't know ...'

'Do you know now?'

'What?'

Willis snorts some cocaine. 'Whether there's a difference between killing for a cause and sacrificing oneself for one?'

I stare at him.

'You were babbling. About Dagestan.'

'Oh ...'

'Well, do you?'

I'll never know. So I growl. 'Death is a lie ...'

'That's your stupid mantra! Not an answer.'

Belkis would know. But she's still hobnobbing with the women on the top floor.

Then I look at Childe Asher, heatedly conducting his disputation. 'Go and listen to my son. He'll know.'

Willis takes a few pills. 'I want *your* answer.'

'For what it's worth, I'd like to believe there *is* a difference. A matter of choosing between Good or Evil.'

'How can we tell which is which?'

'The ethical self tells you.'

Willis guffaws. 'Can we trust whatever that is?'

'It's innate. You can trust it.'

'If it's innate it must vacillate. Everything human vacillates.'

Childe Asher appears at my side. 'Ethical selves never vacillate! If evil frightens them, they run away. If they can overcome fear, they stand shoulder to shoulder with goodness.'

Willis snorts. 'That sounds like religious brainwash. Silver-lined toxin.'

Childe Asher rebukes him gently. 'Only if you keep your head in the sand!'

Then he runs back to his debaters. 'See you, Dad.'

Proud of my son, I turn to Willis. 'There you have it.'

Willis shakes his head. 'There I have nothing.' He points at his drugs. 'Except these short-cuts to never-never land!'

I give him a pitying look and leave.

SATURDAY 17.12

I'm at the Transnational station.

Most Saturdays it's crowded. Not so much with people going away or coming for weekend breaks, but with forlorn souls.

Today, given the tight security mounted for the Grand Mufti's visit, Pinkies and Gendarmerie abound.

In general, a sizeable percentage of travellers carry troubled lives. They've either hit a crisis or hope to escape from one. Often, they find it easier to unburden their woes to strangers. So Belkis and I came here regularly to offer empathetic ears. Hrant compared us to the spirit world's soul-rescuers who help those snatched from this world suddenly or violently and are disoriented in the hereafter.

I've come to empathise with three groups.

The first, Mothers of the Disappeared, comprising women of all ages, gather every day. They sit on the forecourt holding pictures of sons and daughters who, caught in the fringes of politics, have vanished.

When people stop by, they show the photographs and ask if they've spotted the children somewhere or have information about what happened to them. These mothers know that the disappeared are invariably executed soon after their arrest, yet they cling to the hope that a traveller or two may have seen a dazed youth in a corner of the land or in a labour camp. (Throwing detainees into the sea from helicopters is Fatherland Security's favourite method of execution. It can then claim that the youths, assessed as misguided romantics, have not been detained and are either lying low or have fled the country.)

To date, no traveller has come forth with any news. Even if there were some with snippets of information, they would be too afraid to tell. Pinkies meticulously log those who approach the Mothers.

Nonetheless the mothers' plight touches people's hearts. Wives of soldiers killed in action somewhere unknown linger mournfully. Pregnant women and those with kids stop and commiserate. Occasionally some Mothers burst into *Mothers of the Disappeared* honouring the Argentinian women whose children, too, disappeared during the Junta's dictatorship.

Today there are about sixty mothers. The numbers vary, though seldom drop below fifty. The regulars, the group's backbone, are mainly middle-class, intellectual or artistic urbanites. The rest languish in the provinces. Age, poverty, illness, travel restrictions and fear of losing their other children prevent them from getting to the city regularly.

The other groups are inside the station.

One consists of families of soldiers on leave from the current engagement with 'terrorists'. They flock the platform where a train has just brought their men.

The terrorists are the large indigenous minority in our eastern provinces. Numen condemned them to ethnic cleansing for campaigning for an autonomous canton – as in the Swiss confederation – where they can speak their own language and pursue their own culture. To date the conflict has claimed thousands of lives on both sides. Lately Numen has intensified the hostilities.

The reunions are restrainedly joyous. The soldiers maintain their military bearing, yet their eyes are tenebrous from the carnage they've seen and barely survived. Their commanding officer, a paternal Major, tries to animate them, but they – and their families – know that after the brief respite, they'll be back at the front and that the next time they return they might be in body-bags.

The other group, assembled at the adjacent platform, is a gathering of families sending off sons, brothers and husbands to the war zone.

Despite brave miens, horseplay and camaraderie, the atmosphere there is elegiac. The commanding officer, a pugnacious Colonel, hurries his men officiously, occasionally wrenching apart couples trying to prolong their goodbyes.

A year ago, there used to be a fourth group. That, too, was composed of families seeing off loved ones. However, the latter were not soldiers but the weekly crop of liberals indicted as traitors, secessionists, or anarchists, and sentenced to internment in remote labour camps. But as those families and deportees often behaved 'turbulently' these transportations now take place in the early hours of a weekday when the city is asleep.

I approach the Mothers of the Disappeared.

A middle-aged woman, sitting wrapped in a blanket with a thermos flask by her side, catches my attention. Softly humming, she displays a large photograph of a young man hugging a guitar.

I recognise the youngster: the musician Belkis and I met while distributing Amador's poems at the University.

The woman notes my reaction. Her dusky eyes float in a lake of tears. 'Do you know him? Have you seen him? My son, Danny?'

I hesitate.

'Please look … Danny – Daniel Cuenca.'

How can I tell her Danny ended up in a dungeon that usually leads to Via Dolorosa? 'Sorry. I don't think …'

She doesn't want to believe me. 'The way you stared at the picture …'

'He looks like someone I knew.'

She shushes me by wagging her finger. 'Don't say *knew*. Say *know*. He might be alive.'

'He looks like someone I *know*.'

My change of tense doesn't help.

A couple of Pinkies scrutinise us.

I ignore them and squat by Daniel's mother. 'Cuenca – the

name rings a bell. And the guitar. A musician was he – is he?'

'Yes. Songster. Recorded a couple of albums.'

'I think I heard him on the radio.'

Enthralled, she talks breathlessly. '*Cante grande* – that's his genre. Honouring ancestors. Songs of love. Songs against oppression. "You're too political" people kept telling him. I warned him also. But ...'

'Serious art is always political. That's why dictators hate it.'

She clasps my hand tightly with both her hands. 'You think so, too. Brave lad. Not afraid to speak your mind.'

I cringe. Gently trying to extricate my hand I stand up. 'Hardly brave.'

She clings to my hand. 'Don't go – stay a moment. Please. It's good talking to you. Like talking to my son.'

I sit down, deeply affected.

She puts her head on my shoulder. 'Maybe you can answer: why does God kill children? Why does He cut out mothers' hearts and crush fathers' souls? Where's is His love?'

'I don't know.'

'My husband, Emmanuel ... He's a *hazan* – a cantor. He says God has gone to another galaxy and left his apprentice behind. He pities the apprentice – too callow to judge life and death, he says.'

I want to say, 'he may be right,' but I don't.

'He – Emmanuel – won't go to synagogue anymore. When Danny disappeared, so did his faith. Now he just sits by the window, singing.'

She very obviously needs to talk. I engage her. 'Your son's songs?'

'No. Only *Danny Boy*. Non-stop.'

'Irish, is he – your husband?'

'And Spanish from way back.'

'How do you mean?'

She becomes even more animated. 'He knows every detail of his ancestors – all the way back to the Armada. He'd tell you, for instance, after the Armada's defeat in 1588, some ships diverted to the North Atlantic and drifted to Ireland. The detour proved disastrous. Twenty-four sank. His forebear, the First Cuenca he calls him, was an Andalusian Marrano – a Jew who converted to Christianity to survive the Inquisition. This man was a gunner on *La Juliana*, one of the ships wrecked off County Sligo. He managed to swim ashore – helped, as Fate would have it, by dolphins.'

I'm taken aback. 'Dolphins? Really?'

'Yes, Emmanuel says dolphins are famous for saving shipwrecked sailors. Anyway, that's how the First Cuenca ended up in Ireland. And because the Irish didn't persecute Jews, he settled there. Eventually he met other refugees from the Inquisition – this time from Portugal – and found a wife. But he didn't forget his community in Cuenca. The city was infamous for its countless autos-da-fe. So, in commemoration of the Jews burned at the stake there, he took on the name Cuenca. Generations followed. Then the potato famine struck. Some Cuencas – including Emmanuel's ancestors – emigrated here. Which made Emmanuel, as he used to say proudly, a hybrid of three religions: Jew by birth, Islamic by Andalusian lore and Christian by Ireland. That's why he named Danny Daniel: the perfect Jewish-Irish name.'

Her ramble has drained her. She picks up her thermos flask. 'Want some tea? I've got an extra cup.'

I glance at the Pinkies. They've lit cigarettes. Definitely keeping tabs on us. 'That would be nice.'

I watch her pour the teas. So motherly. 'The story about dolphins helping the First Cuenca – how did that come about?'

'From the First Cuenca himself, I imagine. But then families are like fishermen – they inflate sprats into whales.'

Impulsively, as she handed me my cup, I kissed her hand. 'Let me tell you a story about dolphins …'

LA PALOMA

Often Dolphineros's missions ended calamitously. Yet Hrant, relating a lecture by Daedalus, insisted that failures were necessary because they hacked out the paths to eventual accomplishment. Referring to his son, Icarus, who took to the air only to fall into the sea when the sun melted the waxed bindings of his wings, Daedalus maintained that the youth's fate didn't deter the generations that followed from trying to fly. And after ages of countless failures, the Montgolfier brothers opened the horizons with their hot-air balloon. Today we fly everywhere; tomorrow we'll shuttle between galaxies. Thus, in the struggle between Good and Evil, Good's failures guarantee Evil's demise.

Belkis and I suffered several failures. One of which, but for the help provided by dolphins, would have floundered irremediably. It occurred in Honduras, one of the most hostile and dangerous countries in Latin America for human rights activists. We were assigned to smuggle out *La Paloma, the Dove*, Central America's songbird who, campaigning for the emancipation of the campesinos, had become the bane of the Minotaurs in the corridors of power.

Aided by a band of patriots and assisted by a cameraman, she transmitted, every Sunday, a vlog from secluded locations. Starting with her signature tune, *Cucurrucucú Paloma* – the classic ballad wherein a woman laments the loss of her beloved – and ending with her adaptation of Woody Guthrie's *This Land is Your Land*, she belted out a medley of incendiary songs that urged the people to oust the Minotaurs and their accomplices, the drug-barons, before they devoured Honduras's future.

In countries where lawlessness is the law, activists have brief lives. Paloma had so far evaded assassination attempts and though commendably no one had yet claimed the substantial rewards offered for her capture, she was running out of hide-outs. Unless smuggled out soon, the barbed noose with her name on it would claim her.

We flew to La Ceiba three days before the Carnival which, on the third Saturday of May, celebrates the city's patron saint, Isidore the Labourer, and draws some half a million tourists.

We were accredited as ichthyologists attached to Iceland's Reykjavik University sent to assess the damage to marine life by the vast increase of plastic waste. Professor Ququmatz, dean of Littoral Atlantic University's Oceanographic Research Centre – and one of Paloma's most ardent supporters – had volunteered to help us.

Ququmatz is an epithet. Born Antonio Suarez, the name honours him as the reincarnation of the Mayan god who, floating in the primordial sea, created life, the cosmos and water's salvational qualities.

He met us with typically exuberant Honduran welcome. A chain-smoker informally dressed in shirt and slacks, shortish and corpulent with long hair, a tousled beard and strong indigenous features, his face shone with joviality. His students called him Pato, partly because he walked like a duck.

We fell under his spell immediately.

He informed us there was a change of plan. Normally the Carnival provided the drug-barons with a smokescreen to forward their goods to various destinations in the Carribean by using naïve tourists as drug mules. But, since the recent death of a young American backpacker whose bag of cocaine burst in her stomach, the government had imposed ultra-strict surveillance on all aircraft and boats. Under these circumstances, smuggling Paloma out of the Caribbean – as originally intended – would be too risky. We had to divert to the Gulf of Fonseca where the

Oceanographic Research Centre had its Pacific branch. There we would escort Paloma to El Salvador and hand her to a patriotic Honduran cell in exile.

We spent the days before the Carnival sightseeing while Ququmatz made new arrangements with Paloma. Given the secrecy needed to contact her, he conducted communications in Ch'orti, an indigenous language. That in itself presented some problems. In a population of about ten million, Ch'orti, slowly lapsing, was only spoken by about fifty thousand indigenes. This enabled the Security Ministry to monitor all communications, particularly on social media. As latterly many Ch'orti-speakers had been extrajudicially killed by death-squads, those still prepared to risk their lives to support Paloma were small in number.

Finally, Ququmatz arranged to rendezvous with Paloma on the volcanic island of El Tigre a week after the Carnival. The venue albeit not perfect – nowhere in Honduras was safe – had nonetheless some advantages. El Tigre was off the beaten track. Its isolation and small population would enable us to assess the security measures. Most importantly, El Tigre was close to a number of El Salvadorian islands. We planned to sail with Paloma to one of these, called Conchaguita.

@

Before setting out for the Pacific coast, we mixed with the Carnival's celebrants. We had brought our peace props. Belkis played the flute; I the harmonica. We joined the marimba players, guitarists and trumpeters, danced with total strangers, shared peace pipes, rotated Tibetan prayer wheels and offered the children beaded bracelets. We received garlands in return.

One incident marred the enjoyment. Ququmatz, showing unexpected skills as a juggler, was entertaining a group of children. Nearby some campesinos, gathered around a small band, were singing folk songs. When we stopped to watch them, a tall, well-dressed man sidled up to us.

'White gods, I presume?'

Belkis looked at him quizzically. 'That's some greeting.'

He responded gravely. 'That's how Moctezuma, the Aztec emperor, addressed the conquistadores. He thought white Cortés was the god Quetzalcoatl returning as legends had predicted.'

Belkis jested. 'We're of humbler stock. Icelanders.'

'Good. That might keep you safe.'

I faced the man sharply. 'Safe, did you say?'

He smiled impassively. 'Cortés destroyed a great civilisation. Natives haven't forgotten that. Whites don't make good gods. Actually they're no longer white but green – dollar green – gringos.' One of those Anglicised mestizos that pose like hidalgos. With something crawling in his oily smile.

I retorted brusquely. 'Moctezuma and Cortés – that was Mexico. Honduras is Maya-land.'

He chuckled. 'I see you know your history. Still conquests spread. And never leave – like gringos.'

That irked Belkis. 'Are you suggesting we're not welcome?'

A big smile this time – a very smarmy one. 'No. But I think it's important to ask foreigners what they are doing in this hell-hole. Why don't you stay at home? There you won't keep looking behind you to see who's following.'

Belkis riposted brusquely. 'We consider the world our home.'

I interjected. 'And a home that needs lots of repairs!'

The man looked surprised. 'You are here to do repairs? How commendable! I'm Salazar. Businessman. Perhaps I can help. What sort of work do you do?'

Belkis replied coolly. 'Research! PhD work.'

'Lucrative?'

My alarm bells started ringing. 'We make do.'

Salazar pondered a moment. 'I imagine researchers could well do with some manna from Heaven.'

Belkis quipped. 'They could certainly do with a magic wand.'

'Magic wands are what we, businessmen, have …'

I taunted him. 'Are you offering us a job?'

'If you want one.'

'Doing what?'

'Anything. Courier work maybe.'

'You mean drug-mules?'

'Mules – no. More like cranes delivering happiness.'

Belkis fumed. 'You've picked the wrong people!'

'Did I?'

I snarled. 'Definitely.'

Salazar shrugged. 'Pity … *Vaya con Dios!*'

As he walked away a burly man staggered over and started ranting at Belkis. 'Woman with red shirt! Go home! Here red shirt is bad sign! Brings fire.'

Belkis humoured him. 'Like Prometheus? I'm flattered!'

The man pointed at me. 'You, too, carrot-head! Go home!'

I squared up to him. 'You're drunk, man. Just get going!'

My confrontation enraged him even more. He shouted. 'Red means blood!'

The singing stopped. People looked afraid.

Ququmatz, alerted by the silence, rushed over. 'What's going on?'

The man kept shouting. 'Women easy to kill. Soft. Men more difficult, but not too difficult. So vamoose!'

Ququmatz took him by the arm. 'Go, hombre, go! Before I call the police!'

Incongruously the man bowed. But as he tottered away, he shouted again. 'Don't say Diego didn't warn you!'

Ququmatz looked troubled. 'Carnivals – that's when riffraff creep out. They worry me.'

I was worried, too. 'We also had someone asking us to smuggle drugs.'

That troubled Ququmatz even more. 'Oh?'

'I think we should report them.'

'No. Most police are in cahoots with drug-barons. Besides, you're undercover. We don't want to start an investigation.' That chastened us. Then Belkis, seeking to recapture the gaiety we had been enjoying, urged the band to resume playing. I caught sight of Salazar across the road. He was watching us with his unctuous smile.

The next day, we set out for El Tigre in a house trailer bearing the Research Centre's logo and equipped with four beds, a kitchen, a shower and a workable laboratory. The week at hand would give Paloma the time to thread her way to our rendezvous. Bypassing the capital, Tegucigalpa, we drove through the country's mainly mountainous terrain for four days. We visited Mayan ruins and national parks and proceeded to San Lorenzo.

Having made countless such journeys, Ququmatz had become a patriarchal figure in many villages. Wherever we stopped to buy provisions, people, despite their poverty, refused payment. Ququmatz responded by giving donations to community centres. Most impressively, many campesinos, fascinated by Ququmatz's work, kept bringing him uncommon riverine fish.

On the afternoon of the sixth day we reached Coyolito, the hamlet that provided the only regular ferry service to El Tigre. Hours later, Paloma texted that she, too, had arrived and was staying with Nahún, the boatman from Playa Negra, whose cruiser Ququmatz had hired.

Early the next day, a Sunday, we parked the house trailer at the Fishing Cooperative where Ququmatz was much esteemed and boarded the ferry to Amapala with a group of tourists. We took the hikers' route that circles the island and offers slip-tracks to its volcano, fishing villages and beaches. We had decided that trekking in broad daylight would enable us to spot any suspicious activity.

Aware that in the midst of a few hikers, my red hair and Ququmatz's long ebony hair would be conspicuous, we wore hooded cagoules. So cloaked, we felt safe even when a Coastguard helicopter from the mainland circled the island a couple of times.

We reached Nahún's cabana in Playa Negra early afternoon. With its secluded beach and crude jetty, the place had a raw charm. But instead of the boisterous Honduran welcome we expected we met an eerie silence.

Moments later a truck with some men firing submachine guns veered from the road and stopped alongside. Five men and the driver jumped out.

I recognised the driver. 'Diego!'

He wagged a finger at us. 'I warned you!' Hidebehind perched on my shoulder.

Ququmatz shouted at the men. 'Where's Paloma?!'

A man in smart slacks and shirt, also armed, emerged from the cabana: Salazar, the suave businessman from La Ceiba. He spoke amiably. 'She's inside. Come in. Come in.'

Diego prodded us. 'Move!' We stepped onto the veranda.

Haughtily, Ququmatz faced Salazar. 'Now let me guess. You are –?'

Amused by Ququmatz's tone, Salazar saluted like a soldier. 'Salazar, Señor. Coke-king. Patriarch. Jefe. All things!'

Ququmatz, maintaining his arrogance, seethed. 'Paloma – inside you said. Is she hurt?'

Salazar crowed. 'Not anymore. You see, she shouldn't have come. Women should know their place.' Ququmatz ran into the cabana and howled. We rushed in. And froze at the sight of four bodies on the floor.

Raging like a wounded lion, Ququmatz threw himself at Salazar. '*Demonio!*'

Salazar knocked him out with his gun. 'Also, women shouldn't interfere in big business. Certainly, never carry guns like Paloma. That begs for tragedy.'

Diego and his men were blocking us. Belkis pushed them out of the way and went to attend to Ququmatz. I heard Hidebehind chuckle. I tried to think of a way to overpower Salazar and his men.

Salazar, enjoying my impotence, identified the bodies derisively. 'Paloma, the dove. Nahún, the seadog. Itzel, his wife. Esteban, Paloma's cameraman – probably her lover, too. Mature women like young men.'

I stared at the bodies. Nahún and Itzel – tall with striking Mayan faces. Esteban, bearing the glow of mixed blood. And Paloma, lips twisted as if trying to wrench songs that had stuck in her throat.

Salazar scoffed. 'Always surprises me why hand-to-mouth people like Nahún choose hard work when money is so easy to get.'

Belkis, cradling Ququmatz, hissed. 'They're born good – that's why!'

'Good is always a bad choice, Señorita.'

Belkis flared. 'You've killed four saints! Don't you feel any remorse?'

Salazar sneered. 'I did Heaven a favour. Not many saints around these days. So, I gifted a few.'

Ququmatz was regaining consciousness. I helped Belkis pick him up and seat him on a chair.

Salazar pointed at some bottles on the table. 'Take a breath. Have a drink. Honour the dead. Nahún kept a bar for clients. There's bourbon, rum, tequila, vodka, gin.'

Hoping alcohol might clear my mind to find a way to overcome our captors, I swigged some rum. It produced an idea. I faced Salazar. 'Before you kill us – as no doubt, you will – can we bury our friends? In solidarity?'

Salazar snapped his fingers. 'Thanks for reminding me.' He barked at Diego. 'Ándale!'

Diego signalled at the other men. They picked up the bodies of

Paloma and her helpers and carried them out onto the veranda.

Salazar waved a hand. 'I have something better planned – a surprise. You like surprises?'

Belkis taunted him. 'Where we come from, surprises surprise the surpriser.'

Salazar smirked. 'Here's not where you come from, señorita!'

'You'd be amazed where we come from.'

Salazar chuckled heartily. 'You liberals! Always stiff upper lip.'

I sipped more rum. 'Don't underestimate stiff upper lips.'

Salazar dropped his bonhomie and turned feral. 'Look at it this way: Paloma and her sidekicks were at my mercy – as you are. Now they're travelling from dust to dust. That's the reality.'

Ququmatz muttered disconsolately. 'Give me another reality. Who betrayed us?'

Salazar faced him, amused. 'Who do you think?'

'Surely not campesinos!'

'No, not campesinos, Professor. But then they're stupid. They turn into three monkeys to save Paloma. She's holy, we don't betray holy souls, they say. I tell them I'm Jefe – better than holy soul. You live because of me. Because of my gang. I protect you! Make you family! Give you food, shirts, money, guns, drugs, everything! Sometimes I even warn liberals – like Diego and I warned you in La Ceiba. Forget saints, I say. They try to change the systems. But systems can't be changed. Death-gangs, head-honchos they're forever! It's like talking to stucco masks!'

Ququmatz taunted him. 'Stucco masks know right from wrong!'

Salazar poured himself a drink. 'Yes, they do. On the other hand, your stucco masks also have canaries. Put gold around their necks, pearls on their cojones, greenbacks to wipe their arses with and they'll give viaticum to anybody.'

Ququmatz looked puzzled. 'Canaries … Do you mean somebody abroad?'

'More than a somebody, Professor.'

Ququmatz, refusing to believe him, shook his head. 'Why would they? It's safe abroad.'

'Dollar is God everywhere.'

'Even so …'

'You'll have a chance to see for yourself, Professor. They'll be in Conchagüita – where you're going. They'll be the choir for the funerals.'

Ququmatz retorted defiantly. 'Don't bet on that!'

Salazar pointed to the bottles. 'One for the road? For my surprise?' Ququmatz, Belkis and I exchanged looks. Then we – even Belkis – filled our glasses. Salazar became effusive. 'No doubt, you're wondering why I'm not killing you. I would have – if, like Paloma, you pulled a gun. But you're not *guerreros*. You're peripheral. Better to let you sail. It saves me the trouble of killing you.'

Belkis was incredulous. 'You're letting us go? Are you serious?'

'I'm always serious! But I want you to promise you'll hand over Paloma to her canaries in El Salvador. They can build a shrine for her. And eat their greenbacks – shit-scared – hoping that I won't one day get rid of them, too.'

'Then what – after the funerals?'

'Then you go home. Maybe even hang up your boots.'

Ququmatz stood up. 'You should know I don't hang up my boots. You might as well kill me now!'

Salazar shrugged. 'I can vaporise you any time, Professor. Also, with respect, when the authorities hear that you collaborated with Paloma, you'll be untouchable. They'll retire you. No one will risk downing piña coladas with you. No more love-ins with fish. If you're lucky, you'll find a backyard and get hooked on cocaine or señoritas or catamites.'

Diego shouted from outside. 'Preparado, Jefe! Too engrossed talking, we hadn't noticed Diego and his men packing Paloma, Nahún, Itzel and Esteban into body bags on the veranda and hauling them onto the back of the truck.

Salazar finished his drink. 'Let's go, amigos. Don't forget your backpacks.'

By the time we walked to Nahún's cabin-cruiser at the ramshackle jetty, Diego and his men had laid out the body bags on the deck.

Salazar enthused. 'Your yacht. From Noah's time but will get you safely to Conchagüita. Get in.' We boarded the cabin-cruiser. Hidebehind was still on my back, but I felt more confident about getting us to safety. We had a boat and the sea was our domain. Diego released the mooring line. I started the motor. It fired immediately.

Salazar waved his gun. '*Vaya con Dios*!' We sailed off as a few fishing-boats were returning home.

Ququmatz scanned the horizon. 'He's not letting us go, you realise that?'

We concurred. 'Yes!'

He pointed at the sun gliding to set. 'It'll be dusk soon. They'll probably attack then. I imagine a Coast Guard will blow us to smithereens. Some stuff will float – that's why Salazar told us to take our backpacks. News will say we hit an old mine.'

Belkis thought a moment. 'If we can move out of their sight a bit, we can swim to Conchagüita.'

Ququmatz shook his head. 'Not a chance. Besides, Conchagüita is out! You heard Salazar. There are canaries there waiting to tell the world we died in a terrible accident. The neighbouring island, Meanguera, also El Salvadorian – that's your destination.'

'*Our* destination?'

'I've been told you're great swimmers. You should do it! And soon!'

'Are you suggesting –?'

'Staying put, yes.'

I protested. 'Nonsense! We started together and we'll stay together!'

Ququmatz waved a dismissive hand. 'I'm hardly fit for a long swim. Too old, too fat, plus smokers' tarred lungs.'

'We'll help. I can carry you!'

Ququmatz rummaged through his rucksack and brought out two plastic envelopes. 'Take these. Specimen bags. I always carry some in case I find something interesting.'

'What do we need them for?'

'Maps, passport, money. Tie them round your waist. Now undress. Scatter your clothes on the deck.'

Belkis protested forcefully. 'You're coming, too. Oric's strong.'

Ququmatz shook his head. 'I've had a great life – despite all the ills of my country. I don't mind leaving it.'

We disagreed vehemently. 'You won't be leaving it!'

Ququmatz pointed at the sun. 'Sunset soon. Undress now. Please!' We humoured him and undressed. He took off his necklace and gave it to me. 'Find the Oceanographic Centre in Meanguera. I have an old student there: Xavier Lopez. Rock solid. Go at night when it's quiet. He always works late. He'll recognise the necklace – he gave it to me one birthday. St Christopher, travellers' patron saint. Never forsook me – and it won't forsake you. Put it on now.' I did. 'Tell Xavier what happened. He'll get you home.'

Belkis held his hand. 'Your turn to undress! You're coming along!'

'I'm staying with Paloma. I haven't been with her for a while.' We heard a whirring sound and looked up.

Ququmatz frowned. 'The helicopter we saw this morning.' It was flying straight towards us.

'It's coming to bomb.' He rushed into the cabin, came out with two snorkels and handed them over. 'Nahún's always wellequipped. Go now! Swim under water!' As we hesitated, he argued. 'You must admit, I can't swim to Meanguera from here.

Nor would I let Oric carry me. So that's settled!'

Belkis and I exchanged looks. He was right.

He kissed us. 'Go! Now! Please! For Paloma's sake!'

Belkis hugged him. 'One last truth. Death is a lie.'

Ququmatz chuckled. 'That's good to know.'

Disconsolately, we slid overboard and swam away from the boat.

He waved at us. 'Tie your bags! Watch out for sharks!'

We donned the snorkels and dived.

Minutes later, we heard the muffled sounds of explosions. We waited a few minutes then surfaced. No signs of the cabin-cruiser. Just an oil slick and floating pieces of wood and clothes. And no remains of Ququmatz or the body bags.

We caught sight of the helicopter returning to its base.

We swam to Meanguera. On the way, sharks appeared.

When they started circling us, pods of short-beaked dolphins, led by a larger one, appeared. They chased the sharks away. Thereafter, communicating with clicks, whistles, postures and acrobatics, they formed a protective ring around us. Occasionally the larger one nudged us to change course.

We realised they were Leviathans led by Hrant. Some, we presumed, were recent ones: Ququmatz, Paloma, Esteban, Nahún, Itzel. We even imagined that one young dolphin who stayed very close was Childe Asher.

We reached Meanguera around midnight. The dolphins led us to the Oceanographic Centre's pier. There was light in one of the rooms. Assuming its occupant was Xavier Lopez, we went there.

The sudden appearance of two near-naked people astounded him. When I showed him Ququmatz's necklace and related how he, Paloma and her companions were murdered, he burst into tears. Then he promised that although the Honduran media, fully controlled by the Establishment, would not investigate the destruction of Nahún's boat, he'd make sure the world would know.

As Ququmatz had predicted, early that morning, Honduran news services reported that the famous Professor Ququmatz, two of his foreign students and four guests – including the superstar, Paloma – had perished when their pleasure boat hit a mine dating back to the dispute between Honduras, Nicaragua and El Salvador over the Gulf's islands.

For a week, we hid in a lumberyard – 'for our own good' as Xavier put it. We saw him at nights and became great friends.

Early the second week, a Human Rights organisation flew us to Costa Rica's capital, San José.

@

The Pinkies are photographing us with their techsets.

Defiantly, I kneel and rest my head on Daniel's Mother's shoulder.

She strokes my hair. She's no longer tearful. There's hope in her voice. 'When Dolphineros are killed do they really become Leviathans?'

'Yes.'

'And consort normally with people?'

'Yes.'

'My son – Danny …?'

'A Dolphinero, very likely.'

'Maybe a Leviathan?'

'Maybe.'

She laughs softly. 'It would be typical of him.'

I kiss her hand and stand up. 'Remember that. Always.'

She squeezes my hand. 'Your Belkis …'

'A Leviathan now. But by my side.'

'Maybe she and Danny will meet.'

'Why not?'

'And you? Still a Dolphinero?'

'For now.'

She rummages through her bag, brings out a shamrock and gives it to me. 'For good luck. With my love.'

I'm deeply moved.

'I am Esther, by the way.'

'I'll think of you as mother.'

She beams. 'Will you?'

'What better?'

As I move, she calls out. 'When you see Belkis, tell her to tell Danny I know he's alive. That I'm proud of him. Always will be!'

'I'm sure he'd want to hear that from you – when he visits.'

'Playing his guitar?'

'And singing *Cante Grande*.'

She sighes beatifically, then starts singing *Danny Boy* softly.

I leave with the song implanted in my mind.

SATURDAY 17.28

I've reached the old town's rim where creaking tenements, patched up with every conceivable material, hobnob with medieval walls. In olden times this fringe was a ghetto known as Urs-Lāutari and harboured Romani bear-tamers, horse-breeders, musicians and acrobats. Today, still home to some Roma communities, it's also a 'dumpsite' for immigrants. These days, despite the reasonable quota of refugees we initially agreed to admit, our intake, subverted by Numen's antediluvian fixation on 'purity of blood', has been drastically reduced.

Amador, alluding to the artefacts and flint-knappings excavated, imagined the locality as a Stone Age habitat and wrote an epic poem called *Terra Amata*. In this place, he contended, one can hear hunter-gatherers' whoops, agriculturists' rain-dances, women's birthings and euphonies of the thousand-and-one languages hibernating on our tongues. Here those interested in olden times discern countless civilisations and watch history's shadow-plays of happiness and tragedy, wealth and poverty, soldiery and slavery, philosophy and iconoclasm, science and art.

The lanes are festooned with flags, buntings and pictures of Numen and the Grand Mufti in observance of the latter's state visit. Television screens at vantage points show a legion of diplomats entering Xanadu's grandiose banquet hall, where a sixteen-course feast – sixteen representing the years of Numen's rule – awaits them.

I'll spend the night here. Roma hospitality is legendary. And Rajko, a virtuoso of the *kanun*, keeps his doors always open.

The main lane bustles with police cars, bulldozers and diggers.

Moni led by Phral appears. 'Hello again.'

I stroke Phral then ask Moni. 'What's with the heavy machinery?'

'They'll raze the neighbourhood. Starting at midnight.'

'They can't do that! It's a preservation area – by law!'

'Laws evaporate when Numen sides with developers. They plan to poshify the place.'

'What about the people living here?'

'They'll be relocated.'

'Where?'

'Who knows?'

'Can't your pebbles tell?'

'I won't ask them. Won't be good tidings. What brings you here, Oric?'

'I thought I'd stay with Rajko. Get primed for tomorrow's final stand.'

'Rajko – a prince! I'll join you.'

Phral, delighted by the idea, starts leading us.

We skirt round the heavy machinery and the police cars.

I kick one of the bulldozer's tyres. 'I can stop them, Moni. Some sand in the petrol tanks.'

'Don't. They'll blame the Roma and go on a rampage. What's needed is shape-shifters that transform machines into pumpkins.'

'I'll get some from the corner-shop.'

Moni rebukes me. 'Sarcasm, Oric?'

I retort. 'You're a diviner. Can't you shape-shift, too?'

Moni sighs. 'It takes time to learn. Perhaps next reincarnation ...'

A dulcet voice interrupts us. 'We can organise shape-shifters!'

I spin round. Childe Asher and Belkis, both smiling mischievously.

I wink at Belkis. 'Wonderful to have a son who believes the impossible is possible.'

Belkis reproves me. 'You should know – he always means what he says.'

Childe Asher gets excited. 'Should be fun. Leave it to us.'

They vanish.

We've reached Rajko's shack.

Moni knocks on the door.

Rajko, his wife, Lule, and his six children – three girls: Dika, Jaella, Livia; and three boys: Boldo, Nicu, Pesha – come out immediately.

Rajko, a big man with powerful arms, embraces Moni. Then he hugs me and mumbles heartfelt condolences about Belkis; Roma have a deeper understanding of loss.

Despite the eviction hanging over his family, he welcomes us joyfully. 'Good that you dropped by! We're about to celebrate our exodus. Neighbours will join. My Lule has prepared a special feast and I've got enough firewater to sozzle angels.'

We go in.

Lule serves wine to Moni and Phral.

Rajko hands me a huge glass. 'Home brew! Turns kittens into tigers.'

I sip. It's more than firewater; it's lightning. 'Wow!'

Rajko pours himself an equally large glass.

We sit. Elated to be with each other. No words needed.

I watch Phral horse around with the children. A bevy of cats joins them.

Moni starts dozing.

Rajko picks up his *kanun*.

As he plays, I shut my eyes. Invariably, whenever I'm cocooned by goodness, Hidebehind stands at a distance to remind me he's biding his time. I've learned to live with that. I think of my journal. It emphasises the goodness of goodness.

PAX MUNDI

One of our missions sent us to work with *Pax Mundi*, an association that campaigns for world peace and organises free cultural encounters in countries where entrenched hatreds wreak social disorder and wars.

Founded in Berlin by an international caucus of artists and backed by several foundations, it promotes the theory that art, even when tyrannised by religious, ethnic, racial and nationalistic dogmas, can melt these malignancies by sustaining humankind with beauty, harmony and spiritual transcendence.

At this time, *Pax Mundi* wanted to focus its attention on the persistent persecution of the Roma in many European countries. With Hrant's blessing we decided to serve as assistants in a forthcoming encounter.

As impartial scholars would assert, historical accounts are rarely, if ever, objective. Historians, bound by their ethnicity, nationality, religion, culture and ideologies, tend to tint their narratives with their biases. Annals, whether recorded by victors or vanquished, are consistently divergent. Also, chroniclers often neglect tangential factors such as poor harvests or water shortages and fail to emphasise that history is moulded by migration – not only of displaced peoples but of tribes seeking better pastures, of armies invading honeyed lands, of prophets, rebels, ideologues and humanists trawling for converts.

The history of Romani migration is one of the most neglected. Europe's largest minority, the Roma, have been maligned, scapegoated, ostracised and slaughtered for over a millennium. Unwelcome in many countries, seldom allowed to settle in cities and villages, they've been condemned to perennial nomadism. Like their Jewish counterparts, they barely survived *Porajmos*, 'the Devouring', their Holocaust.

As the globe rattles with a new tectonic phase of migration, antagonism towards them has intensified.

For its Roma encounter *Pax Mundi* organised six groups to cover those countries most hostile towards the Roma.

Every group was allocated trailer-trucks large enough to haul tents, platforms, musical instruments etcetera and decorated with Romani motifs. Fitted with mod-cons, each truck also provided excellent accommodation for six people.

The groups drew lots.

We drew Hungary – a country which increasingly subjects its large Roma minority to social and economic exclusion. Recently its Supreme Court, decreeing that educational segregation of Romani children was legal, encouraged schools to bar them from canteens, gyms and remedial classes.

Our group comprised eight artists and twelve assistants. In addition to recitals, the artists were to conduct masterclasses. The assistants would act as stage managers, handle odd jobs, liaise with the crowds, help with the catering and drive the trucks.

We set out from Berlin in five trailer-trucks: four allocated as male and female dormitories; the fifth to store the props and to serve as greenroom, galley and dispensary.

Given *Pax Mundi*'s ethos none of the artists demanded top billing. But as their figurehead they elected Mai Montañés, the flamenco superstar, nicknamed La Terpsichore after the goddess of dance and song. Convinced that the soul of flamenco was Gypsy music – a fact that she believed explained Spain's better treatment of the Roma – she personified, as Lorca put it, '*the Gypsies' flame and universal truths*'.

The other artists were: Chiyoko Ishikawa, a Japanese wunderkind and the best living interpreter of Chopin's works – those 'cannons buried in flowers' as Schumann described them;

Ghislaine Weber, the German harpist, called 'Seraph' for her ability to 'colour music with heavenly hues'; Serena Saracino, the Italian soprano whose voice entices chandeliers to sing; Hayyan Habeeb, the Palestinian master of woodwind who causes 'the leopard to lie down with the kid'; Dakota Reed, the American balladeer 'born with the songs of all peoples'; Tomek Waclawski, the Polish painter whose works conjure 'a clement parallel world'; and Manoush Baxtalo, master zitherist 'who translates what hearts say'.

Nick Dewar, a wiry ex-rugby international, one of the new generations of Scots who wear kilts as everyday clothes instead of on special occasions, joined us as our doctor. Lastly, the ever-serenading Neapolitan, Fortunato Umiliani, the Italian football team's chef, pitched in to keep the group wellfed and wellwatered. We all bonded immediately and journeyed in an atmosphere of laughter, bonhomie, music and anticipation. After several autobahns we reached Passau, the Bavarian City of Three Rivers straddling the confluence of the Inn, the Ilz and the Danube.

We had planned to spend a day sightseeing the old town's mix of gothic and baroque architecture and visit St Stephen's Cathedral, famous for housing the largest church organ in the world.

Instead we met many refugees from Syria and Afghanistan who had walked all the way from Turkey hoping to build new futures in Germany. Some other European nations, vilifying the refugees as economic migrants, were beginning to refuse them entry. Aware of this, Ghislaine prompted us to visit the Refugee Reception Centre – a sub-camp of World War Two's infamous Mauthausen – to show that many Europeans still cared for displaced persons. While Fortunato conjured a cordon-bleu banquet, our artists staged an impromptu performance. The refugees, enlivened, joined in with their own songs, dances and narratives. We hoped the poignant interlude might induce these outcasts to believe that spirits can be repaired, that the metamorphosed Mauthausen can promise life instead of chasms.

From Passau, driving straight through Austria to Hungary, we saw many more refugees plodding towards the German border. In Hegyeshalom, the Hungarian border town, we met Manoush Baxtalo who would direct our encounters. Burly, decked with rings, earrings and a pendant with an engraving of a colossus holding aloft a rainbow, he had coal-black eyes that appeared to have seen everything.

We – particularly Mai – took to him immediately.

Doborján, Franz Liszt's birthplace, was the venue of our first encounter. The choice delighted Chiyoko, a sublime interpreter of Liszt who, she insisted, while much influenced by Romani music, had also been greatly inspired by Chopin's lyrical romanticism.

Initially this first encounter was scheduled to take place in the grounds of Liszt's house – now a museum. But as we would raise the curtain at noon and press on for the rest of the day, we needed a more spacious site for our stage and tents. Serena, radiating her diva's charm, persuaded the municipality to switch the venue to the town's Athletic Field.

We erected a large stage. Instead of a set we hung a backdrop painted by Tomek which featured cartoons of the artists as musical instruments bearing olive branches and flying among clef signs, crotchets and quavers.

Watching a multitude – including countless Roma – flock to the Athletic Field, Manoush worried that the Roma presence might cause trouble.

He needn't have. The venue emanated a festive spirit. People, seizing a respite from the prevailing austerity, displayed no signs of antagonism as they settled where they could, or grouped around the food and drinks stalls.

At noon sharp, the artists assembled on the stage.

Chiyoko began with Liszt and then streamed on to Chopin, playing a series of mazurkas, polonaises and the 'Revolutionary

Étude'. Finally, returning to Liszt, she ended with the *Rákóczi Marsch*, Hungary's unofficial national anthem.

Manoush followed her. Starting with Anton Karas's theme for *The Third Man* – a film that captured the apocalyptic days of the Cold War – he burst into several compositions by his fellow-zitherist, Félix Lajkó. He ended with a potpourri of Romani songs.

Next, it was Ghislaine, jumping from mood to mood, with Ravel, Ellis, Mendelssohn and de Falla. She ended spiritually with Schubert's *Ave Maria*.

Dakota Reed went on after her. A Sioux cult figure with a vast repertoire, he introduced himself as a world citizen. Strumming his guitar and expertly navigating his idiosyncratic harmonica – yoked to his mouth with a metal frame – he presented, as his homage to the diversity of nations, some official and unofficial anthems: *Himnusz, Scotland the Brave, Land of My Fathers, La Marseillaise, Fratelli d'Italia, Marcha Real, The Star-Spangled Banner, Deutschland über alles, Russia our Holy Nation, Hatikva, Nkosi Sikelel' iAfrika* and *Waltzing Matilda.* He then enthralled the audience with such classics as *Amazing Grace, La Paloma, Greensleeves, Danny Boy, Umm Khulthum's Thousand and One Nights, Hava Nageela, Kalinka, Sakura* and *The Lion Sleeps Tonight.*

Serena, lauded as the greatest soprano since Maria Callas, next enthralled the audience with a selection of Mozart, Puccini and Verdi opera arias. She ended with her own arrangement of the Hebrew slaves' chorus '*Va pensiero*' from Verdi's *Nabucco.* She chose this most dolorous lament – originally composed in support of a unified Italy – as a plea for the emancipation of all peoples.

Hayyan started his recital with classical flute sonatas. Then, declaring that he, too, was a world citizen, he switched to different instruments. With oboe and clarinet, he presented bitter-sweet songs of the Roma diaspora; with various trumpets he took the audience to Africa; with arghul and zurna to the Middle East; with Kalyuki and Zhaleika to Russia; with Pungi, Shehnai and Alghoza, to India; with Bawu and Mangtong to China; with Nohkan and Kagurabue to Japan; with a range of sicus to South America; and with a didgeridoo to Australia.

Finally, Mai, in a vibrant traditional Andalusian dress, wafted onto the stage. Clicking castanets, gliding across the floor, ensorcelling the audience with magnetic eyes, she imposed a breathless silence. Then she danced. At times she appeared to levitate; at other times her feet pounded the boards in preternatural percussion. Whenever she stopped to sing dolorous *cantes*, Manoush picked up a Spanish guitar and provided the *toque*, the fiery accompaniment that elevates flamenco to dramatic heights. Tomek, Belkis and I, acting as stage managers, also strode onto the stage to perform the *palmas* and the *pitos*, the handclapping and finger-snapping.

After almost six hours – with brief intermissions – we reached the grand finale.

As Mai ended her performance with muted foot-tapping, Manoush joined her with the delicate steps of a Hungarian folk dance. Hayyan proceeded by dancing the Assyrian *khigga*. Chiyoko floated with a geisha dance. Dakota stomped a Sioux strut. Ghislaine clapped and struck the soles of her feet in Tyrolian *schuhplattler*. And Belkis and I, somehow unintimidated, shimmied.

The artists' exuberance spurred many in the audience to dance with us. Most satisfactorily, we noticed that as they swirled about some Hungarians and Roma clasped each other unreservedly.

In the evening, after an hour's interval, we set up the masterclasses. Those, too, proved most rewarding.

Music lovers thronged to Mai, Manoush, Chiyoko, Ghislaine, Serena, Dakota and Hayyan.

Tomek emerged as the star. People flooded his workshop. As he remarked later, as long as the planet lives there'll never be a shortage of talent.

The encounter ended at about ten p.m. It could have gone

on, but we had to strike camp and drive the following day to our next destination.

It had been an exhausting day, but we felt jubilant. Except for the odd instances when some hoodlums heckled us, the encounter had confirmed that art did melt away animosities, that whatever the differences between peoples and cultures, the joy of humanness overpowered the hatreds concocted by deranged power-merchants.

From Doborján, resting every alternate day, we travelled to Szeged, the 'Sun City'; from there to Debrecen, Hungary's second metropolis; then to Miscolc, the industrial town famous for its glass works; and finally, to the capital, Budapest, for our last encounter.

Travelling and working as a dedicated group, we became a tight-knit family.

And Cupid fired his arrows.

Mai and Manoush fell in love. Inevitably, Belkis and I thought. But since Manoush was married and doted on his three children, their ardour remained platonic. When they danced, their longing for each other became as manifest as the mid-air acrobatics of courting eagles.

Chiyoko, who dabbled in ink-wash painting, sought Tomek to improve her technique. Tomek, enthralled by her Buddhist philosophy which urges the painter to capture the subject's spirit before limning its appearance, happily took her under his wing. Within days they became inseparable.

Although our encounters had caught the nation's imagination, Budapest, Hungary's capital and one of Europe's most beautiful cities, welcomed us with some reserve. There was expectation in the air, but we also sensed a distempered atmosphere.

Pax Mundi had arranged with the civic authorities to present our encounter in Józsefvarós's renovated Mátyás Square, near the city centre. But just outside Budapest we were stopped by municipality officials and told that permission to perform in

Józsefvarós had been rescinded. Our new venue would be in Budafok, at the city's south-western fringe.

No reason was given for this change. But Manoush was pleased by the relocation. Irrespective of the fact that the new venue was close to his *kumpanya*, Józsefvarós, he explained, was predominantly inhabited by Roma and other minorities and had become a target for ultra-nationalists. While latterly the neighbourhood's diversity and renovation had made it a popular locality, particularly for tourists, it had remained an eye-sore for chauvinists. Reminding us that we had received abusive reactions from racists, moving the encounter to another venue was a wise decision that reduced the possibility of a disturbance.

Situated on the Tétényi plateau with slopes cossetting the Danube, Budafok was a major viticultural region. The people were friendly – even to Romani *kumpanyas* encamped on uncultivated patches.

Our venue would be the Market Square where vintners organised a yearly fête to promote their wines.

The night before the encounter, the artists – except for Manoush who had gone to his *kumpanya* to be with his wife and children – became restive. Some could not sleep. Others played solitaire. Yet others sat by the trucks, drinking, smoking, reading or watching the stars.

Despite Mai's reassurances that disquiet was common in performers psyching up for a tour de force, we kept sensing something else discordant.

The day rose fresh and sunny.

The Market Square filled up long before noon.

The overcrowding not only obliged the television crews to set up screens and loudspeakers in the surrounding streets, but also, to Manoush's delight, restricted the racists to the peripheries.

As usual Chiyoko started the show. Belkis and I thought we had never heard her play better.

Emulating her, the other artists reached sublime heights.

Mai and Manoush, particularly, whirled and soared into dimensions only a few performers can ascend.

At the end of the show, complying with the demand for encores, Manoush played and sang his version of *Gelem, Gelem*, the paean for the unification of the Roma which until then he had omitted from his repertoire.

'Oh Roma, Oh Romani youths!
We were once a great family.
The Black Legion murdered them.
Arise with me, Roma of the world.
The roads have opened.
Now is the time!
Arise with me dark grapes of dark faces and dark eyes!
Come back to travel the roads.
Oh Roma, Oh Romani youths!'

@

Manoush's performance electrified the audience. As if freed from dungeons, the communal dancing, singing and socialising became even more harmonious.

As the crowd seemed determined to see the evening out, we cancelled the workshops.

Only those members of Manoush's *kumpanya* who had attended the show left. They would prepare a *pachiv* – the ceremonial feast that would smooth our paths as we went our different ways.

At some point, Dakota and Manoush became blood-brothers.

Belkis and I witnessed the ceremony, in which they sucked the blood from each other's thumbs.

Twilight, always short-lived yet always a reminder of the Universe, encircled us.

We had a bit of time before going to the *pachiv* and had gathered around the trucks, relaxing, smoking, drinking and chattering about how good the last performance had been.

Suddenly we heard explosions and saw columns of flames and smoke in the distance.

Manoush bellowed. 'It's my *kumpanya*! I must go!'

I sprang up. 'I'll take you!'

So did Belkis.

Dakota, Hayyan, Tomek, Nick, the doctor, and Fortunato, the chef, joined us.

I drove the truck furiously.

The *kumpanya* was quite large – about twenty-odd caravans. Some of them were on fire.

People rushed about with buckets of water.

Dogs, goats, lambs and chickens scurried in panic.

Tethered horses neighed in terror trying to break loose.

Eerily, the *pashiv* tables on the green – many set with flowers, cutlery, plates and bottles – stood undamaged.

There didn't seem to be any casualties.

As we jumped out of the truck, Manoush pointed at one of the burning caravans. 'That's mine!'

He raced towards it shouting the names of his wife and son.

We ran after him, also shouting their names.

Suddenly Manoush froze. He pointed at a shoe by the steps up to the door. 'That's Florica's! They're in there! The twins must have been sleeping!'

In panic, he staggered towards the caravan.

He bolted into the burning home.

A moment later, the caravan blew up.

The blast catapulted us.

Burning shards rained.

Later, while the firemen doused the burnt-out caravans, an ambulance took away the charred corpses of Manoush, his wife and his children.

The paramedics treating people for shock – with Nick busy by their side – wanted to hospitalise Belkis and me, too, but having suffered only minor burns, we refused.

Manoush and his family were the only fatalities.

My last view of the devastation was Mai smearing her face, hands, arms and feet with the still-wet ashes of Manoush's caravan.

Next morning, *Pax Mundi* flew us to our countries and made arrangements to transport the trailer-trucks back to Berlin.

Official communiqués reported that the atrocity had been perpetrated by a gang of neo-Nazis armed with crude Molotov cocktails. But for a paraffin cooker that exploded just as Manoush had rushed into his caravan, he and his family might not have been harmed.

To date the file on this crime remains open.

Hayyan, Tomek, Dakota and Nick are still trying to trace the *kumpanya*. So far all they have gleaned is that its members have joined the queues of vilified refugees.

@

It's almost midnight.

We're tense, waiting to be evicted.

On the settee Lule cuddles her daughters.

Rajko, surrounded by his boys, softly prays as he lights candles for Manoush, Florica and their children, Gyorgi, Tobar and Talaitha. 'May their earth be plentiful, and may they rest in eternal light.'

Moni stares with his blind eyes into domains only he can see.

Phral is equally solemn. No doubt seeing what Moni sees.

I swig some firewater.

The feast is barely touched.

The cats have left. Maybe they prefer to be sad alone.

The neighbours, made mournful by Manoush's fate, have left, too.

Rajko pours himself a drink and sits next to Lule. His sons sit by him on the floor. 'What about the other artists, Oric?'

'They're coping.'

'The trauma?'

'Indelible.'

He nods. 'As always.'

'But one good thing: Chiyoko and Tomek are one breath now. They've settled in Berlin.'

'Other good things, too, Oric. Manoush lives on – in his music.'

'True.'

'What about Mai? We don't hear about her.'

'She never performed again. She stopped believing art heals. Decided humans are terminally evil.'

Rajko shakes his head. 'She's wrong!'

'I can see her point.'

'No. No! Music is Creation's sound. It was here before words. It will still be here even when the Universe is destroyed.'

Moni surfaces from wherever his mind has been. 'It's also evolution's hosanna. It proclaims there'll be an end to killing.'

I taunt him. 'You see that in your pebbles, Moni?'

Moni bristles. 'What I see is a poem by Amador, a painting by Rembrandt, a symphony by Beethoven. And the billions of masterpieces that help us navigate.'

Phral snuggles up to Moni.

'But evolutions can stop abruptly. A galactic cataclysm, a Saviour spewing Intercontinental Ballistic Missiles – *the end*!'

Moni upbraids me. 'There's no *the end*! Something always survives and *begins* again.'

Rajko grabs my hand. 'Listen to Moni, Oric! He speaks the truth. Tell Mai that. Beg her to dance and sing again.'

'Too late for that. After Budapest, she went home to Granada. Tidied up her affairs. Then climbed Mulhacén – that's Spain's highest mountain. Climbers found her weeks later. At the summit. Naked. Frozen. Fire turned into ice.'

Rajko and Lule cross themselves. 'Why didn't we hear about that?'

'It was reported. Briefly. News is short-lived.'

A sudden commotion from the street interrupts us.

We rush out thinking the demolitions have started.

On one side of the road, engineers are arguing. They can't switch on the arc-lights or start the bulldozers. The generators can't tap into the grid.

On the other side, residents jeer.

Police try to use jump-leads to start the machinery, but they, too, fail.

A mechanic curses. 'Gyppos!'

An engineer mocks him. 'You think Gyppos savvy technology?'

Rajko guffaws. 'Good, eh?'

I look at him in disbelief. 'Is this your doing?'

'With all the police around?'

Moni, chuckling, joins us. 'You wanted good tidings. There you have it. Say "thank you", cats.'

Rajko and I stare at him. 'Cats?'

'Phral saw it all. Every cat in the neighbourhood got together. They dug the earth and pissed on the grid. That corroded the conductors and shifted the electro-magnetic fields. It'll take ages to sort things out!'

Phral confirms this by barking happily.

'The cats are still there. Look!'

There are hundreds of cats up and down the street – including Rajko's lot. They're being pampered by Belkis and Childe Asher. I'm dumbfounded. When we wished for shapeshifters Childe Asher said: 'leave it to us.' I should have listened to Belkis: the boy always means what he says.

I cheer and roar. 'Well done, my loves!'

They give me the thumbs-up.

Rajko puts his arms around Moni and me. 'Looks like no eviction tonight. Time to honour Lule's feast!'

SATURDAY 18.00

The National Pantheon – last stop before Xanadu.

I'm spruced up: suit, shirt, tie, shiny shoes.

The Pantheon has two sections: The Sanctum, a copy of the Pantheon in Rome, and the Poppy Memorial.

Belkis and I avoided the Sanctum. It's a temple that glorifies cannon fodder in a quasi-Japanese rock garden. Rows of marble slabs engraved with the names of 'those who made the ultimate sacrifice' stand as sentries to the Unknown Soldier's Tomb in the domed interior. Visible from most parts of the city, this spurious edifice in a spurious garden is meant to reassure the people that our Spartans will stop the barbarians at our gates.

The Poppy Memorial's tranquility, on the other hand, offers a sense of Life's beatitude.

Both sections are festooned with portraits of Numen and the Grand Mufti.

I sit on a bench in the Poppy Memorial.

The flowers' ruddiness, Saviours profess, is a reminder that death is Nature's price for peace. How can they be made to comprehend that Nature is none other than Pachamama and that Her objective is to create, never to destroy? But am I, a callow sophist, really convinced that She'll perfect evolution? Don't I know that since the Universe is constantly expanding there will never be an end to evolution; that the best Pachamama can achieve is a work in progress? So how can I believe that one day She'll persuade the wolf not to kill the lamb?

I'm rambling. No surprise when my hour is nigh, and my mettle is still suspect.

I sense Hidebehind's presence. That's not surprising, either.

I watch a couple of gardeners weeding the poppy beds.

Nearby some municipality workers are replacing the posters of Numen and the Grand Mufti that have faded in the sun.

Belkis and Childe Asher appear.

Hidebehind, peeved, slithers off somewhere.

Belkis embraces me. 'I thought you'd be here.'

'You just chased away Hidebehind.'

'Can't wait, can he?'

'Early bird catches the worm.'

'He'll never catch you, Oric.'

'He already has.'

'That was my fault. I lost my head.'

'You keep saying that – but it doesn't help. I lost my *Self* – the *Self* I thought I had.'

Belkis smooths my brow. 'Hidebehind doesn't think so. That's why he's here so early. Psychological assault. He's worried. He wants to undermine you. He knows how strong you are. I'd say he fears you – more than you fear him.'

'Then he overestimates me. As you do.'

Childe Asher interjects. 'We don't, Dad. You've always been strong and brave – a true Dolphinero!'

I wince. 'Strength and bravery don't last forever. They wane. Think back to the missions Mum and I went on. Many failures. Few successes. Same old world. Nothing changes. Evil continues to rampage.'

Childe Asher rasps. 'You're talking through the wrong orifice, Dad.'

That makes me laugh. And sadder. I don't deserve their trust. Not yet.

One of the municipality workers lights a cigarette. He notices the gardeners' covetous looks, saunters over and offers them one. They accept. He waves away their thanks and leaves them his pack.

Generally, no matter how harsh life is, people are generous. But no Saviour would offer cigarettes to menial workers.

As usual Belkis reads my mind. 'Saviours wouldn't even give their sins away – unless they get back more power!'

'I wouldn't give away my sins either. They'd crush the recipient.' She laughs.

Childe Asher shakes his head reprovingly. 'Have you forgotten what *sin* is – and its equally cruel twin, *punishment*? Saviours' wily fabrications! Rooted in *original sin* – the biggest Big Lie ever. We struggle to give life continuity. Saviours seek to erase that continuity and make death permanent. They realised long ago that carnality – our sexual drive – is our life force, is Love's fountainhead. So they mutated it, reconstructed it as sin because otherwise they wouldn't be able to control it. It's up to us to debunk that Big Lie, to expose the Saviours' soullessness. To show the world that Love will always defeat them.'

We stare at him, surprised by his outburst.

He continues passionately. 'No place for *sin* and *punishment* in Pachamama's mind. Her sole objective is eternal life for every Life – and to provide the resources Life needs. Thus, She gave us, humans, one wondrous gift: the ability to see what's right and what's wrong and the acumen to detect the myriad disguises behind which what's wrong hides!'

My son already a Demosthenes. I turn to Belkis, overwhelmed. She beams. 'Like they say: out of the mouth of babes.'

She grabs Childe Asher's hand and they disappear.

❧

I gaze at the poppies.

I detect faces: Hrant, Moni, Phral, Belkis, Childe Asher. And a disjointed silhouette – Hidebehind presumably.

They're examining a body.

I shiver. It's my body!

Moni declares: 'Bodies are just vehicles. here we have a dead man. A serene visage. A good man in quietus. Then suddenly he's wan, blank, just a face. Soul gone. But not to worry, it's gone only to find another body to home in and reincarnate.

I agitate. 'What if I can't find another body? What if there are no bodies left?'

'You all right?'

I look up, confused, shaken. It's the gardeners. 'What?'

'You were shouting.'

I've been talking to myself. 'Sorry. Dozed off. Bad dream.'

'You sure?'

'Yes.' I grab my cigarettes. 'Smoke?'

They show me the pack the municipal worker gave them.

I light one for myself and offer my packet. 'Keep yours. Have one of mine.'

They hesitate. They're tempted. Then they take one.

I light the cigarettes. 'Where're you from?'

They waver. 'From … ahh …'

They'd rather not say. I move along to make room for them on the bench. 'Have a seat.'

The first shakes his head. 'We're okay.'

'Don't worry, I won't question you.'

The other mumbles. 'We … can't stop. Must work. They watch.'

'Who? The police?'

'The boss.'

'You're entitled to a break.'

The first one laughs. 'He forbids.'

'He can't grudge you a smoke.'

'You don't understand. He owns us. If we stop work, he stops food. And money and bed. Throw us out.'

I should have guessed. Illegals. Shouldn't this be repaired, too, while we repair the world? I dig out a few coins. 'Here. Have a pint on me.'

They step back. 'Thanks. No. We can't!'

'It's all right.'

The second one explains. 'Boss also check our pockets. Make sure we don't do other work.' They shuffle away.

I watch them as they get busy with the poppies.

I pick up my journal.

GEZI PARK

On one occasion, we went to Istanbul to join the demonstrations in Gezi Park.

Located in the city's heartland, Gezi Park had become the retreat where Istanbullers could raise their spirits with glimpses of sunny skies or showers from gamin cloudbursts or the bosomy silence of heavy snow. Other features like fragrant flowers, shady dream-catching trees, freshly cut grass evoking primal tales were additional delights.

Yet Turkey's Ustan Guc, that mimicker of piety, had decided to raze Gezi Park and erect on its site a mosque superior to all others. Moreover, eager to prove that Turkey, albeit devoutly Muslim, was in step with Western customs, he also planned to build a grandiose shopping mall, a braid of luxury hotels, some exclusive clubs and an enclave of ritzy pieds-à-terre where his vassals could romp with courtesans. Finally, as the jewel in its crown, this Ustan Guc would maintain ultra-modern barracks for his Security Forces and a monolithic nerve centre that would outshine Lubyanka.

The Gezi Park demonstrations started when some office workers, on their way to work, came upon contractors uprooting the Park's trees. Shocked by this infraction, they rushed to the Park and formed a human barrier in front of the bulldozers.

In a short time, families with children, students, artists, academics, businessmen, blue-collars, shop keepers, even old people, for whom Gezi Park symbolised freedom, flocked in support of the protesters. As the euphoria of solidarity spread, the ranks swelled.

Predictably the Prime Minister's reaction to this illegal gathering was to warn the protestors that unless they disbanded the Security Forces would eject them forcibly. The protestors, by then numbering thousands, defied him with an increasingly festive spirit. Some raised banners stating that peaceful manifestations were a basic human right. Countless groups, inspired by youngsters, danced to bongo drums, guitars, violins, flutes, saxophones, clarinets and ouds. Some elders sang songs by Victor Jara and Atahualpa Yupanqui whom they had extolled during Chile's and Argentina's dark hours under military juntas.

We joined a group of academics and, consuming bottles of raki, discoursed on the persecution meted out to campaigners for freedom of expression and governmental transparency.

Near dawn the next day, Hrant became restive. Sitting like Buddha in a Nepalese outfit – a long *tapalan* shirt and tight *suruwa* trousers – and endeavouring to spread spiritual blessings by spinning a Tibetan prayer-wheel, he vented his apprehension. 'About a thousand years ago, the Syrian poet Al-Ma'arri observed that two species of Saviours had hijacked history: the first with brains but no hearts; the second with hearts but no brains. Both, in their particular ways, fomented endless conflicts. People, if not reduced to weapons-fodder, perished with their dreams in pillages, rapes, deportations, famines and summary executions. Yet many while drawing their last breath, gazed at the world and marvelled at the beauty and benevolence it had so generously provided for them. And they prayed that one day both species of Saviours would wither and leave humanity to attain its birthright to life, love, freedom, equality, fraternity, happiness and natural death.'

Just then Ustan Guc struck. His security forces turned Gezi Park into an inferno. Harsh arc lights from helicopters obliterated the dawn. Water cannons churned the grounds into a mire. Salvos of bullets, pepper sprays, CR and tear-gas followed.

All the while loudspeakers indicted the protestors.

'Traitors!'

'Terrorists!'

'Infidels!'

'Apostates!'

The people, shocked out of their sleep, slithered helplessly in the mud. Many, choking on pepper spray and tear-gas, collapsed. Some hit by bullets fell on others injuring them, too.

Hrant grabbed us and, as if in possession of a magic carpet, steered us out of Gezi Park into a nearby hotel where panicking personnel were barricading its entrance.

He led us onto the hotel's roof restaurant.

Early risers, petrified by the mayhem in Gezi Park, huddled under the tables.

Hrant ranted. 'I was about to conclude. These days a new species of Saviour has risen, without brains and without hearts. Take a good look! We've entered the age of killing without rhyme or reason.'

@

The municipal workers wave at the immigrant gardeners and leave.

I watch the posters sway in the wind. I hadn't looked at them closely. Now I do.

The Saviours are in various attires: in presidential array – Numen in tuxedo and gold chain of office; the Grand Mufti in silken *thawb, bisht, ghutrah* and *agal* – peacocks displaying tails. Also, humbler poses: piously at prayer; as doctors auscultating; in cap and gown receiving honorary degrees; music buffs at concerts; engineers in hard hats; grimy miners with head-lamps; farmers threshing; picnicking with their families; handing cups to football teams. And larger portraits as bemedalled commanders-in-chief: Numen trooping the colour like a British sovereign; the Grand Mufti in the cockpit of an F-14 on his aircraft carrier.

The last reminds me of a conversation we had with Hrant on our return from Saudi Arabia. Mercifully, he said, luck was on our side for undertaking our mission before the King appointed his son, the thirty-two-year-old Crown Prince Amyr, to run the country. Since then absolutism has ruled the Kingdom. Soon after, Amyr, having seized control of the armed forces, shut down the country and incarcerated some 500 top dogs – including eleven princes – in Riyadh's palatial Ritz-Carlton Hotel on the pretext of stamping out corruption and reclaiming some 100 billion dollars appropriated from the Treasury. Simultaneously promising to end 'terrorism' and to institute comprehensive human rights, he covertly forged a formidable security web. To fulfil his 'promise' he pursued whosoever dared to criticise, even mildly, his governance. He arrested and executed these innocents – killing on one occasion forty-seven of them in one day. And all the while he escalated Saudi's participation in Yemen's War which killed hundreds of thousands of civilians – a large percentage of them children – with aerial bombings, starvation and deadly epidemics.

It should also be noted that Amyr is a mogul himself. In addition to his undisclosed wealth, he owns an ultra-modern yacht, a French chateau and Leonard da Vinci's portrait of Christ worth, respectively, 500, 300 and 400 million dollars.

Under those conditions, Hrant stated, all of us in JJ's team would have been slain soon after setting foot in the Kingdom.

That conversation with Hrant left me – not Belkis, never Belkis – wondering whether we can still believe that Pachamama's children – we Dolphineros and Leviathans – will eventually defeat Hydra's brood. Can the world be repaired ever? Can power be defeated? Or is power omnipotent as it has always claimed to be?

If so, why am I still resolved – assuming I can defeat Hidebehind – to confront Saviours?

For a grand last stand?

Can that excel the peace of Picayune, our magical island?

Dolphineros' last stand or Picayune?

Can't feel Hidebehind's presence. Does that mean Picayune?

A commotion interrupts my thoughts.

A tall amputee dressed in a bodysuit and balancing on one crutch is pointing to the poppies and shouting at the gardeners. 'They're the Four Horsemen of the Apocalypse! In disguise! Look – there's Pestilence. Behind it: Famine, War, Death. I, Don Quixote de la Mancha, have cornered them at last. One strike with my halberd – they'll be six feet under!'

The gardeners try to reason with him. 'But sir – these are only flowers.'

He pushes towards the poppies. 'Charge!'

The gardeners block him.

As he raises his crutch to hit them, I jump up to intervene.

But Belkis and Childe Asher are already by his side. When did they reappear?

Childe Asher holds him by the waist. 'It's all right, valiant knight. I'm here. Sancho's here!'

'You see them, my man? Evil. Evil!'

'Yes, sire. But they're running away. These poppies are their victims. Felled by them.'

The man's eyes go cloudy. 'Felled, you say? Felled …?'

'Look! Their blood. Redder than red.'

The man stares at the poppies. 'They felled me, too. Tore me to pieces.' He shuts his eyes to banish the past. 'But I pulled myself up …'

'As veterans always do.'

The man looks around him in frustration. 'Run away again, have they? You'd think they'd have guts, stand and fight.'

Childe Asher takes his arm. 'Come, dear knight. We'll find them. Let's saddle Rocinante.'

'Oh, yes, my horse. Where did I leave him?'

Childe Asher leads him away gently. 'Just around the corner.'
Belkis whispers. 'We'll take him to Jujube Palace.'

I nod.

One of the gardeners mutters. 'Maybe madness is better for him – safer world.'

'Maybe.'

I return to the bench and open my journal again.

WALLENBERGS VI

Belkis and I were inducted into Wallenbergs VI.

We were to rescue Zoha Iqbal, a young Pakistani woman sold into servitude in Saudi Arabia. The mission included JJ himself, his team-member, Enoch, and four Saudis: Shahid, Nasser, Tariq and Rashid. The *Magi* alerted Zoha through their channels.

And Belkis and I, furnished with Foreign Labourer documents supplied by an Omani counterfeiter at a hefty price, travelled in a workers' bus from Jordan's Red Sea resort, Aqaba, to Riyadh, the Saudi capital. There, in a safe house, we joined Shahid and Nasser who supplied us with Municipal Cleaner tags that they had procured by bribing a contractor.

Taking turns, we surveyed the grandiose mansion where Zoha was confined. The mansion belonged to Qadi Seyfullah, a prominent Sharia judge. Not surprisingly, his lofty standing generated a continuous flow of petitioners seeking favours. For poor Belkis the surveillance, particularly during the day when she liaised with Zoha while Zoha emptied the dustbins, proved torturous. Dressed in a hijab that free-spirited dolphin could barely tolerate Riyadh's dessicating heat.

Some days later, travelling as folklorists interested in Arabian music, JJ and Enoch flew in from Cairo to Abha, a mountain retreat in the southwest, popular for its temperate climate and Summer Festival.

Concurrently, Tariq and Rashid, carrying identities of trainees from a German ornithological organisation assigned to chart the biodiversity of the peninsula's birds, arrived in Haql on the Gulf of Aqaba – about ten kilometres from the Saudi-Jordan border. The

Magi had established that whereas Saudi Arabia maintained high alert at most border-posts, particularly at ports and airports, the long frontier with Jordan, except for the official Durra Crossing, was perfunctorily patrolled.

JJ and Enoch rented a holiday villa in Abha and waited for us to bring Zoha. Thence, from Abha we would drive on minor roads to Haql and meet up with Tariq and Rashid who would have picked out a suitable entry point into Jordan. Travelling to Haql from Abha instead of directly from Riyadh had been deemed safer as it would avoid the motorways and most of the checkpoints.

Unexpectedly, the mission hit a snag. Following a Jihadist attack on the Prophet's Mosque in Medina which killed four police officers, the Saudi authorities promptly reinforced their Jordanian border with squads of SANG, the National Guard – reputedly a law unto themselves.

Since attempting to slip into Jordan under these circumstances would have been too risky, we had to resort to Plan B: the sea route. Haql is a small holiday resort aiming to gain popularity. It has a few hotels – two posh ones – and a Marina with a mini-industry for sea-sports. But, conveniently for us, there are numerous secluded coves down the coast, where shellbacks, in cahoots with coastguards, flipped in and out like flying fish with their contraband.

Eventually, after punctilious groundwork, the *Magi* recommended a smuggler affectionately known as Tonton – real name: Theodul Baptiste Manumichon – a Martinican ex-Foreign Legionnaire who had served in France's former colonies. When discharged with a cluster of medals, he had turned to the more profitable trade of smuggling. He resolutely abided by the old adage 'my word is my bond' and never extorted customers during a job. JJ immediately engaged him to pick us up from Haql.

At the end of our second week in Riyadh, Zoha's captor, Qadi Seyfullah, accompanied by his family and entourage, travelled to

Switzerland to spend the summer in his Alpine chalet. He left Zoha in charge of his mansion confident that, having confiscated her passport, she could not decamp.

The next day we made our move. We rented two cars – a limousine and a saloon – from different car-hire companies. The saloon had the imprint of a well-known logo whereas the limousine, devoid of any insignia, looked like the sedan of a dignitary.

Early that night we moved to a side street near the mansion.

Zoha, instructed by Belkis during the garbage collection, locked up the mansion and came out to water the lawn, her last chore of the day.

When the neighbourhood went quiet, she slid out.

We handed Zoha her forged ID papers and placed her in the limousine with Belkis and Shahid. We waited briefly for Belkis and Zoha to change into suitable clothes, then set out for Abha.

Nasser and I followed at a distance in the saloon. Driving where possible on minor roads and stopping for petrol only at remote service stations, the thousand-plus kilometres trip to Abha took the best part of two days.

At the Al-Alfaj and Wadi ad-Dawasir checkpoints – unavoidable as they controlled major junctions – the religious police stopped the limousine. On both occasions, having verified that Belkis and Zoha were properly dressed in *niqabs* and that their papers proved adequate, they questioned them about the purpose of their trip. Shahid's story that they were taking their sick sister to convalesce in Abha – very convincing given Zoha's emaciated condition – satisfied them.

Thanks to our car's well-known logo, Nasser and I received a cursory glance and were waved through.

Zoha, enlivened by Belkis's empathy, recounted the events leading to her bondage.

Born in a village near Lahore, she had lost her father and three siblings to a cholera outbreak when she was five. But, doted on by her mother, Mahnoor, a cotton gin operator, she had enjoyed a happy childhood. A studious girl, she decided at an early age to become a teacher – an ambition that antagonised the tribal elders enmeshed in Sharia laws. Believing that Allah's words imparted everything a Muslim needed in life, these patriarchs saw contemporary trends, especially the craving for emancipation, as profane. Moreover, entrenched in shariatic misogyny, they regarded female education as the path to apostasy. Zoha, studying single-mindedly – and getting excellent grades particularly in English – failed to notice the alienation she incurred.

But her mother noticed. Mahnoor even thought of moving to another province but feared that, as an uprooted and ageing single mother, she would remain an outsider wherever she went and find it impossible to get a job. Two years later, Mahnoor's fears materialised.

One afternoon, a gang of juveniles from prominent families attacked and raped Zoha on her way home from school. Traumatised and for once rejecting her mother's advice to pretend that nothing had happened, she reported the assault. The rapists vehemently refuted the accusation and demanded to be tried in a Sharia court where four witnesses must attest to the offence. Four men, chosen by the rapists' families, not only testified against Zoha but also alleged that she had wantonly seduced the youths. Zoha was charged with *zina,* premarital sex. The verdict prompted the rapists to demand *rajm* – public stoning – as the only punishment that would restore their honour.

Zoha's sentence caused divisions in the community. The poor folk, familiar with rich families' connivances, appealed for Zoha's sentence to be annulled. Humanists clamoured for clemency or at the very least the right for an appeal at a civil tribunal. But the rapists' families, goaded by Islamist hardliners, rejected these demands arguing that Sharia's verdicts were immutable.

At this juncture, a Qatari, Yasir, introducing himself as a well-connected 'interagent', approached Mahnoor. Commiserating with Mahnoor as an enlightened man who deplored the brutal sentences of the Sharia, he offered to help Zoha. He stressed that, in the prevailing atmosphere, Zoha would not be safe even if the authorities decided to commute her death sentence; the Islamists would stone her extrajudicially. Consequently, Zoha's only chance of survival was to leave Pakistan. He could arrange to take her to neighbouring Iran where through his contacts he would find her a decent job. Naturally transactions for such measures would be costly – certainly beyond Mahnoor's means – however, he was prepared to finance the move himself as the commission he would receive from Zoha's employer would cover his expenses as well as give him a small profit.

Mahnoor, desperate to save Zoha, agreed.

In Iran Yasir exploited Zoha by arranging a series of Nikâh al-Mut'ah – the contracted marriages of short duration that Iran's Twelver tradition permits to men needing the comforts of a 'temporary wife'. As Zoha's youth made her very marketable for such liaisons, Yasir amassed substantial 'bride prices'. Around that time, Mahnoor fatally injured herself while adjusting the saws of a cotton gin.

Despite her repugnance for her new life and the desolation of her mother's death, Zoha managed to pursue her studies. Libraries became her refuge – especially during *iddahs*, the prescribed intervals of sexual abstinence between 'temporary marriages'. She began to write. In due course, under a pseudonym, she wrote a treatise, *The Jahannam of Piety*, which, indicting the dehumanisation of women, chronicled the transformation of a vibrant religion into a nefarious one. No publisher – Eastern or Western – dared publish this book. And the few manuscripts that she sent out ended up shredded by Iranian censors.

Four years later, misfortune struck again. Zoha's latest 'temporary husband', Jahangir, an opium addict, enraged by his inability to have sex in his drugged state, accused Zoha of reneging on her duties and stabbed her several times before collapsing in stupor. Zoha managed to call for an ambulance and miraculously survived.

To Yasir's dismay, the attack ended Zoha's career as a 'temporary wife'; the scars criss-crossing her body rendered her undesirable even for casual sex. Furthermore, as Jahangir's defence that Zoha had brought the assault on herself by failing to comfort him was upheld by the public court, she was denounced as a harridan.

Yasir, not one to discard a golden calf until it was cadaverous, resorted to the lesser – but still profitable – market of organ sales. He coerced Zoha into donating one of her kidneys to a rich Bahraini needing a transplant.

After the operation, resigned to the fact that Zoha was no longer a lucrative chattel, Yasir sold her 'body and soul' to Qadi Seyfullah.

@

Even the best analysts can overlook a tiny detail on an aerial map. Thus, the *Magi* failed to notice that one of Qadi Seyfullah's neighbours, a cleric, was obsessed with gardens.

We had barely joined JJ and Enoch at Abha when this neighbour, noticing that the Qadi's lawn looked parched, went to urge Zoha to water it. Finding the mansion deserted, he alerted the authorities. Zoha's sudden disappearance prompted Seyfullah to rush back from Switzerland. Infuriated by the perfidy of a woman whom, he claimed, he had charitably taken into his home and treated as family, he accused her of being a sorceress. As proof he stated that he remembered occasions when Zoha's eyebrows manifested 'strange undulations'. Now, reviewing past cases of *sihr* – witchcraft – he realised that the undulations had been messages from malevolent jinns. It was imperative to apprehend her and subject her to *ruqyah* – the ritual exorcism that imposed special prayers, potions of 'holy water', floggings and, as a last resort, execution.

His influence in both religious and governmental circles prompted a nationwide search for Zoha. Broadcasts and social media published her photograph with warnings that she was a threat to Islam. As the alert circulated, we heard that a *Mutaween* informer had filed a memo about a 'seclusive' group roosting in a house normally rented to holidaying families.

We had to decamp at once. Since our cars' details would have been recorded at checkpoints, our only option was to footslog to the coast and rendezvous with Tariq, Rashid and Tonton somewhere safe. Weaving separately through the Festival crowd, we bought, from different shops, as much water and canned rations as we could and reassembled in the countryside.

There, following consultations with Tariq, Rashid and Tonton in Haql and the *Magi* in London, JJ decided to proceed to Al-Birk, a small coastal town situated at the tail end of an ancient lava field, of interest only to Palaeolithic researchers – hopefully a destination the *Mutaween* would *not* expect us to choose.

We would trek the hundred or so kilometres in three stretches: at daybreak before search parties, if any, deployed; whenever the terrain offered adequate cover during the day; and at night when searches would be unlikely. Barring mishaps, we anticipated reaching Al-Birk in about six days – ample time for Tonton to sail down with Tariq and Rashid from Haql.

Our hopes that Saudi security might disregard Al-Birk as our possible destination were soon dashed. Early next morning, motorised SANG patrols and surveillance helicopters began to scour the volcanic desert. We coped well the first day by taking cover in sepulchral lava formations. But on the second day, JJ, who had been suffering from headaches in Abha, developed paroxysms of feverish shivers. Zoha diagnosed malaria.

Fortunately, our first-aid kits included quinine. But the *Magi* insisted that only a combination of *lumefrantine* and *artemether* would help JJ. We contacted Tonton and urged him to get these somehow. Tonton promised that he would obtain the medication through an associate in Israel, assured me that the diversion from Haql to Eilat would not be a problem, and said he would reach Al-Birk in time for our rendezvous.

In the event, Tonton's detour made little difference. JJ's enfeeblement slowed down our progress and it took us another five days to make it to Al-Birk. When we finally rendezvoused with Tonton, Tariq and Rashid at a secluded beach, we had run out of water and food and had to be helped onto the boat.

Tonton proved a loveable seadog. A gentle giant with grizzly Rastafarian dreadlocks, he smuggled anything except arms, drugs and slaves. Those trades, he contended, were not only abominations, but also would dishonour his genial nickname, the French word for 'uncle'. For some three decades, he had cast anchor just about everywhere in the Near East and the Indian Ocean smuggling gold, jewellery, haute couture, alcohol, cigarettes, films, household goods and electronic gizmos. Since most of the goods he shifted were either banned or luxury stuff, he had secured collusion, even protection, from the region's coastguards by greasing their palms generously and regularly. The only inconvenience he faced was steering clear of the trigger-happy Iranian ships delivering arms to Yemen.

After picking us up, Tonton made full use of the night. By dawn, before SANG helicopters began searching again, we were out of Saudi waters and in a Sudanese inlet.

Thereafter, we spent the days anchored at secluded coves where Tonton could hole up before unloading his contraband.

Despite the sweatbox heat, being cooped up in Tonton's cabin expunged our exhaustion. It also helped JJ to begin to recover with the medication Tonton had brought from Israel. Belkis, who helped Zoha tend JJ, soon sensed that the two had become very fond of each other.

The nights on the deck were blissful. As we chugged along relishing the balmy breezes, we ate, drank, sang, smoked and listened to Tonton who was especially endearing in his arak-hued moods. He would wax lyrical about the sea – or 'briny', as he called it, a term he'd appropriated from a British sailor – as his most passionate inamorata whose many caprices he could predict and lovingly humour. And as was the prerogative of old-salts, he had two other paramours: *Undine*, his motorised *baghlah*, built to his specifications in India; and *Edith*, his sound system named after Piaf, the French singer. But, he boasted, briny never got jealous of these courtesans: after all, *Undine* always nestled at briny's bosom and *Edith* was the cupbearer every solitary soul needed.

He also mesmerised us by 'swinging the lamp' – another acquired British slang – with his reminiscences: the singular blessings of his women in every port and the saintly rogues from many lands, races and faiths who he called his 'nephews'.

By way of punctuating these narratives, he regaled us with songs from The Beatles, Bob Dylan, Umm Kulthum, Theodorakis, Livaneli and Piaf. In fact, Piaf's *Milord*, which he accompanied with his deep voice, had become his anthem; he sang it whenever he had to say good-bye to those he had come to love.

On the fifth day we were forced into yet another change of plan. the *Magi*, constantly monitoring Saudi communications, reported that the Saudis had heightened their search for Zoha. Alleging that Zoha's ability to avoid capture proved not only that she was a witch but also that she was the mastermind of a Zionist spy-ring, the Qadi arraigned the Council of Ministers for betraying the jihad against the Jews. As a result, additional SANG units and patrol boats were deployed to scour the Red Sea.

This escalation, Tonton explained, ruled out going through the Straits of Tiran to either Aqaba or Eilat. It also precluded Sharm el-Sheikh, the Egyptian resort at the southern extremity of the Sinai Peninsula as that, too, would be closely watched. Our safest course was to divert to mainland Egypt.

Thus, at daybreak the next day, we landed at Marsá al 'Alam.

Kamal, one of Tonton's middlemen, summoned post-haste, took charge of us.

Tonton refused the hefty bonus JJ offered him for his gallantry. Instead he declared that having acquired new 'nephews' he was now richer than Croesus.

Then, hugging us all, he sang *Milord*.

'Mais vous pleurez, Milord!
Souriez-moi, Milord!
Allez, riez, Milord!
Allez, chantez, Milord!'

We sang and wept with him. Then Kamal drove us to the airport. Picking up the tickets procured by the *Magi*, we flew to Hanover. Shahid, Nasser, Tariq and Rashid travelled with us. They would continue their Dolphinero work in Europe. JJ and Enoch escorted Zoha to the USA.

I'll end on a happy note.

JJ and Zoha were married in JJ's hometown.

A year later they were blessed with their first child, Mahnoor, named after Zoha's mother.

A year later Zoha launched her book which, supported by JJ, she had written again. Published in many countries, it now stands as a beacon for human rights and gender equality.

@

I hear music. Beethoven's ninth.

I look up thinking Belkis has come to bolster me for the demo with her spirit.

She's not around. Nor is Childe Asher.

The music comes from an old couple's sound system. They're at a nearby bench, eyes closed, holding hands, softly humming.

My cobwebs clear.

I remember Hrant talking about *light-workers*. Many saw them on 9/11 flashing through the dust as New York's twin towers collapsed. Two emotions guide us: love and fear. We spurn the first and embrace the second. *Light-workers* do the opposite: they overcome fear with love and help souls to slip through destruction into light.

The old couple have opened infinity's door.

Maybe they're my parents. I can't discern their faces. But I can see light – soft, dazzling light.

Ode to Joy ends: *This kiss is for all the world …*

The old couple shuffle over.

The man touches my arm. 'Sublime, eh?'

'Absolutely.'

The woman points at the Poppy Memorial sadly. 'It makes one wonder – why do we kill when we have Beethoven?'

The man comforts her. 'Don't fret. Not even vengeful gods can kill music.'

I snarl. 'There are no vengeful gods. Only ghouls in armour craving godhood. But they'll end up destroying each other. And we'll repair the desolation they've left behind.'

'Who're "we"?'

'Creation. Pachamama. Leviathans. Dolphin children. You two. Just about everybody.'

The man is impressed. 'Are you a seer, young man?'

The woman chides him. 'He's more than that. He repairs – puts things right.'

They wave their frail hands and totter away.

Hidebehind cackles somewhere.

I cackle back.

I feel I'm Atlas. And the world I'm carrying – normally too heavy – now weighs no more than the light on my face.

SUNDAY 08.45

I reach the Archaeological Park where Numen built his Xanadu.

The Palace's Pavilion, Numen's venue for sealing international treaties 'in full view of the people', is where He and the Grand Mufti will sign the duumvirate concordat.

The Park is a UNESCO World Heritage site endowed with two cultural treasures: the Rock-Art enclave bearing several Neolithic pictographs; and a replica – one of the very few extant – of the eighteenth-century Maltese-style Windmill Redoubt. While the Maltese fought the French, the original mill, restructured as a blockhouse, not only never stopped grinding grain, but also proved an impregnable stronghold.

Nowadays its function is placid: it entertains with its sorcerous allure countless visitors and offers a café-cum-gift-shop where they can be lulled by the euphony of its swishing vanes.

The windmill is my destination.

It's still early. But security teams are already in situ.

Police units are setting barriers at the Park's entrances and along the inner lanes and walkways. At the Spectators Enclosures some twenty metres from Xanadu's boundaries, Gendarmes with sniffer-dogs check for explosives.

There are three Spectators Enclosures. The main one faces Xanadu's Gate, an eight-metre high wrought-iron structure which, despite its ornamented trellises and filigrees, has the solidity of a portcullis. Blazoned in gold letters at the Gate's crest lies the iconic sign: The Buck Stops Here – a prime example of Numen's sly bathos.

The other two have been raised on the eastern and western boundaries.

There's no enclosure at the northern boundary. That sector, harbouring a heliport and patrolled by the Dragon's Teeth, is protected by a moat and a no-man's land beyond it.

By the water-cannons positioned behind each enclosure Scythes horseplay as they equip themselves with gas masks, pepper sprays, truncheons, teargas and assault rifles.

From Xanadu's Gate, an Italianate garden leads to Numen's vainglorious 1150-roomed Palace – so aptly nicknamed The Ziggurat.

The Pavilion, a baroque extravaganza inspired by the Dianatempel in Munich's Hofgarten and flanked on both sides by Bernini-style marble fountains, lies halfway up the gardens. Numen's imitation of familiar masterpieces is meant to affirm his cultural refinement.

What compelled me most when I suggested Xanadu as the better location for our demo is the fact that whereas pavilions normally stand on a knoll beyond the palace, Xanadu's Pavilion is central and faces the Maltese windmill. (Numen sentimentally declared that he chose the site in order to gaze at the windmill and reminisce about his father, 'a humble miller'.)

The Spectators' Enclosures have been declared clear.

The police are ushering in the early arrivals.

A pellucid mist of sand-motes – at this time of the year drifting from the Sahara – varnishes Xanadu with an iridescent sheen.

Stiletto jabs on my neck warn me that Hidebehind is close-by.

A dog licks my hand.

Phral – with Moni in tow.

I stroke Phral. 'What brings you here, Moni?'

Moni shrugs airily. 'It's Sunday. Rest day. I thought I'd have a look-see.'

'Best you don't see what's likely to happen.'

He purses his lips. 'Witnesses can't be choosy. I also thought I might bump into you and pick up your journal for Childe Asher. You forgot to give it to me at Rajko's.'

Again, I think Moni is a Leviathan. 'Stupid of me.' I take out my journal and give it to him.

He bends over Phral. 'Strange thing to say, eh Phral?'

Phral whines in agreement.

Without the journal I feel unburdened, weightless. As if I've shed my life. But then I have, haven't I?

'Want to walkabout, Oric?'

'I'll hang around – soak in the atmosphere.'

'Right.'

Nearby Hidebehind sneers.

'One thing, Moni.'

'Yes?'

'Do you foresee any good news from this jamboree?'

'I'll have to consult my pebbles.'

'Try your gut-feel.'

Moni ponders. 'Good news, you say?'

'Like what should be done will be done. What should be said will be said.'

'Isn't that what you normally do?'

'Only when I can avoid Hidebehind.'

'Haven't you always?'

Hidebehind snarls. My spirits rise. 'I have, haven't I?'

Moni shuffles away with Phral. 'Take care.'

I grin. 'Sure.'

An escadrille of helicopters alights on the heliport. More Dragon's Teeth jump out and spread out between the Pavilion and the heliport.

A few metres in front of Xanadu's Gate there's a three-tiered structure known as Scold's Bridle – a name coined by old hacks that campaigned for free speech and ended up mute. It refers to a medieval torture device, an iron muzzle that enclosed the head and, with a bridle-bit inserted into the mouth, disabled the tongue.

Offering a grandstand view of the Pavilion from each of its tiers, Scold's Bridle provides lounges for national and international correspondents who adhere to Numen's censorial laws. All television, film and photographic cameras are checked before they can be taken in. No deviant lensman can show Numen as an emperor without clothes.

As perks the lounges, lushly fitted and encased by thick-glass windows, provide well-stocked bars, sumptuous buffets and nubile Pinkie waitresses.

An array of electronic detectors scans the turnstiles at the entrance.

Gendarmes stand guard. Those armed cosset their submachine guns as if breast-feeding them. The unarmed, nylon-gloved and wearing medical tunics over their uniforms, conduct the queueing reporters into portable cubicles for body-checks.

As I stop and watch, an elderly man in the queue jests. 'You look surprised.'

I look at him, puzzled. 'By what?'

'The security.'

'Good thing, isn't it?'

The man introduces himself. 'Charlie. Cameraman. From Down-under.'

'Oric.'

'First assignment?'

'Shows, does it?'

'Your togs – spiffy.'

I smile sheepishly. 'I thought one had to look smart.'

'Not if you're pen pusher or crew. We're not star tv-commentators – just also-rans.' He gestures towards the Gendarmes conducting body checks. 'But then they strip down everybody anyway and search every nook and cranny. And I mean every nook and cranny. Some Bruces bring hygienic pads in case of emissions.'

'I see.'

'You greenhorns, you get the lowest tier. Bit claustrophobic. My ilk, we get the top tier. Plenty of ozone. Audio-bods are okay, too – they're on the second. On the other hand, perks are free for all. Bars to drive Hemingway loco. Canapés à la Joséphine. Cocktails bewitching like sheilas. And if you're a smoker, grab a cigar or two

– Cuban, Fidel's brand.'

I look impressed. 'Sounds great! But I'm not going in.'

'Why not? Stringers aren't excluded.'

'No accreditation yet. The Boss says I'm still a tyro.' I point at the western Spectators' Enclosure. 'That's my place – with the huddled masses.'

'With Panurge's sheep, eh?'

I'm surprised by his subversive remark. I could be a Pinkie.

He notes my cautionary look. 'Don't get me wrong. Huddled masses are dinkum.'

I tease him. 'Sure – like sheep.'

He offers a wry grin. 'I'm vegetarian."

'Healthier.'

'Yeah.'

I make a move. 'Better be on my way.'

'Sure. Have a good day.'

'You, too.'

I amble to the western boundary.

Some people, mainly elderly women, are walking their dogs. Beyond, a professional trainer supervises his socialite clientele's aerobics.

These people intrigue me: so close to a national event, yet carefree. What if Pinkies finger them as unpatriotic for ignoring Numen's pageant? On second thoughts: why should Pinkies bother with them? Lotus-eaters in hushed homes never threaten the Saviours. That's how democracy slips into dictatorship.

Clusters of citizens are moving into the Spectators' Enclosure. Among them a couple of cerberuses lead a group of waifs in institutional garb.

Orphans are saddened by orphans. I'm no exception.

I reach the windmill. The flurry in the Pavilion suggests the concordat will be signed soon. The windmill is closed for the day. But its café-cum-gift-shop is open. On the patio, a couple, pestered by children eager to get into the Spectators' Enclosure, are sorting out their backpacks.

I go into the café. It's empty. There's only one attendant. I buy an orange juice and sit on the patio.

Hidebehind lances my spine with his icy dagger.

I hold still.

I hear a bark. Phral is running towards me. Hidebehind jumps off my shoulder and scoots. Phral comes up. I stroke him.

'Good fellow! You scared Hidebehind off.' Phral gurgles happily. 'Where's Moni?'

Phral turns his head towards the Spectators' Enclosure, where I see Moni waiting patiently. Phral puts his front legs on my shoulders as if to cuddle me then runs off to join Moni.

On the patio, the couple and their kids hurriedly leave for the Spectators' Enclosure.

I go into the café and hand my empty bottle to the attendant.

Then I saunter to the door at the back which opens to a corridor where the toilets are situated.

The toilets also serve the windmill and can be accessed directly from there, too.

Belkis and I had verified that when, reconnoitring for Plan B early in the week, we walked unchallenged into the mill's living quarters – left exactly as it had been a century or so ago – and hid a megaphone in the galley's elemental stove.

I slip into the windmill through its toilet's door.

I dart into the galley and pick up the megaphone.

I then move up to the Cap and crawl to the windshaft.

I open some slats behind the vanes to give myself enough room to squeeze out.

I've timed it well.

Numen and the Grand Mufti have come out on to the Pavilion's terrace for the ceremony.

The people at the Enclosures applaud tactfully.

The Grand Mufti spreads his prayer-mat. His Imam announces that whatever the occasion, the Grand Mufti never misses the Salat, one of the obligatory daily prayers. These, he explains, together with Faith in Allah, Charity, Fasting and Pilgrimage to Mecca constitute the Five Pillars of Islam.

The crowds fall silent as the Grand Mufti goes through his ritual of standing, bowing and prostrating.

While Numen respectfully stands by, his Dragon's Teeth survey the crowds arrogantly. They look like clones of the Easter Island Moai – same megalithic presence, same fixed minatory expression. They're supposed to be anonymous, almost invisible. But since asininity never consorts with logic, they proudly flaunt their threatening demeanour. I've even heard them boast on television that as Numen's shields they're the Nation's unsung heroes.

Hidebehind's dagger hacks at my spine.

Again, I wonder: why won't he face his prey? He'd be bloodcurdling if he did.

Maybe he fears people as much as people fear him. Or fears them more than they fear him. Maybe he knows eyeball-to-eyeball he'll be exposed as the cowardly bully he is.

He is cackling again. There's a breeze in his voice. He's outside. Somewhere …

Rage possesses my body. An erupting rage that I've never known before. It compels me to face him come what may!

I wriggle out onto the vane's sail.

I shout. 'Afraid to look me in the eye?'

He snarls. I can feel him slithering around the sail.

He's cornered.

And at last he materialises!

His face, if it's a face, is like a blank headstone. In fact, it's not a face. He doesn't have a face. Nor a body. And the headstone is not solid but a gelatinous mass that can't take shape or have eyes, ears, nose, mouth, forehead or chin stippled on it. But there are reflections, phlegm-green, that seem to rebound from shards of a broken mirror.

I stare at my faces staring back at me.

And I see …

A naked baby.

Twisting and turning in distress.

Screaming, wailing, crying.

Turning away its face as if to protect itself from a blow.

It's uttering words. But they are incomprehensible.

What is it trying to say? 'Mama?' 'Dad?' 'Belkis?'

Or yelling at the wind: 'why have you forsaken me?'

How many mes are there, for Goodness' sake!?

Hidebehind hoots. 'Saviour against Dolphinero, Oric!'

The pathos of the baby on the shards breaks the dagger in my spine.

I spit at Hidebehind. 'You're on!'

He hoots. 'Saviours always win.'

'Until they self-destruct.'

'They never do.'

'Yes, they do. And often.'

'You delude yourself, Oric! Big Lies versus Truth. Irrationality versus Reason. Brutality versus Love. Doomsday weapons! Dolphineros don't stand a chance!'

'You forget the scorpion's sting.'

He stops hooting. 'Scorpion's sting? What's that?'

'The kamikaze syndrome.'

He gambols up and down the sail dancing the *Dance of Death* in a grotesque travesty of Amador and Belkis dancing *The Dance of Life* at Amador's wake. 'Dream on, Oric.'

To shut out the vision I evoke Belkis's return as a Leviathan.

After I left her Agapé I went to the spot where she'd fallen. It was still tinted with her blood. Not even the municipality's bleaches had washed it off. Rather, they'd given it a russet sheen.

Doesn't that prove Dolphineros transmute into Leviathans?

I scan the Pavilion's terrace.

The Grand Mufti has concluded his prayers.

Gripping tightly the megaphone, I balance myself.

Hidebehind continues to cavort triumphantly.

I kick him off the sail.

The air devours him like the cindered smoke of a steam locomotive.

Incredible! Was that all that was needed all this time? Just a kick?

I hang onto the windmill's sail like Da Vinci's *Vitruvian Man*.

The wind tousles my hair.

I am a tiger burning bright, ready to finish unfinished business.

One of Hrant's narratives chimes in my head.

@

On the Appian Way a Leviathan and a Dolphinero scurry in opposite directions.

The Leviathan, Jesus, Son of Man, is rushing to Rome.

The Dolphinero, Peter, fisher of men, is fleeing Rome.

Jesus doesn't see Peter. He inhabits a world which is this world as it should be.

Peter spots him and runs over. 'Master! *Quo vadis?*'

Jesus, pleased to see his disciple, pats Peter's shoulder. 'Nice coincidence, Rocky.'

Peter asks again. 'Where're you going, Master?'

'Rome. Where else?'

Peter agitates. 'Don't! Centurions are out looking for you. You'll be crucified.'

Always a teacher, Jesus corrects him. 'You mean recrucified.'

'Yes!'

'And you, Peter? Where are you off to?'

'Anywhere far away.'

'To Samarkand?'

Peter looks at him uncomprehendingly. 'Samarkand? Where's that?'

Jesus strokes Peter's panic-scourged face. 'A tale, Rocky ...'

'I must run, Master.'

'Listen! In Baghdad's market a servant is buying victuals for his Amir. Inadvertently he brushes against a fellow. The fellow looks askance at him. The servant recognises the fellow: Thanatos!

'He rushes to his Amir. Jabbering he tells him that Death has eyed him menacingly and would surely seize him. So, he begs for a horse to escape to Samarkand – which is many leagues away.

'The Amir gives the servant his thoroughbred.

'Later that afternoon, in the city square, the Amir comes across Thanatos and berates Him for giving the eye to his servant.

'Thanatos refutes the accusation: "I didn't give him the eye. I was surprised. I didn't expect to see him in Baghdad. I have an appointment with him tonight in Samarkand."'

Peter begins to weep.

Jesus kisses Peter's brow and resumes his journey to Rome. 'See you, Rocky.'

In despair Peter looks up and down the Appian Way.

Then he follows Jesus.

Numen leads the Grand Mufti to an ornate table where two leather-bound portfolios are laid out for their signatures.

They sit imperiously while authorised photographers jostle to take pictures.

Free of Hidebehind, I am elated. I whisper. 'Belkis, my love, I'm here. No more fears. Free to be what I should be.'

Numen and the Grand Mufti start signing the concordat.

If my judgement is correct, the windmill would be the last place the Security teams would expect to find a seditionist. It will take them a few minutes to sweep the Park and locate me.

Rotating the vane, I bellow into the megaphone. 'Friends! Compatriots! Freedom-lovers! This is Oric, a nemesis of self-appointed Saviours.

'In their quest for godhood these Saviours have processed a mutagen they call fear and with which they blight our Ethical Selves, our gifts of love, our compassion, our enlightenment and our creativity.

'In pursuit of godhood fantasy, these King Kanutes in purple and fine linen cook the age-old recipes of racial, ethnic and religious toxins. Thus, they crown themselves with wars and genocides!'

A thick silence descends. Only the Security Forces' muted deployments can be heard.

I'm galvanised. 'But they can't blight *all* the people. Countless free spirits evade their webs and nets to become beams of Light and illumine wherever shoots of Goodness emerge.

'For these free spirits know that blight is *not* eternal. They know humankind's agonies can be repaired! *Will* be repaired when they expose Evil in all its guises! When Goodness melts down the mutagens, then the Saviours will realise that everywhere their rule of hatred has turned to dust. They'll see there's no place in the Universe where they can be gods.

'And cursing their fantasies they'll implode!'

I spot Scythes and helicopters zeroing on me.

I blare with even greater fervour. 'Friends! You have a choice! To remain blighted or to be free spirits! Lights unto the world!

'The first condemns you to the rule of fear! To rapacity, extortion, tyranny, dungeons, torture, concentration camps, dismemberments, beheadings, executions! Your heads will be trepanned, and your minds will be tinselled with Big Lies that appear more dazzling than Truth! You'll be ordered to push the world off its axis!

'The second will provide you with love, compassion, creativity, the Ethical Self! It will restore your inalienable rights to liberty, equality, justice, peace, humanhood! It will guide you to live in Light until it's time for the cosmos to collect your souls! It will enable you to save the Word from immolation!

'That's the choice!'

Bullets whizz.

I'm ripped to pieces.

I summon my last breath. 'Death is a lie!'

EPILOGUE: ETERNAL HOPE

A blue aura cocoons me.

A sea-mist descends.

An albatross plucks me.

Its wings coddle me. I remember legends about their wings.

This albatross bears the persona of Kāne, the bird-god that escaped the total darkness of Po and created the first human.

We soar.

My blood that burst like sunspots stops dripping.

My torn flesh mends.

I am alive: broad-shouldered, flame-haired.

I have shed the skin where Hidebehind used to sit.

I haven't deserted.

The sea-mist disperses.

We land on the grotto.

Belkis is on the pool's ledge.

So is Childe Asher with amber almond eyes.

Hrant, too. Sombre as ever.

Belkis kisses me. 'Hello Leviathan.'

Childe Asher embraces me. 'Ready for your Agapé, Dad?'

Belkis caresses my hand. 'You didn't stay for mine. You won't miss yours.'

A dog barks: Phral.

Holding onto him: Moni.

They, too, climb onto the ledge.

Phral licks my hand.

Moni grins.

I laugh. 'Leviathans also.'

Moni holds up my journal. 'I promised to give this to Childe Asher.'

'It wasn't that urgent!'

'We move fast.'

Phral barks in confirmation.

Moni gives my journal to Childe Asher. 'Cherish it.'

Childe Asher whoops. 'Thanks, Dad.'

The grotto expands.

Becomes a vast Agora that stretches towards infinity.

Hordes of Leviathans appear.

They're singing *Journey's Start*. Amador's poem composed as a song by La Paloma.

> *... so here we are*
> *spreading ourselves*
> *on*
> *the wind*
> *the rock*
> *the spring*
> *the sun*
> *when we rise again*
> *we shall rise*
> *as*
> *breath*
> *land*
> *river*
> *hearth ...*

Moni waits until the horizon teems with Leviathans.

Then he steps forward. 'We have good tidings! When they felled

Oric, people chose to be free spirits – Lights. They vaulted over the barriers. Smashed Xanadu's Gate. Swarmed to the Pavilion. Security, even the Dragon's Teeth, froze. Before they could raise their guns, they were overpowered. The snipers in the helicopters did manage to fire, but only briefly. They had to get back and pick up Numen and the Grand Mufti who had run to the heliport. Both were flown to the Grand Mufti's aircraft carrier and sailed immediately.

'That's not all! The country, watching the events on television, also rebelled. They stormed the jails. Freed the patriots and the intelligentsia. Disarmed the Police, Riot Gendarmerie, Scythes, Intelligence Agents, Dragon's Teeth, Pinkies. Arrested all Numen's bootlickers.'

The news cheers the Leviathans. They throw their hats, chapeaus, tams, berets, skullcaps, turbans, coats, beads and rings into the air.

I am stunned. 'That's good tidings indeed!'

Moni continues. 'Here's the latest: Numen has been given asylum by the Grand Mufti. But, he warns, he and the Grand Mufti have proxies. They will deploy them. The duumvirate will grow from strength to strength and conquer the world.'

Hrant takes a deep breath. 'They'll find us and the Dolphineros ready for them!'

The Leviathans thunder 'Aye!' and burst into the *Ode to Joy*.

Slowly the Agora drifts into the aether. The Leviathans have left. Agapés must be brief. Repairing the world leaves little time for joy.

Childe Asher turns to Hrant, Moni and Phral. 'Don't you think Mum and Dad should have some time together ...?'

They agree and quickly leave.

I turn to Belkis. 'Do you think we'll ever stop the Saviours?'

She replies passionately. 'That's our belief.'

'Will you keep inspiring me?'

'Doubting again?'

'Conflicts never end. Peace never comes. Hatred always survives. The end of one horror always spawns the beginning of another. Can we defeat hatred – ever?'

'Yes, my Oric. We can. Believe me!'

'I will.'

'Tomorrow let's start looking for new Dolphineros. Today is ours.'

We swim out, gambol like flying fish and ride the waves like the Dolphin children we once were.